TEMPLE

The Prophecy of the Hidden Treasure

Bill Thompson

Published by
Ascendente Books
Dallas, Texas

Temple: The Prophecy of the Hidden Treasure
All Rights Reserved
Copyright © 2017
V.1.0

Published by Ascendente Books

ISBN 978-09979129-20
Printed in the United States of America

Books by Bill Thompson

<u>Brian Sadler Archaeological Mysteries</u>

THE BETHLEHEM SCROLL

**ANCIENT: A SEARCH FOR THE LOST CITY
OF THE MAYAS**

THE STRANGEST THING

THE BONES IN THE PIT

ORDER OF SUCCESSION

THE BLACK CROSS

TEMPLE

<u>Apocalyptic Fiction</u>

THE OUTCASTS

<u>The Crypt Trilogy</u>

THE RELIC OF THE KING

THE CRYPT OF THE ANCIENTS

GHOST TRAIN

<u>Teen Fiction</u>

THE LEGEND OF GUNNERS COVE

This book is dedicated to my late father Charles E. Thompson, a strong Christian and a student of eschatology, the study of the end times and God's final judgment for those on earth. He never went to Israel but he would have loved it.

My dad enjoyed every minute he spent with Dr. O.S. Hawkins, his pastor and next-door neighbor back in Oklahoma. I'm told they had many stimulating conversations about the Second Coming.

My wife and I were privileged to make a trip to Israel with O.S. and his wife and it was the most wonderful place I have ever visited. You'll see a glimpse of O.S. in one of the characters in this book (one of the good guys)!

————

Thanks to my faithful beta readers whose comments and suggestions always provide valuable insight and guidance.

————

My next novel will be available in the coming months. You can sign up to be notified in advance and get pre-release specials as available.

Just go to
billthompsonbooks.com
and click "Sign Up for the Latest News"

And I will give you the treasures of darkness,
and hidden wealth of secret places,
in order that you may know that it is I, the Lord,
the God of Israel, who calls you by your name.

Isaiah 45:3 (New American Standard version)

Author's Note

Although this is a work of fiction, the places in Israel that I mention all exist. Beth Shean (Beit She'an) is a fascinating archaeological site in the north, with acres of ruined, ancient buildings, their majestic stone columns standing like soldiers reaching to the sky. The spectacular Dome of the Rock sits atop the Temple Mount and is one of Jerusalem's most recognizable landmarks. Many scholars believe it stands on the very site of the Second Temple, which was destroyed by the Romans in AD 70. Others think the sacred Islamic shrine is close to the place where the temple stood, but not directly above it.

I use the terms al Qaeda, al Qaeda in Syria or AQS interchangeably throughout this book. Earlier that group was called the al Nusra Front and today it is sometimes known as Tahrir al-Sham or the Levant Liberation Committee.

Al Qaeda and ISIS are closely aligned at the very least, and some experts on the politics of the region believe they have now become a single jihadist organization.

Biblical prophecy has always fascinated me because I believe that every time it is fulfilled – as it has been time and again throughout the centuries – it proves the existence of a higher Being who is and always has been in control.

Isaiah prophesied that King Cyrus of Persia would free the Israelites and help them build the Second Temple. Isaiah 45:3, the verse on which this story is based, predicts the words of God to Cyrus, a man whom Isaiah called by name a hundred and fifty years before he was born. It was Cyrus to whom the treasures of darkness were given – the holy relics stolen from the Jews. The prophet Ezra predicted that Cyrus would help the Israelites rebuild their temple. And it all came to pass, just as Isaiah and Ezra had prophesied.

This is significant because many Jews and Christians believe that the Third Temple must be rebuilt, rising like a phoenix from the spot where the Second Temple stood long ago. This will signal the end times – the war of Armageddon and the end of things as we know them. The political tension between Palestinians and Jews over rebuilding the temple makes it impossible to imagine that the Dome of the Rock would be razed just so the Jews could have their site back. Some biblical scholars think that it will be destroyed by natural causes to make way for the new structure. But what if the site of the Second Temple is on the Temple Mount, but not exactly where the Dome stands? If that were the case, the Third Temple could be erected alongside the Muslim shrine.

The notion that there will be another temple in the end times comes from the book of Ezekiel. Today it is part of thrice-daily Jewish ritual prayers and is a fundamental aspect of Christian eschatology. According to an article entitled "Time to Build the Third Temple,"* in January 2017, the reestablished Sanhedrin asked the leaders of the USA and Russia to assume the role of Cyrus, fulfilling prophecy by helping the Jews rebuild their temple.

The article further states that a member of Israel's Knesset, Rabbi Yehuda Glick, who attended President Donald J. Trump's inauguration, has had discussions with prolific Turkish Islamic author and television personality Adnan Oktar, who has called for Jews and Muslims to unite in building the Third Temple next to – but not in place of – the Dome of the Rock. He has met with members of the Jewish Sanhedrin on this subject.

I love the thrill of adventure and I hope that someday the treasures of the Second Temple will be found. Could they have been whisked away on that night when the Romans sacked Jerusalem and burned the temple in AD 70? Perhaps in the end times – when the Third Temple is rebuilt and Jesus Christ comes again – we will learn the secret!

*Brinegar, R. and Robins, D. (2017, March 2). *Time to Build the Third Temple*. Retrieved from http://www.endtime.com

CHAPTER ONE

Jerusalem Post, Sunday, May 2

US VP Case to visit Jerusalem, dine with Lukin.
First American leader on Israeli soil since Embassy moved
from Tel Aviv

There will be dramatically heightened security as American vice president Donovan Case arrives in Tel Aviv tomorrow for a two-day state visit. Case has a packed schedule of meetings and luncheons, and on the last evening he will dine with Prime Minister Avraham Lukin and his wife, Aya, at the American Colony Hotel in Jerusalem.

Tensions have been high in Israel since President William Henry Harrison IV implemented the Jerusalem Embassy Act four months ago. He ordered the facility relocated from Tel Aviv to Jerusalem. The embassy will temporarily share space in the building presently occupied by the United States consulate general's office. The ambassador and nearly two hundred staff are currently working in Jerusalem. The remainder of the embassy employees – several hundred people – will move here when a new compound and ten-story office building under construction in West Jerusalem are completed next year.

Although the Jerusalem Embassy Act has been law for two decades, every American president since Bill Clinton refused to implement it, citing concerns over national security. And those concerns now seem to be valid. Violent outbursts, rioting, protests and threats against leaders of both Israel and the United States have occurred almost daily since the move. Palestinians in Israel and Arabs in border countries are angered by America's move, which they describe as an attempt to legitimize Jewish control over Jerusalem.

The vice president will be staying at the American Colony Hotel, which will be under tight security during his visit. Streets around the building will be blocked all day Tuesday in advance of that evening's dinner. Sources close to the matter told the *Post* that all guests who were staying at the American Colony will be moved to other venues for security reasons.

———

Jerusalem Post, Tuesday, May 4

Tensions high as American VP's motorcade is attacked;
Hundreds of protesters arrested over two days as PM
refuses to cancel dinner

On Monday afternoon, a motorcade transporting US Vice President Donovan Case was attacked by an angry mob near the King David Hotel in Jerusalem. The protesters threw rocks, eggs and tomatoes at the vehicles and some broke through security lines, striking the American leader's SUV with their fists before being subdued by security officers and police.

According to a person who spoke on condition of anonymity, some members of the Knesset urged Prime Minister Avraham Lukin to cancel Wednesday's scheduled state dinner with Case at the posh American Colony Hotel, but Lukin refused. That source revealed that both the vice president's security detail and Lukin's have expressed concern at the numbers of protesters taking to the streets and the heightened level of anger and violence they are displaying. Nearly three hundred people have been arrested since Case arrived on Monday, mostly Palestinians but also Syrians and Lebanese nationals who apparently came to Jerusalem solely to join the movement protesting the state visit of the American vice president.

"In its short history, Israel has faced bigger challenges than threats from a group of rabble-rousers who have no valid claim to our land and who refuse to obey the law," the prime minister said. "Having the American embassy in Jerusalem after all this time is the culmination of years of struggle. This city belongs to the Jews, and our American friends have helped make that clear to the world. God willing, Vice President Case, my wife and I will have our dinner Tuesday evening and no rock-throwing hoodlums are going to force us to cancel it."

The head of the Palestine Liberation Organization, Mohammed Kahn, termed Lukin's remarks "incendiary and dangerous," adding, "Retaliation by those whose legal right to these lands is challenged by Israel and America is both understandable and inevitable." When asked by a *Post* reporter if that remark meant he supported violence against Lukin or Case, he refused to answer.

When the embassy was moved to Jerusalem a few months ago, the PLO revoked recognition of Israel as a nation, breaking the terms of the Oslo Peace Accord to which the PLO was a party. In the months since President Harrison's decision to relocate the symbolic seat of American government in Israel, violent protests, car bombings and threats against leaders have dramatically increased.

CHAPTER TWO

One Day Earlier

Brian Sadler and his wife, Nicole Farber, sat in the expansive bar of the David Citadel Hotel in Jerusalem. Through the massive windows past the patio they could see the Tower of David and the Old City standing in ageless grandeur in the distance. The last rays of sunlight gleamed on its ancient, historic walls as though the fingers of God were reaching down from Heaven to bless that sacred spot.

A couple of patrons in the bar stopped by their table, introducing themselves to Brian and saying how much they loved his TV specials on the History and Discovery networks.

Bijan Rarities had already been a well-regarded Fifth Avenue antiquities gallery when Brian became its owner. He had significantly expanded both its reputation and his own by relentlessly promoting archaeology as an adventure, not a boring dig in the sand. The tedious work at hot, dusty sites was a factor in amazing discoveries, but Brian capitalized on the exciting parts – times like that morning when Howard Carter first gazed upon the golden treasures of King Tutankhamun and called them "wonderful things." He created immensely successful television documentaries that had been seen by millions around the globe and at the same time transformed himself into an instantly recognizable celebrity.

After the tragic bombing of his New York gallery a few years ago, Brian had moved to Dallas to join Nicole, who would later become his wife. He established a shop there, using it as his base and traveling frequently to his other locations in London and New Orleans.

He was also an adventurer, often visiting sites in Central and South America, exploring ruins and learning more about the mysterious people who had built enormous skyscraper temples while having only rudimentary tools with which to work. Many of these journeys had ended up as fodder for his television specials.

His wife, Nicole, a solo-practice lawyer in Dallas, occasionally accompanied him on his adventures, and she'd been especially excited about this trip. This was her first time to Israel and Brian's second. He had enjoyed their week and loved accompanying her to the sites they'd read about in the Bible since they were children.

They stood as Vice President Donovan Case strode confidently through the room, flanked by Secret Service agents. He gave them a wave as he approached their table and the three agents peeled away, taking up positions that allowed them to observe the surroundings.

"Hey, guys," he said as he hugged Nicole, then Brian and pulled up a chair. "Sit! Sit! Great to see you both! Thanks for working with my schedule so we could get together. I'm sorry there's not much time, but you know how it is."

Brian and Nicole had arrived in Jerusalem a week earlier. Although the primary purpose of his trip was to attend tomorrow's auction of relics from the time of Jesus, they'd allowed plenty of time to visit the historic sites. When they heard Don was going to be in town, Brian had asked his scheduler if he could spare time for a quick drink.

"Mr. Vice President," Nicole began, but Case shook his head and wagged a finger in her face.

"After what we've been through, I'll always be on a first-name basis with you both."

"Don," she began again, "we've been fortunate to have time here for sightseeing. Do you get a chance for any of that on these state visits?"

"Occasionally, but usually it's such a hassle on both sides that it isn't worth it. I've always wanted to visit the Temple Mount, for instance, but your friend the president screwed that up for me. Since he moved the embassy from

Tel Aviv to Jerusalem last spring, the Dome of the Rock's now off-limits to firebrands like me." He chuckled, but they knew he was serious.

A few months ago, President Harrison had ordered the embassy moved from Tel Aviv to West Jerusalem, the actual capital of Israel. Knowing there would be a tremendous firestorm over the act – one that had been approved by Congress years before but never implemented – the president had secretly prepared the ambassador and consul general well in advance. On the morning that the president made his announcement from the Rose Garden, semitrailer trucks were already on the road, hauling furniture and equipment from Tel Aviv to the consulate general's compound in Jerusalem. His existing staff would be shuffled around to make room for over a hundred and fifty newcomers who had been lodged in Jerusalem hotels the night before the announcement. There would be cramped quarters for months while a new compound was built, but it was business as usual in the new Jerusalem embassy the morning after the president's press conference.

Prominent Jews in Israel and the United States had praised the president, calling the move an act of courage. Prime Minister Lukin said it was a bold step in the right direction, but his opinion was not universally shared. Within minutes after Harry's speech, there was a hastily arranged press conference from the Capitol, where minority leaders of the House and Senate assailed the president for his decision. They called it a foolish, dangerous move that would needlessly incite anger. There was no reason to relocate the embassy, they railed. But it had been too late.

As expected, inflammatory, bitter criticism had been leveled at Harry by the chairman of the PLO and the heads of state of many Arab nations. The president of the European Union was more diplomatic in her remarks, although it was clear that she and other allies felt this was an unnecessary, volatile move, one that would create far more problems than if he had simply left it alone, as his predecessors had chosen to do.

While in Israel, Brian and Nicole had seen firsthand the anger some citizens felt. They had hired a former Mossad officer's security company – one recommended by the embassy – to arrange a guide for their excursions in Jerusalem and around Israel. He was fluent in English, well-versed in the Christian and Jewish history of the sites they visited, and – as evidenced by distinct bulges under his jacket – ready for a problem if one arose. It was comforting yet disconcerting, given the unrest they saw everywhere.

Over the past few days there had been rioting in parts of Jerusalem and things had escalated when the vice president set foot on Israeli soil. Arab demonstrators, furious that the American embassy now occupied a plot of land claimed by the Palestinians, chanted and threw rocks at Case's motorcade. There had been dozens of arrests, and Brian and Nicole occasionally felt uneasy outside the hotel, although they didn't let the situation ruin their adventure. Things happened in Israel now and then. It didn't mean you should stay at home. It simply meant you should be careful.

"I'm glad the president ordered the relocation," Case continued. "It's been a law for twenty years, but until now no chief executive wanted to open what was going to be a huge can of worms. Despite what good friends he and the prime minister are, and despite how strongly Israel has urged every president since Bill Clinton to move it, it was a bold and risky step. The Arabs are furious. Everyone knew they would be, but my trip here is intended to show that America is Israel's ally, period."

The last time they'd seen Don in person was at their wedding in the East Room of the White House last year. The president had served as best man, just as Brian had done long ago when Harry and Jennifer, his first lady, were married. They reminisced about the unsettling time when they all worked together against Chambliss Parkes, the former speaker of the house who was now on death row in Indiana. Case had been director of the CIA while Parkes had briefly led the nation before being sentenced to death for treason. After a harrowing set of events, Don had been instrumental in the dramatic return of Harry Harrison to the presidency, and Harry had chosen him as his running mate.

Their conversation turned to the increasing violence in the Middle East following yesterday's announcement that the United States was focusing its efforts on taking out Syria's most deadly terrorist organization, a coalition called Tahrir al-Sham. Known in the West as the Levant Liberation Committee or al Qaeda in Syria, its ruthless leader was a young man known as Tariq the Hawk, who was on Interpol's most wanted list. Tariq had played a key role in the Chambliss Parkes affair, and he harbored intense hatred for President Harrison and the American people.

"Frankly, I didn't agree that we should reveal our plans to wipe out the Syrian terrorists," Case explained, "but I totally agree that Tariq has to be eliminated. He's head of the deadliest group on earth and holed up in the most unstable country in the region. Prime Minister Lukin's very concerned about how Syria will respond. At the very least, it's a challenge – a threat. At worst, they could consider it an act of war. With Syria next door and itching for a fight, Israel's leaders *should* be worried. And so should we, although that can't stop us from helping our friends and battling killers like Tariq."

Brian eased the subject into something lighter. "Are you heading back on Wednesday?" he asked, knowing from this morning's news that the vice president was scheduled to dine with Israel's prime minister and his wife tomorrow night.

"We'll leave right after the state dinner, actually. Tonight I'm having dinner with Ambassador Sheller at the embassy. Tomorrow I'll be in Tel Aviv, meeting with government officials and doing an industry tour. Then it's back here for dinner and we'll take off after that, around 10:30 p.m. I'll be back in DC the next morning."

"You're staying at the American Colony Hotel, right?"

Case nodded.

"I was supposed to be at an auction there tomorrow afternoon. Thanks to you, now it's moved down the street. I can't imagine how tight the security will be in that place with both you and the prime minister there at the same time."

After an hour and with profuse apologies for rushing away, Don Case left for his dinner at the embassy. Brian and Nicole would never see him again.

CHAPTER THREE

The Next Evening

One single item – a chalice – stood on a table at the front of the room. It literally radiated brilliance, glistening as the light reflected off its golden veneer. The auction catalog described it as "a wedding cup of Cana." Three of them had been uncovered near the site where Jesus was believed to have performed His first miracle, changing water into wine at a marriage feast. It was in perfect condition – there wasn't a scratch or a dent anywhere on the twelve-inch-high goblet. It might not have been touched by Jesus Himself, but it was nevertheless significant and very rare. Only because there were two more, each equally pristine, was it allowed to be put up for auction by its discoverer, who had been awarded the relic as his reward. Forty people sat in the petite salon of Jerusalem's Olive Tree Hotel and observed the battle for the last item – the most prized piece of the event.

The auctioneer announced, "Three twenty-five. I have three twenty-five. Do I hear three fifty?"

Like a back-and-forth tennis match, every head in the room moved to the right as a paddle rose into the air and quickly dropped.

The auctioneer acknowledged the bid with a nod. "Three fifty. I have three fifty. Now three seventy-five?"

All eyes shifted to the left. There was no reaction from the man on the other side of the room.

"Mr. Malouf, the bid is three fifty. Do I hear three seventy-five?"

The man sat impassively for a moment before raising his paddle. "Four fifty," he said in heavily accented English.

There were gasps from the spectators. The auction estimate had been two hundred thousand dollars, but the bidders had sailed past that mark several minutes earlier. Where there had once been five contenders, now there were only two.

Brian Sadler stared stonily into space, his face devoid of emotion. Damn, he had wanted that piece and he had come here intending to have it.

"Four fifty to you, Mr. Sadler. Will you bid four seventy-five?"

Thirty seconds went by. Then fifteen more. There wasn't a sound in the room.

The auctioneer had no desire to rush the bidder, but in fairness to everyone, it was time for a decision. "Mr. Sadler, will there be another bid?"

He shook his head. "No." There was enthusiastic applause from the assemblage as the winner exhaled in satisfaction. He gave Brian a brief wave and got a nod in return.

"Mr. Malouf, you are the winner at four hundred fifty thousand dollars. Congratulations. That concludes today's auction, ladies and gentlemen. Thank you for coming and thank you to all our bidders."

As Abdel Malouf walked to the front of the room to complete the paperwork for his purchase, Brian was approached by an attractive woman in her twenties. "Mr. Sadler," she said, "I'm Miriam Rosen with the *Post*. Could I have a moment?"

The last thing Brian wanted right now was to subject himself to a reporter's questions, but this was part of the game. Win or lose, the public deserved to know the thoughts and emotions of people who could offer a fortune for an artifact, only to see it go to someone else when the gavel fell for the final time. He'd done these interviews a hundred times since becoming owner of Bijan Rarities, often as winner but sometimes, like today, on the losing side. Brian's attendance at auctions always piqued the public interest, given his notoriety and his close personal relationship with Harry Harrison, the president of the United States.

"I need a word with my colleague first," he told her. "I'll be back in a moment."

Malouf was seated at a small table, reviewing the sale document with a representative of the auction house. He stood as Brian approached and offered his hand.

"Congratulations," Brian said sincerely as he shook the Arab's hand. "I had hoped to take that magnificent chalice home, but it wasn't meant to be." He'd never faced this adversary before, but he knew the man by reputation. A Syrian, Abdel Malouf was perhaps the most famous purveyor of biblical relics in Israel. His shop in the Muslim Sector of the Old City was a showplace of fascinating rarities.

"I'd like to invite you to come by my store for a cup of tea before you leave Jerusalem," Malouf offered. "It would be good to know each other better."

Brian was about to accept when he heard a rolling sound like thunder. There was an enormous rumbling *whump*, then another. From the hallway outside the salon came shouts of alarm. A security guard rushed into the room and yelled, "Evacuate! Now! Go out through those emergency exits!" He pointed to a series of French doors along the side that opened into a garden and guided everyone toward them.

A representative of the auction house grabbed the chalice and whisked it outside as Malouf yelled to the guard, "What's going on?"

"There's something happening down the street! It sounded like a bomb! Get out!"

Brian had a sickening feeling. Car bombings happened periodically in Jerusalem. But a bombing down the street, today? He glanced at his watch. It was 6:13 p.m.

Surely this isn't about ... Dear God, don't let this be what I think it is. The state dinner was set to begin at six, just fifteen minutes ago. At this very minute the vice president, the Israeli prime minister and his wife should be sitting in the dining room of the American Colony Hotel a few blocks away.

Brian left the room with the others and was directed to the sidewalk by a hotel employee. He hurried across St. George Street, cut through the Addar Hotel, jaywalked across Derech Shchem Road and turned onto Louis Vincent Street, where the American Colony Hotel sat. There was a thick black plume of smoke rising into the air left of the hotel's main entrance two blocks ahead of him. In the distance, he heard a wail of sirens growing louder and louder.

The American Colony Hotel was a very unusual place. Unlike most of the real estate in Jerusalem, which is fervently claimed by both Arabs and Jews, this nineteenth-century oasis had always been considered neutral. Owned by neither Arab nor Jew but instead by foreigners, it was a quiet fortress where both sides could gather in peace. Ambassadors, representatives of the United Nations and diplomats worldwide stayed and conducted business in a safe, comfortable setting. This venue had been chosen for Vice President Case's stay and tonight's state dinner since this was the first time an American leader had set foot in Israel since the embassy was relocated and things were sure to be tumultuous at the least.

At precisely the moment Abdel Malouf had won the bid, the American vice president was being seated in the American Colony's dining room at a table already occupied by Prime Minister Avraham Lukin and his wife, Aya. The Israeli leader knew Case, having met him earlier in Washington.

Servers poured wine and offered menus as the leaders chatted amiably. The room was quiet since there were no other guests. Besides the waitstaff, the only others present were two dozen Secret Service and Israeli security guards along the walls. They were silent sentinels, alert to every movement in the room.

Because of the event, there were large numbers of soldiers and security personnel stationed inside the hotel and out. Now it seemed as if they were flying about in every direction, screaming instructions and brandishing a variety of weapons from handguns to automatic rifles. Secret

Service agents and Israeli security guards barked orders amid the chaos, establishing their jurisdictions and ordering local police to secure the streets around the burning structure.

"Halt! Stop right there!" a cop yelled as Brian approached, raising his Dror light machine gun menacingly. Five more joined him to form a human barrier across the street. Behind them the hotel was a scene of frightening confusion. From here, Brian could pinpoint the exact location of the black smoke he'd seen. It had grown denser than before, a sign of the blaze's intensity, and it bellowed forth from the northwest corner of the building. Another huge burst of flame shot over the top of the retaining wall encircling the hotel.

Brian knew the layout. He and Nicole had had lunch last week in the same room where tonight's dinner was set. He glanced at his watch again; if things were on schedule, the state dinner would have begun twenty minutes ago in the room that was now a blazing inferno.

His mind raced with fear and diminishing hope. With all the security concerns, could the venue have changed at the last minute? Was there a possibility the leaders might not have been here at all? Could the explosion have been an accident?

Brian's cellphone rang. He looked at the screen, saw the code name "WHH4" and knew the answer.

William Henry Harrison IV, the president of the United States, was calling. This wasn't good news.

CHAPTER FOUR

The president shouted, "Brian! Where are you?"

"I'm at a barricade a couple of blocks away from the American Colony Hotel."

"What? You're at the *hotel*? What the hell are you doing there? Were you at the dinner?"

"Hang on a sec, Harry. It's not that at all. It's a coincidence. I was at an auction down the street when everything started, and I walked over here to see what happened. Nicole and I had a drink with Don Case yesterday. Are he and the prime minister okay?"

"I don't know. I'm in the elevator, heading to the Situation Room, and I wanted to check on you and Nicole before things got crazy."

"She's back at our hotel. We're fine. What's happening?"

"I'm not sure. We'll have choppers overhead in a few minutes. But from early reports, it looks really bad."

At that moment, it seemed that every emergency vehicle in Jerusalem arrived simultaneously. The clashing scream of a dozen sirens was deafening. Brian kept the president updated as a truck filled with barricades pulled up. A team of soldiers began blocking off the streets as medical workers with gurneys ran toward the hotel's front entrance and a dozen fire trucks came off the main highway onto narrow Louis Vincent Street, taking up positions around the hotel and beginning the battle to bring the situation under control.

"I can't stay where I am," Brian advised. "The soldiers are pushing us back."

"I'm in the Situation Room now. I want to put you on speaker for a minute. Everyone, this is Brian Sadler, a friend of mine who's outside the hotel in Jerusalem. Brian, tell us what you can see. We're being told the entire left front quadrant is engulfed in flames."

"I saw the same thing when I got here, but it's impossible to tell what's happening now," he told Harry. "That's where the dining room is; I'm sure you know that already." He explained that the hotel was surrounded by a privacy wall. Because of it and the acrid smoke that was becoming more and more dense, it was difficult to see anything inside the grounds. "There's a helicopter coming," he advised.

"That's ours," Harry replied, and Brian saw the American flag on the door of an Apache Longbow chopper now hovering fifty feet off the ground about a block away. "We're getting feed from them now and I must go. Stay safe and keep in touch."

The last time a hotel in Jerusalem had been bombed was over seventy years ago when a Zionist group attacked the King David Hotel, killing ninety-one people. That building had been the headquarters of the British military command, and the bombing was in retaliation for the arrests of Jews who were accused of seditious acts.

There were flare-ups of violence and mayhem in Jerusalem on a regular basis as terrorist organizations struck against what they considered the illegal occupation of Palestine by the Jews. But today's attack was different. If the American vice president was dead, the United States would undoubtedly unleash its full fury whoever had committed this horrific atrocity. The Israelis would do the same if their beloved prime minister and his wife were gone.

At 10:30 p.m. local time the Israel Broadcasting Authority and major American networks aired simultaneous news conferences from Tel Aviv and Washington. President Harrison and the head of Israel's Knesset solemnly informed the world that Vice President Donovan Case, Prime Minister Avraham Lukin and Lukin's wife, Aya, had been murdered in a bombing at the American Colony Hotel during a state dinner. Twenty-seven others were killed, mostly hotel staff and security personnel. Fourteen of the dead were Secret

Service agents assigned to guard the vice president. No group had claimed responsibility, and the American president promised to do anything he could to help Israel bring the perpetrators to justice.

As they watched the newscast from their hotel room, Brian and Nicole saw the grim resolve in Harry's face and the way his hands gripped the podium like a vise. He was obviously struggling to restrain himself and not doing a very good job of it.

Six hours later the Syrian state news network RTV aired a live press conference from an undisclosed location. A man whose face was covered in a black mask stood outdoors next to a tank and read a brief statement in Arabic. Tahrir al-Sham – al Qaeda in Syria – was proud to claim responsibility for the assassination of the evil leaders of America and Israel. It had taken place because the American embassy had been moved to West Jerusalem – land that rightfully belonged to Palestine.

"How dare the infidels think they can challenge Allah's chosen people?" the hooded spokesman concluded. "May they rot in hell for eternity. *Allahu akbar*. God is great."

By morning the world waited to see what the United States and Israel would do next. A full-scale military response was possible, White House sources said, although striking Syria would surely unite the Arab nations against a common enemy. If that happened, first-world nations would join their allies. Once sides were chosen, lines were drawn in the sand and someone issued an ultimatum, World War III could follow.

In today's environment where several nations had the weaponry to destroy the planet, the next great war could truly be Armageddon, the final battle between good and evil. According to the Bible, God's wrath would be unleashed against the forces of Satan in a literal war the likes of which man has never seen. It would happen in the Jezreel Valley south of modern-day Haifa in northwestern Israel, and it would be the end of everything on earth.

And it could really happen. Very soon.

Around eight a.m. the next morning, a somber group of senior embassy officers gathered at the Tel Aviv airport to bid a fallen comrade farewell. A squad of Marines carried a casket to a huge Boeing 757 with *United States of America* emblazoned on its fuselage. They snapped to attention and saluted as the coffin was loaded, standing in silent vigilance as Air Force Two rolled down the runway, carrying Vice President Donovan Case on his final trip back to the United States of America.

———

Experts from the CIA, the Mossad and other agencies painstakingly combed through the rubble in the American Colony Hotel, examining everything they came across to determine how the attack had occurred and what explosives were used. Agents pored through employment files and background information on every hotel employee. They retrieved the logbooks that notated every delivery van and maintenance truck that had arrived in the past two weeks, and calls were made to confirm the vehicles were legitimate.

It didn't take long to piece together what had happened. The material the terrorists used was called Torpex, an abbreviation of the words *torpedo explosive*. More powerful than TNT, the same stuff was used in the 2008 bombing of Pakistan's Islamabad Marriott Hotel, where fifty-four people were killed. Some world leaders blamed al Qaeda for that act, although no group ever claimed credit for it.

This time around, the Mossad was aware that AQS had stockpiled Torpex somewhere in Syria, so it made sense that the group could have been responsible. Getting it inside the hotel compound had been simple. Video recordings showed the service gate opening at 5:47 p.m., just thirteen minutes before the dinner was to begin. At that time, the prime minister and his wife were already seated in the dining room and the American vice president's entourage was arriving at the hotel's front entrance.

A white delivery van from the hotel's liquor distributor sat idling at the gate. Secret Service agents spoke

TEMPLE

with the driver, checked his identification and looked underneath the vehicle with mirrors. A bomb-sniffing dog was led around the truck. They opened the rear doors, examined the contents, and closed them, and waved the van through. From records the investigators saw, everything was normal. The delivery occurred around the same time every Tuesday, Thursday and Sunday, and it was always the same van and the same driver. There was nothing unusual except that a state dinner was under way one floor above the loading dock. The agents could have turned the van away, but investigators later determined that the explosion would have had the same result if the driver had detonated his load at the gate instead of the dock. At that point, it made no difference.

As usual, a hotel security guard directed the driver to back his van down a ramp to a loading zone that connected to the hotel's vast storage rooms. From there, service elevators led to the kitchen and dining room one floor above. The dock camera showed the driver exit the van, shake hands with the guard and open the back doors of his truck. He took out a two-wheeled dolly, loaded five cases of wine, made a trip inside and repeated the process several times. At 6:13 p.m. he closed the doors, waved to the guard and got back into the truck.

At precisely that time, the video footage stopped. That was the moment that the explosion occurred, and the loading dock had been ground zero. Investigators looking at the almost completely demolished van found traces of Torpex. After reviewing the video, they at first thought the bottles of wine were filled with it, but that wasn't correct. Based on the evidence, they finally concluded that several hundred pounds of Torpex were concealed somewhere in the van. It was a material that bomb dogs wouldn't pick up unless they were specially trained for that specific chemical, and it had not been detected by visual inspection. It had most likely been hidden under the rear floor.

The liquor distributor's driver had been on the company payroll for two years. He was a Palestinian whose record of attendance and dedication to his customers had earned him commendations. His thrice-weekly route included the American Colony Hotel, and he had made deliveries there for months. He knew the dock supervisor and other employees – all of whom had perished – by name. There had been nothing to arouse suspicion. He was a perfect terrorist, imbedded so deeply into society that he had become part of its fabric.

CHAPTER FIVE

These were challenging times for Israel. Attempting to stabilize things, the Knesset quickly selected a new prime minister. After unprecedented calls for cooperation among its members – and a plea from Israel's allies to act quickly – the speaker called for a vote the day after the bombing. Daniel Shigon, a hawk who was a decorated military veteran, was elected with broad support from inside his own party and out.

Seventy-two years old, Shigon had spent his career in the military, beginning as a young officer in the 1967 Six-Day War and eventually reaching the rank of general. He had been an elected member of the Knesset for ten years. He was brave and steadfast, an outspoken hawk and a champion for the future of his beloved country. Even those whose beliefs differed from his knew him to be fair, honest and willing to listen to both sides before forming an opinion. Polls showed that Jewish citizens considered him the perfect man to guide Israel in these difficult times.

Shigon's wife Karen was an American. They had met at university in London, married in 1964 and lived in Israel ever since. Their adult children were spread from New York to London to Tel Aviv. Despite her heritage, the new prime minister had no affection for the United States. He had observed how often America offered the carrot – defense and financial alliances – followed by the stick – demands for cooperation and peace with the Palestinians. The Jews had fought these same enemies for thousands of years and that war would continue until the last war on earth. While this prime minister was in charge, the USA wasn't going to bully Israel into doing something against its best interests.

His first act as commander-in-chief was to mobilize the armed forces and prepare for war. As in the 1967 battle, it wasn't Israel's plan to strike first, but the country must be prepared for anything. Shigon and his defense minister also advocated seizing the Temple Mount to retaliate against the Arabs, but the Knesset wisely vetoed that course of action. Tempers were short enough already between Palestinians and Jews; now wasn't the time to make a move that would only incite more anger. Instead, checkpoints were set up at the Old City's entrances. APCs were moved into place and armed soldiers interrogated every person and checked every vehicle seeking entry. The lines of people waiting to enter became snarled nightmares and snaked for blocks. Some hardy tourists waited it out, but most gave up, disappointed that they wouldn't see some of their religion's most important sites. That angered shopkeepers inside the walled city, who depended on tourism for much of their revenues.

Sporadic fights between soldiers and pedestrians broke out as tempers flared. An Arab man was shot to death at the Lion's Gate, the entry to the Muslim Quarter, when he pulled a long knife and unsuccessfully tried to stab a soldier who was wearing a bulletproof vest. A minor riot occurred and twenty people were arrested before it was quashed by soldiers with batons and pepper spray.

The increasing tension threw a kink into Brian and Nicole's plans. Always optimistic, he still held out slender hope they could visit some of the places they hadn't seen yet. "Tomorrow we were supposed to go to Tiberias and spend the night," he advised. "We were going to sail across the Sea of Galilee to Capernaum to see the very spot where Jesus preached. I've always wanted to go there –"

She interrupted, and this time she wasn't mincing words. "Seriously, Brian? Do you think it's safe to travel on the highways now, especially to Galilee? Did you see the same newscast I did this morning? Did you see the map of the Sea of Galilee that they showed? Syria's like five miles away and there's about to be a war! Tell me you're not still thinking we should take that trip."

As happened so often, Nicole tempered her husband's enthusiasm with a reality check. The news this morning was alarming, as Israel prepared for its first full-scale conflict in fifty years.

The problem with going to the north was that the Golan Heights on the eastern shore of the Sea of Galilee was just five miles from Syria. The area was teeming with military activity; Syrian troops were taking up positions, and no one knew what might happen next. Syria could strike first, as could another of the Arab border nations. There was too much uncertainty and too much potential danger. There would be no sightseeing trip to Galilee this time. Anyway, he told her, there were a lot more important sites they hadn't visited in Jerusalem.

"We'll stay around here. Do you want to leave a day earlier than we planned."

"That's up to you, but if we can finish up early, I say let's get the hell out of Dodge."

"Let me work on it," he said as his phone rang. He mouthed, "It's Harry."

They chatted for a couple of minutes and then she saw Brian's face turn serious as he listened without responding. He said, "I don't have a problem doing that. We're going back early, FYI. I'm going to try to book us out on Saturday, but that gives me tomorrow and Friday to see what I can find out."

"What did he want?" she asked when the call was over.

"If we have time, he wants me to see Abdel again briefly and talk about his past. The CIA thinks he might have been involved with one of the jihadist organizations when he was young. Lots of Syrians did that – it was a noble thing to fight for freedom – but once al Qaeda and ISIS became what they are today, many of their followers wanted out." Harry had explained that quitting wasn't ever an option. Some who looked like they were no longer with AQS had become sleepers, and the CIA thought Malouf might be one of those.

"All he's asking is that I get him to discuss politics," Brian explained. "You can come with me – I'll offer to buy lunch tomorrow. It won't take much time out of our sightseeing agenda."

"Let's do it. I've never met a terrorist."

"And I doubt you're meeting one this time. This guy's as meek as a mouse. I don't get Harry's concern, but I also will spend an hour if it might help our fight against al Qaeda."

He changed their return flight to Saturday, two days earlier than their original schedule. They had already planned to spend a couple of nights in London; now they would make it four. He explained that they'd head to the airport around 1 p.m., take the British Airways flight at 4:30 and arrive at Heathrow around nine.

"We'll go to the flat, have a nightcap, go to bed and be up for a fun Sunday in London!" he added with a smile.

"Sounds like a plan," she replied, relieved that they had a firm date to leave all this unrest that seemed to be everywhere she turned. She was looking forward to London and knew he was even more than she. She already knew what they would do when they got up that first morning. It had become a routine, one that she enjoyed almost as much as her husband. They'd stroll the streets, window-shop and take in the sights he loved in his favorite city. They'd end up having lunch at Dumpling Legends, a restaurant in Chinatown that was always her husband's first dining destination. Going there was a ritual, and although she wasn't crazy about the place or the food, she indulged her husband's wishes because he loved it.

After lunch, they'd go to Bijan Rarities, Brian's gallery in Old Bond Street, and visit with Cory Spencer, the manager. She'd piddle around while Brian did a little business. In their four days there, they would take in a show or two and try out new little restaurants and wine bars. While Brian spent mornings at Bijan, she'd stroll the city's quaint neighborhoods and verdant, serene parks. London was a relaxing place and she couldn't wait to get out of Israel before something else bad happened.

As hard as it was for Brian to admit, she was right about leaving early. He had been looking forward to tomorrow's trip to Tiberias and the north, an area so rich in early Christian history. He had arranged a trip across the Sea of Galilee on a boat that was similar to one Jesus might have taken. The voyage would have ended in Capernaum, one of the cities where He preached and taught.

It was nearly ten a.m. by the time they went to the patio for coffee and pastries. Consulting the dog-eared pages of the Fodor's guidebook he had lugged everywhere, Brian tossed out a proposed itinerary for the day. They'd start at the Shrine of the Book at the Israel Museum, where the original Dead Sea Scrolls were displayed. Going to Qumran, where the scrolls were found in 1947, had been tops on his list for this trip, but a road trip was off now. Visiting a museum wouldn't be the same as going to Qumran, he admitted, but it would be a substitute until the time when he could come back.

"After the museum, I have a surprise for lunch," he said. He'd found a place that sounded totally different than the norm, he added teasingly. She smiled; her husband was a master at finding special places and she enjoyed surprises.

"What about this afternoon?"

"I'd like to go back to the Temple Mount. There's a tunnel we can visit, way down underground where the ancient street level was. It has viaducts and cisterns and the guidebook says it runs below the Muslim Quarter for more than five hundred yards."

"I can't imagine why you of all people would want to see that," she quipped. "It totally sounds right down your alley, Indiana!"

They spent an hour in the dark, eerie rooms of the Shrine of the Book, seeing the largest collection of Dead Sea scrolls in the world. Back in the blazing sunlight, he hailed a cab and told the driver they wanted to go to the Notre Dame pilgrim center.

"What's that?" she asked. "I thought lunch was next."

"It is. Just wait."

They arrived at a large impressive building dating from the 1800s that stood opposite the Old City. Brian paid the driver and they walked to its entrance.

"This looks like a monastery," she said.

"It is. It's owned by the Vatican and it's called Notre Dame of Jerusalem Center. It's for Catholic pilgrims – a place for rest and repose, I guess – and its restaurant is famous for one of the best rooftop views in the city. Let's go!"

They took an elevator to the roof and stepped out onto a wide veranda dotted with dining tables shaded by umbrellas. The views in every direction were spectacular, but the most impressive was the southern vista overlooking the walls of the Old City. The Dome of the Rock shone splendidly and the scene was straight from a travelogue. They shot pictures and had a waiter take theirs too.

"This may not have been our best lunch in Jerusalem," she said as they finished their bottle of wine, "but it absolutely is the most spectacular. I loved sitting out here with the ancient city laid out in front of us. Good job, honey!"

They walked across the street, entered the Christian Quarter through the New Gate and walked to the Temple Mount. Consulting the guidebook, he led them to a stairway tucked into an alcove. They paid a fee, hired a guide and walked down into a narrow complex called the Western Wall tunnel. Their guide explained that they were seeing original walls from the time of Herod that survived the destruction of the temple in AD 70. They saw streets built by the Romans that led to the Temple Mount two thousand years ago. Brian was enthused and Nicole had to admit it was very interesting and completely unexpected.

Forty-five minutes later they exited near the Via Dolorosa and stopped for a coffee. "I'd like to make one more trip to the Temple Mount," he told her. "I may never get here again and I want to take it all in once more." She was as excited as he, and soon they were standing on its broad platform a few hundred feet north of the Dome of the Rock. There were groups everywhere, wearing translation headphones and listening to guides explain everything. Nearby he heard a commanding voice speaking in English, explaining the features of the area where they stood.

He turned, nudged Nicole and whispered, "Do you know who that is?" She saw a handsome, distinguished-looking man with a shock of gray hair, speaking English to a group of people she presumed were Americans.

"No. Who is he?"

"That's C. R. Faulkner. He's a well-known Southern Baptist preacher."

Nicole nodded. "I've heard of him." Since he was somewhat of a celebrity himself, she was surprised to see how enthused Brian was to see the religious leader.

"He's been pastor of some of the biggest churches in the United States, including one in Dallas," he continued. "I've known of him since I was a kid. He preached in the Baptist church in Longview one time and my parents took me to see him. He was well-known even back then. Let's listen for a minute. I'll bet he knows Israel like the back of his hand."

They stood at the back of his group of maybe twenty-five people, mostly in their fifties. Faulkner was explaining his own theory about how the Third Temple might be rebuilt in the end times. From years of research and more than fifty trips to Israel, he was saying, he had come to believe that the original temple once was on the exact spot where they were standing now.

"We're about three hundred feet north of the Dome of the Rock," he continued, turning their attention to a small canopied structure supported by four pillars. "I believe – as do many experts and scholars – that this is really where the Second Temple actually stood. This small building is Muslim – it's called the Dome of the Tablets. It's not mentioned much, but there are good reasons to believe the temple could have stood here."

Pausing for effect, he continued. "What would the big deal be if it were here instead of under the Dome of the Rock?"

Brian whispered, "It could be rebuilt without destroying one of Islam's most sacred sites."

Most of Reverend Faulkner's group came to the same conclusion, and he joked, "I'm glad you've been listening to me these past few days!" He directed them next to the southeastern corner of the Temple Mount, where he would explain about a building called Solomon's Stables. As the people walked away, Brian approached the pastor and introduced himself and Nicole.

"I'm glad you stopped me," Faulkner said, slapping Brian on the back and explaining that he was hosting a group from his church in Miami. "I'm a huge fan. You've brought so many ancient things to life and allowed people a glimpse into the past. I love all that, and since we're here on the Temple Mount, I hope it means a documentary about Israel!"

"You can count on it!" Nicole replied with a grin. "Neither danger, nor bombs, nor threat of war shall keep my husband from his appointed rounds!"

The pastor laughed heartily, wished them God's blessings for the rest of their trip and left to join his parishioners.

"It was nice meeting him," Nicole said as they strolled back, hand in hand.

"Even more than that, I'm glad I got to hear his ideas. If there ever ends up being a documentary about Israel, I should include Faulkner's comments about the location of the temple."

As I told that pastor, there's no doubt about his making a documentary, she thought to herself. She could see his mounting enthusiasm with every step they took. Whether on this abbreviated trip or another one someday soon, he would discover something interesting and show this magical, holy land to the millions of viewers who avidly followed Brian Sadler's adventures.

She had no idea then how quickly – and how terrifyingly – he'd fulfill that prediction.

CHAPTER SIX

The tension was palpable as Brian and Nicole walked along King David Street back to the hotel. People still strolled arm in arm, laughed over a glass of wine and a cigarette, and took dogs for walks. But in just two days, things had changed discernibly. There was a nervousness in the air that was exacerbated by soldiers standing on every corner, keeping a vigilant watch with automatic rifles cradled in their arms.

At the hotel, he called Abdel and asked him to join them for lunch tomorrow. He couldn't come, but advised he had been going to call Brian later today. "Would you like to see something far more exciting than the chalice? Would you like to see a vast hoard of relics that will make your heart jump when you consider its beauty and historical significance?"

"Absolutely," Brian replied eagerly. "Tell me more!"

"Read Isaiah 45:3 and call me back."

He described the call to Nicole. When they were in the hotel lobby, he pulled up the King James version of the Bible on his phone and read the verse out loud. "And I will give thee the treasures of darkness, and hidden riches of secret places, that thou mayest know that I, the Lord, which call thee by thy name, am the God of Israel."

Oh, my God, Nicole thought to herself, knowing exactly what he was thinking. *Here he goes again.* "We're leaving Saturday, sweetie, really early. That's two days from now. There's no time –"

"Maybe he can show me today." He was already returning Abdel's call.

"Put it on speaker," she demanded. She didn't intend to sit alone in their room while he trotted off somewhere in the boondocks. "I want to hear the conversation."

"I read the verse," he said when Malouf answered.

"Are you intrigued, Mr. Sadler? Do you want to see the treasures of darkness that God spoke about?"

"Yes, but we leave first thing Saturday and I promised Nicole we'd visit more sites in the time we have left."

"Then a visit may not be possible. It is in a cave some distance from Jerusalem. It will require a few hours' travel by car. I have been in the area before, and I assure you that you will be safe with me if you choose to amend your plans and stay to see it. You will also be amazed beyond your imagination."

"Why me? Why are you willing to show it to me?"

His answer was convincing. "I have followed your career in the antiquities field. There are few of us with the credentials you and I have. You were also a worthy opponent in our little bidding war last Tuesday evening. You deserve the opportunity to see it. Maybe someday the public will learn of its existence, but perhaps not. It could be your only chance to visit a truly unique place."

"When would we go?"

"Tomorrow, Allah willing, or perhaps another day. It will take time to make the arrangements and it is not for me to say when we go. It is possible you could make your flight on Saturday, but I won't know that until I make a call."

"Let me talk to Nicole," Brian said. "Set up the trip and call me back."

He disconnected and turned to her. "This is a once in a lifetime opportunity —"

She interrupted him with more ferocity than he'd seen in all the years they'd known each other. "Of course it is! It's always like this with you. You can't resist, can you? It doesn't matter that this whole damned country is about to be attacked by every Arab nation on the planet. It doesn't matter that the vice president of the United States was assassinated here two days ago. You don't even care that I'm in danger too. All that matters now is that some Arab you hardly know threw you a bone and you're salivating all over yourself to find out what the secret is."

"Don't you think you're overreacting?"

As soon as they were out he knew those insensitive words had been a mistake.

She jumped up and thrust her face directly into his. "As dangerous as Israel is right now, you're willing to go with this stranger somewhere that's a few hours away. He won't tell you where it is. You could even be going to another country. Let's see. Which one of the vacation spots on Israel's border will it be? Syria, Lebanon, Jordan or Egypt? Pick your poison. Every single one is pissed at Israel – and America too – but it'll all be okay because brave Brian Sadler wants to go see some treasure. Well, darling, I wish you well. I can't stop you from being an idiot. How many times have we done this? I give up. I'm going home tomorrow. I'm not going to London – I'm going home. It's no fun going somewhere I love without you. Put me on the quickest connection to Dallas, and as usual I'll see you when you're finished playing Indiana Jones."

"I'm sorry –"

Her face was red with anger. "Don't you dare say that to me! You're not sorry! You're so excited you're about to piss in your pants. I know you. Don't you understand that by now? It doesn't matter what I say."

"Yes, it does. You're my wife. If you say don't go –"

"If I say don't go, then for the rest of my life I'll be the one who stopped you from seeing Abdel's damned treasure of a lifetime. You may never mention it, but the resentment will always be there, seething just beneath the surface."

"That's not true, Nicole. I don't have to do this."

Sighing deeply, she took his hands. Her voice softened and a tear ran down one cheek. "Yes, you do. I love your spirit and your enthusiasm. I guess God's taken care of you all this time, but I'm not sure why. So far, no matter how bad things have gotten, you've managed to come back to me. You're in God's country now and you want to see His

43

treasures. I get it, Brian. I'll never fully understand it, but I get it. The excitement you feel is part of who you are and I love every bit of you. I just get tired of saying the same thing over and over. Come home, Brian. Don't leave me."

"Just one or two days. I promise."

"You also have to promise to keep Harry informed about your whereabouts." Brian's close relationship with the US president had helped him in the past.

He said he would. Abdel called shortly and advised the trip was set for Friday morning and he'd provide details later.

He knew what her answer would be but he had to ask anyway. "Since the trip's on Friday, you could wait until Saturday and fly to London with me like we'd planned."

She gave him an incredulous look and shook her head. "I'm out of here as soon as possible."

He booked a seat for the next morning on a Delta flight from Tel Aviv to JFK, where she would transfer to American for the rest of her trip. She'd leave the hotel at 4 a.m. and be home in Dallas tomorrow night.

"Ready for bed?" he said, turning out the light.

"Yeah, since one of us has an early wake-up call."

"I'll go to the airport with you."

"It's over an hour each way. You don't need to go with me and waste all that time. Just go see your damned treasure on Friday and come home."

Their lovemaking was slow and deliberate at first, but it became frenzied and wild toward the end. Steamy and sweaty, she clung tightly to him as if it would stave off the worry that was flooding her mind. Then he held her in his arms until he felt the measured breathing that meant she was asleep.

He loved this woman more than anything and wouldn't ever hurt her. *She understands me,* he reasoned, using her own words to convince himself that the chance to see something like this overruled the danger that might exist. *She's okay with this,* he said over and over until he fell asleep himself, hoping by repetition to make it true but knowing deep inside that it wasn't.

She lay next to him, pretending to be asleep but angry at herself for wanting to make love instead of withholding sex to punish him. Every time they were at this point – when he was preparing to go on another adventure – his adrenalin levels shot through the roof. His voice and actions always gave away his growing excitement. Other things grew too – his passion for adventure also affected his testosterone. The thought of another exciting trip stimulated him so thoroughly and completely that their lovemaking was a huge turn-on for her too. The sex was never better, more intense, more innovative and more thrilling than when he was about to head off into parts unknown.

I'm sending him totally opposite signals from what I should be. My own sexual desire is helping fuel his enthusiasm for something I desperately wish he wouldn't do, she admitted to herself. Then she rolled over toward him, ran her hand down his chest and shuffled down under the covers. Within minutes they were both passionate, then exhausted and satisfied, contentedly falling asleep at last in each other's arms.

Outside the hotel at 4 a.m., he kissed Nicole goodbye as she entered the limo to go to Ben Gurion Airport. She hugged him, but she didn't hide things this time. Her words were brief and cool. "Come home, Brian. Just come home," she said as she closed the door. She turned and waved through the back glass as the car pulled out of the David Citadel's porte cochere.

Upstairs, he tried to go back to sleep, but he was too excited. He searched the Internet for Isaiah 45, reading the passage in several versions, each of which described things slightly differently. He found the words *hidden treasure, riches stored in secret places, concealed wealth, treasures from dark places* and *hidden stockpiles.*

The verse in Isaiah was also cross-referenced to Matthew 13:44 in the New Testament. It was one of Jesus's parables and it spoke of treasure hidden in a field, found by someone and then reburied. He located an interpretation and read that Jesus was supposedly discussing the value of the kingdom of Heaven, a treasure of unspeakable worth. But was it truly a parable, or was Jesus describing a real hidden treasure?

A treasure of unspeakable worth. Hidden treasure stored in a secret place. A hidden stockpile from before the time of Jesus. He could hardly contain his enthusiasm.

Nicole texted him just after seven to say she had boarded. Half an hour later she texted again to say the doors were closed and they were ready to depart.

"I love you," she said.

He wrote that he loved her too and would see her Saturday. He clicked on a tracking app and followed the plane as it taxied to the runway and left for New York at 7:58 a.m.

Once he knew she was really gone, he felt an overwhelming, immense feeling of regret, as though he had deliberately shuttled her off so he could satisfy his own desires. He tried to rationalize his staying behind. She was his wife and she understood his needs. She had vigorously and willingly made love with him last night, just like always. She wasn't mad or worried or angry.

But part of him – the rational part – kept invading Brian's mind with the truth. He was forcing her to do all the giving in this relationship. *But I am a good partner,* he told himself, all the while knowing he wasn't, since her only issue with him was his indifference to his own safety.

As soon as I'm back home ... he promised himself, just like so many times before.

Abdel called around noon. "I will be in the lobby at six a.m. You will be back by three, Allah willing."

"What should I bring?"

"It will be quite warm outside, but it will be cool in the cave. Dress accordingly."

Brian booked the same itinerary for Saturday as Nicole's today, then he walked to lunch at the nearby outdoor café where he and Nicole had shared wine several times over the past week. He checked the progress of her flight, thinking how lonely it was without her. The Delta plane to New York was already halfway across the Atlantic.

At 5 p.m. his time, ten a.m. in DC, he placed a call and heard a familiar voice.

"Cynthia Beal," said the president's longtime personal assistant and most trusted aide. She had been a huge help to Nicole in planning their wedding at the White House, and the three of them had become good friends.

"Good morning. It's Brian Sadler."

"Hi, Brian. How are you and Nicole?"

"We're fine, thanks. Are you doing well?"

"As well as can be with all that's going on. What a tragedy about the vice president. You guys were with him the night before, weren't you?"

"Yes, briefly. What a great man – he'll be missed. It's really crazy here with all that's happening."

"You're still in Jerusalem? Why are you still there? I can't imagine how worried Nicole must be with everything going on."

"She left this morning and she's on the way home as we speak. I was here for an antiquities auction and I'm staying another couple of days to meet with a dealer who wants to show me some relics. That's what I was calling Harry about. Nicole made me promise to let him know what I was doing, but I can only imagine how much he has going on and I shouldn't waste his time. Just tell him I'm going with Abdel Malouf early tomorrow morning to a location he's keeping to himself. He says it's a cave that has some artifacts. It has something to do with Isaiah 45:3. Tell Harry I'm just following my wife's orders and checking in!"

She laughed. "I'll drop your message in his inbox. And have you checked in with the embassy? If not, I'll let them know your whereabouts."

Brian hadn't and said he would appreciate her doing that, even though he didn't think he would need any assistance from the ambassador's staff. It never hurt to keep in touch, he agreed.

When the president returned to the Oval Office later that morning, she told him about Brian's call. They had last spoken shortly after the bombing and he didn't realize Brian was still in Israel. The message surprised him and he called his scheduling assistant.

"I need half an hour ASAP with Stan Kendrick and Bob Cruickshank over at Langley. Tell them it's about Abdel Malouf." Two hours later the CIA boss and his Mossad chief were sitting in the Oval Office.

"With everything going on in Israel, I'm sorry to pull you away," the president began, "but I think we have something to consider. Stan, you know Brian Sadler, but, Bob, I'm not sure you do."

He nodded. "Yes, sir. I know him by reputation. Mr. Sadler's pretty famous."

Like millions of other armchair adventurers, Cruickshank knew quite a bit about Brian. His gallery, Bijan Rarities, had locations in Dallas, New Orleans and London, and his clients included some of the world's wealthiest people. The documentaries Brian had hosted for History and Discovery were devoured by people like him who loved the way Brian could weave an intriguing story around fascinating objects that had been hidden for centuries. Cruickshank also knew Brian Sadler had been the president's best friend since their college days and that Harrison had served recently as his best man.

"He's in Jerusalem," Harry said, to Cruickshank's surprise. "It was a coincidence – he was there with his wife to attend an auction. They had drinks with Don Case the night before the bombing. Earlier I asked Brian to have a chat with Abdel Malouf before he leaves Israel. He knows the guy as a colleague and they were bidders at an auction the same evening Don was murdered."

He continued. "Sounds like Brian did better than I'd hoped. He left a message a little while ago. Tomorrow morning Malouf is taking him to a secret location a few hours from Jerusalem to see something. That'll give Brian time to feel him out."

Kendrick asked, "What are they going to see?"

"Brian says it's some relics. And Brian says Abdel asked him to read Isaiah 45:3 before they went."

Cruickshank raised his eyebrows. "Isaiah 45:3? Now that *is* interesting. Do you think Mr. Sadler or Abdel Malouf know what it means?"

Harry was surprised. He'd intended to ask them to find out about it, but it was obvious that the Mossad desk chief already knew. "I looked up the verse after Brian told me, but I didn't get much from it. What do you think it means?"

"Well, sir, there have always been rumors in Israel about hidden treasure that used to be in the Second Temple thousands of years ago. Many scholars believe Isaiah 45 isn't a parable – it's a reference to real treasure."

"Interesting," Harry commented. "This changes things. I originally asked you here to see what else we can find out about Abdel Malouf. I don't want Brian getting into something way over his head. The threat of war and his bullheadedness is bad enough. I want to know anything you can dig up about Malouf and ties to AQS."

He paused and then said, "And you might as well dig into Isaiah 45:3 while you're at it. Let me know if you find out anything pertinent."

CHAPTER SEVEN

The ringing of his phone jarred Brian out of a deep sleep. He fumbled for the nightstand and grabbed it on the fourth ring, just before it would have gone to voicemail.

"Yeah?" he slurred, glancing at the bedside clock. It was 3:30 a.m.

"I know it's the middle of the night there," Harry said. "Do you know what's happened?" His serious tone and clipped words brought Brian fully alert.

"No. What's going on?"

"The airport in Tel Aviv was destroyed two hours ago. Nicole left yesterday – is that right?"

"Yes." He mentally calculated the time difference. "She went to New York and changed planes. She should be in Dallas in a couple of hours. Thanks for asking about her."

"We believe they deliberately planned the attack for today because it's the Sabbath. The terminal building was destroyed, and so were three planes from European cities that were docked there. Early estimates are maybe four hundred people dead, but that'll rise, I'm sure. Israelis, Americans, Europeans – lots of nationalities were there, like always in Israel. Since it happened about 1:15 a.m., the casualties were less than if it had been in the daytime, but there are flights in and out of Tel Aviv all night long. The place never shuts down."

"All that loss of life – it's tragic, Harry. What kind of bomb was it?"

"It wasn't a bomb. It was a Bulgaria Airlines Airbus 320 flown by a pilot and copilot who had been with the company for several years. The plane left Sofia with 158 passengers on its usual biweekly run to Tel Aviv. There was nothing unusual until it was on final approach. At the last minute, it pulled up and rammed the terminal. It looks like no one on board survived."

"What do you think happened?"

"It might have been a hijacking – the Mossad's checking passenger manifests. If some group claims responsibility, maybe we'll know what's going on. Meanwhile, the country is locked down and every airport's closed. There won't be flights for a couple of days, maybe longer. The government will have to decide if they're going to convert a military airfield to civilian use, but right now that's the last thing on the PM's list. He's determined to stop all this and I've committed that we'll help."

"The USA is going to get involved?"

"One way or another. Our fleet in the Mediterranean's on full alert. It all depends ..." He paused. "Hold a minute. Something's happening."

As he waited, Brian turned on CNN and watched the carnage just an hour's drive from where he was. The airport was a smoldering ruin and emergency vehicles were everywhere. Those who were lucky enough to survive and could walk were being herded to safety. EMTs were attending to others. The destroyed airplanes looked like the aftermath of an angry kid playing with his toys.

"Al Qaeda in Syria's claiming responsibility," Harry said when he came back on the line. "Do you recall who its leader is?"

Brian said he, Nicole and Don Case had talked about Tariq over drinks the night before Don was killed.

"This creates a new situation as far as the USA's concerned. The AQS statement says two of their people breached the flight deck and martyred themselves for Allah. We must get involved now because this isn't just about Israel anymore. Tariq's hated America – and me personally – ever since we caught him in his cozy deal with President Parkes. We should have taken the bastard out then. As the head of AQS, he's more powerful than ever. His men murdered Don Case four days ago. We'll figure out the best way to help Israel. Until you can get out, I want you to move to the embassy. I'll make a call and they'll contact you. Hopefully they can get you moved tomorrow morning. The David Citadel's a secure hotel but so was the American Colony and look what happened there."

Brian had his heart set on seeing whatever treasure Abdel was going to show him. What Harry was saying was right – simply being in Israel now was dangerous, but he was intent on seeing the treasure. If he turned himself in at the embassy, he was sure he'd end up a virtual prisoner in the compound for his own safety.

"Did you get my message about going to see –"

"I did," Harry interrupted. "I was all for it at first, because it would give you time alone with Abdel to feel him out. But that's all off now. I'm asking – no, I'm *ordering* you not to do it. It's just too risky. Don't even think about it. Get with the ambassador and get on the next flight out of there. Charter a plane if you have to – anything."

"You're *ordering* me, Harry? You're beginning to sound like Nicole," he said, trying to be funny while he watched his adventure slipping away.

"This isn't a joke, Brian. Don't you see how the airport bombing changes everything? Israel was already preparing for war but the PM has declared that any strike now will be retaliatory, not preemptive. Do you understand the implications of that? Israel could strike first and I can't argue with that line of reasoning."

Harry wrestled over whether to tell him more about the man he was meeting. Most of Abdel's file was still highly classified. Surely he could talk Brian into getting out of Israel instead of going with the Arab to God knows where.

Brian, on the other hand, was consumed with this adventure. He used the same hollow words he'd said to himself time and again in these situations. *This is just who I am.* But he also knew the truth – he was as much an addict as a heroin user.

He trusted Abdel, a man he'd never met until a few days before. He rationalized that they were members of a very small group of men and women whose galleries had handled some of the world's most significant rarities. Malouf had been in business in Jerusalem for years, and Brian convinced himself there was a kinship.

"It's not that far away," he explained, minimizing what Abdel had told him. "We're leaving at sunrise and we'll be back after lunch. They're not going to start a war today, Harry. Of all people, you know politics doesn't work that way."

"In Israel and under the circumstances, it'll work a hell of a lot faster than you think," the president replied sternly. "I'm surprised at you. I'm surprised I'm trying to talk you out of this when, as smart as you are, you should be agreeing with me that the dangers far outweigh whatever relics this guy's trying to show you. Malouf's not who you think he is, Brian. I can't tell you more and I must leave it at that, but I'm strongly advising you not to go with him. We can't offer you protection if no one even knows where you're going."

"I know he's a Syrian. If that's the thing you can't tell me, I already know it. I've known him by reputation ever since I got into this business. I've never heard anything bad about him. He's been an Israeli citizen for decades. I lost a bidding war to him Tuesday. He wrote a check for four hundred and fifty thousand dollars, so he obviously also has financial resources. Harry, if he's a terrorist then tell me. But if he's an antiquities dealer like me who just happens to be Syrian, I want to go see this cave."

"I've registered my concern. I can't force you to do anything. Does Nicole know about all this?"

"Leave her out of it!" Brian shot back more forcefully than he intended. "She knows and she's not thrilled either, but she's okay with my going. She understands." That was a lie and Brian knew it. She didn't understand and she never would. Sometimes he didn't either. Occasionally in times like this - okay, being totally honest, almost always – he let his enthusiasm outweigh caution and reason. It had always worked out before and as fear and doubt crept into his mind right now, he replaced them with confidence and excitement.

After the call, Brian tracked Nicole's flight. It was scheduled to land in Dallas in ninety minutes. He hoped

Harry wouldn't call her – as much as he appreciated his concern, he needed just twenty-four hours to see whatever it was Abdel wanted to show him. He rationalized that he couldn't leave now anyway – Harry had said the country was locked down. But that didn't worry Brian. His biggest concern was if the cave wasn't in Israel. With the borders closed, how would they get to it?

It was already 3:45 a.m. and they were set to leave at six. If the trip were off, he'd have heard from Abdel by now. There was a new adventure brewing. He convinced himself his tinge of fear was nothing but nervous jitters.

Before returning to bed, he left a voicemail for Nicole, explaining that the Tel Aviv Airport bombing had led to a lockdown of the borders. He was going with Abdel in a couple of hours and would be back at the hotel by mid-afternoon. He promised to contact the embassy then and ask them how he might leave Israel. If commercial flights weren't an option soon, he'd try to charter a private jet.

CHAPTER EIGHT

Brian was in the lobby early, sipping a coffee he'd brewed in his room. When Abdel walked in, he asked if the trip was still on.

Abdel nodded. "The driver checked the route. There are two ways to go north and we are taking the faster one. It runs close to the border, but so far there are no closures. We may encounter checkpoints along the way; you should take your passport."

Brian patted his shirt pocket. They went outside, climbed into an older model Land Rover and pulled away. The first pink streaks of dawn painted the skies over the Temple Mount as the driver headed out of the city.

"This is Mohammed," Abdel said from the front passenger seat. "He drives for me often and he speaks no English."

"You said we're going north. I heard the borders are closed, so I presume we're staying in Israel."

"You are asking questions I cannot answer. You will be safe, as I said earlier. You must cover your eyes for the last of the trip. For now, the exact location must remain a secret."

"That's fine," Brian replied with a shiver of doubt. Once they were out of the city, he clicked his watch to digital compass mode and saw they were going east. By the time the sun was completely up, they had passed through Jericho and were traveling north on Highway 90, a route Brian had earlier been cautioned to avoid. The guide they used had said that the new Israeli toll road was a safer, more comfortable alternative to the border road they were on today. These days it could be riskier, but it was still the fastest route to the north – if it was open.

They drove for a couple of hours, often within sight of the border. When they were close, they saw lines of Jordanian tanks and trucks and hundreds of soldiers setting up camps. Almost the only other traffic on the two-lane highway was convoys of military vehicles moving into position on the Israeli side. The heightened activity made for a tense ride, and Brian's enthusiasm was tempered – but only a little – by a feeling that this could get dangerous.

Abdel brought up the bombings and expressed his disgust at the assassinations. He told Brian he had moved from Syria twenty years ago and had built both his gallery and his reputation in the Muslim Quarter of the Old City. He admitted that while he enjoyed Jerusalem, he had no love for the Jewish people. Regardless, there was no honor in committing terrorism and murder, he said.

Brian asked if things would be different under Prime Minister Shigon. Abdel thought things would change, but not in a good way. The choice of Shigon was a knee-jerk reaction by the Knesset, he added, but Shigon's hawkish, insular stance would only increase tensions between Jews and Palestinians and incite the Arab nations that surrounded Israel.

"Pardon me for saying so," he continued, "but your friend President Harrison's decision to move the embassy to Jerusalem didn't do anything to help the situation. It infuriated the Palestinians even more and achieved absolutely nothing for America. Other presidents have left the issue alone. It was a slap in the face to everyone except America's friends the Jews."

Brian was acutely aware of how inflammatory the subject was. He and Harry had discussed it several times, most recently as they were engaged in a lively debate about one of Harry's favorite subjects, eschatology – the study of the end times as predicted in the Bible. Harry strongly believed that God was on Israel's side in a war that had gone on for two thousand years and that would continue until the day in the valley of Megiddo when Armageddon – the great war between good and evil that would end the world – would take place.

Brian was surprised when Abdel commented about his friendship with Harry. It certainly was no secret, but it wasn't something he or the president talked openly about with others. However, with the Internet and a plethora of cable networks today, there were no real secrets left in the world, he told himself, hoping that was how Abdel knew.

Abdel interrupted Brian's thoughts. "Israel is closer to war at this moment than at any time since 1967," he suggested. "I worry about what will happen to my gallery if the Jews lock down the Old City. I'm afraid looters would take everything. I want to move out some of the more valuable pieces, but I have nowhere secure to store them."

"If there's any way you think I could be of assistance, I'd be happy to do so," Brian offered. It would be simple to create an agreement under which Abdel could ship his relics to one of Brian's galleries until things cooled down. It would be less simple to work out the physical part – how to move fragile, priceless and bulky objects through the narrow, crowded streets of the Old City and then sixty miles to the airport in Tel Aviv once it eventually reopened. Brian's offer was sincere – he knew other dealers who had done similar things for colleagues who had troubles, and he knew others would do it for him if he needed help.

Abdel seemed genuinely touched by the offer and quickly accepted it. "We should talk more about this back in Jerusalem. Perhaps you can come to my shop tomorrow evening to work out the details," he said.

After they'd been driving two hours, Abdel turned, handed Brian a hood made of black cloth and said, "It's time. You won't wear it for long."

It'll be all right, he assured himself from under the hood as he felt goosebumps on his arms. *Just stay calm. Abdel's a friend.*

When the SUV rolled to a stop, Brian felt a rush of warm air as the driver lowered his window and spoke to someone in rapid Arabic. Abdel had insinuated they weren't leaving Israel, although he hadn't said so directly. Now he began to worry. This could be a problem.

We're at the border.

"Are we still in Israel?"

"Yes. We are not leaving. Just a few more minutes."

The Land Rover lurched forward. Now they were off the paved road and driving on what felt like cobblestones. Brian bounced up and down for five minutes and the vehicle stopped again.

"You may take off the hood and get out," Abdel advised, and Brian was ready. It was getting hot as hell under the cloth and he needed fresh air. They had parked on top of a hill. He walked to the edge and his fears disappeared. He looked down a valley where the rays of the morning sun illuminated a sprawling, ruined city. There were stately rows of ancient columns twenty feet tall that were reminiscent of Greece or Rome. He saw temples, baths and a huge amphitheater, all connected by streets paved with flagstones. For more than a mile in every direction, he saw debris from hundreds of stone buildings long ago destroyed by war, neglect or abandonment. Then he noticed a modern feature – a parking lot lay in the distance. There were people walking around here and there; the place appeared to be a tourist destination.

Where the hell am I?

"Okay, what is this incredible city?" he asked, but Abdel only smiled and shook a finger at him.

"Be grateful that I allowed you to see the vista below us. I knew it would intrigue you, even though you don't know what it is. I could have taken you directly to the cave without stopping at this wonderful ancient city, but we are professionals, after all, and you deserve to see it."

"The construction is obviously Roman. Do I see Byzantine too?"

"It's a bit of both, actually. It is one of the oldest cities in this region. It was already ancient when the prophet Isaiah wrote about hidden treasure. Now we must go in the car again and you must don the hood for five minutes. Soon you will see something even more wonderful than the city below us."

When the car stopped and one of the front doors opened, Brian reached for his hood, but Abdel said, "Leave it on for another few moments. I must lead you to the place we are going."

He took Brian's arm and guided him down a slope, gripping him tightly when the soil became slippery. "Be careful," he cautioned. Brian clumsily plodded downhill through trees and scrub. Abdel slowed his pace, then stopped for a moment.

He took Brian's arm again, pulling him into thick, waist-high brush.

"Can I see where I'm going so I don't fall?" Brian asked.

"Allah is with the patient. I am looking for something. We are almost there."

Moments later they stopped and Abdel removed his hood. It was just the two of them; the driver must have remained with the SUV. They were standing on the edge of a steep rock face that overlooked a valley below.

"It is more difficult from here," Abdel said, pulling aside the branches of a tall, sturdy shrub and wrapping his fingers around a rope. "I will go first. It's only twenty feet. Are you afraid of heights?"

Brian wasn't, and he watched Abdel shinny down the knotted rope and then call for him to follow. At the bottom, there was a wide ledge covered in brush. Abdel pushed a thick bramble aside and pointed to a dark hole about four feet in diameter. "In there," he said, handing Brian a headlamp.

Just past the opening, the cave widened to about ten feet high and five in width. Behind them dim sunlight filtered in from the entrance. Just ahead was a corridor heading off into the darkness, its entrance flanked by a pair of extraordinary objects.

"What the hell are these doing here?" Brian asked, astounded to see two life-sized Egyptian statues carved from stone. "It's a pharaoh," he muttered, thinking he could easily be in the Giza plateau instead of somewhere in Israel. "That's Ramesses III, isn't it? How did these get here?"

"Your knowledge of ancient things continues to surprise me, Brian. You are correct. It is the pharaoh

Ramesses himself. As you may know, what is now Israel was once part of the land of Canaan. There were several wars, the last of which ended in victory for the Israelites, who have occupied this land off and on ever since.

"You pointed out Roman and Byzantine construction in the city I showed you. If you were to walk its ancient streets, you would see Egyptian influence there as well. In the city there are statues, a sphinx and other things that confirm the Egyptians coexisted with the Canaanites. You also find them in other cities such as Jaffa and Hazor."

"How long ago was that?"

"Ramesses III ruled in the middle of the twelfth century before the common era, about three thousand two hundred years ago. He was the strongest pharaoh of his time. In the hundred years after his reign, there were several more rulers named Ramesses, each of whom was weak and unable to challenge the Canaanites. So that is the reason you see the influence of Egypt – particularly Ramesses III – here in this ancient city. What are two statues doing here in this cavern? We likely will never know. The place I am about to show you is a storehouse for wonderful things. These statues lead me to conclude that it could also have been a hiding place for sacred Egyptian objects as well and perhaps even a burial site. But I am getting off the subject. We should go now; we only have an hour here."

Abdel led the way down the narrow passageway past the two statues. They walked a hundred feet along a descending corridor and came to a fork. To the left the path continued down a passage as large as the one they'd just traversed. The corridor to the right was simply a crawl space. And that was the way Abdel pointed.

"From here the passage is very tight, but it isn't far and I promise you'll find it worth the effort." He bent over and went into the opening, shuffling along as Brian followed. Being a couple of inches shorter, Abdel maneuvered more easily beneath the five-foot ceiling than his tall American friend.

Brian had been in his share of caves and he wasn't typically claustrophobic, but his heart began to race as the walls narrowed, creating a tight viselike corridor. His arms touched the sides and he was forced not only to keep his back bent but now he had to turn sideways and sidle through, his backside against one wall and his head an inch from the other. It was damp and clammy. *It's like a tomb*, Brian thought, forcing himself to concentrate on what lay ahead. Abdel seemed to be fine, skittering down the dank passageway with no apparent discomfort.

"How much longer?"

"One minute – maybe two," Abdel's muffled voice in front of him responded. "Are you all right?"

"Yes." He was sure he could last that long, but he was getting goose bumps as he wondered what would happen if he couldn't go any farther. What if the passageway ahead of them had become blocked since the last time Abdel was here? It was so cramped there would be only one way to get out – dropping to his knees, lying on one side and shuffling backwards up the narrow tunnel like an earthworm. Cold beads of sweat formed on his forehead and he noticed a sickening acidic taste in his mouth.

Just then Abdel spoke, his voice clear now, and Brian could see his light. He had reached the end and turned around. Thank God! Brian scrambled out, his bones cracking as he stood upright and stretched. It was markedly cooler; there was a breeze wafting through the corridor now that it wasn't blocked by humans.

Abdel noticed the sweat pouring off Brian and asked again if he was okay. Brian assured him things were fine now and he turned to look at the place where he stood.

All thought of the stress and effort it took to get into this subterranean grotto vanished as he slowly moved his eyes from one end to the other. Even though the only light in the large chamber came from two tiny headlamps, there was no way to mistake the significance of what lay in front of him. There was gold everywhere – incredible, priceless artifacts lying in piles as though they were rubbish in a landfill. There were surely hundreds of pieces, perhaps thousands. Statues lay on the ground, their faces staring in timeless grandeur. He saw chests and torahs, flatware and scrolls, ornate screens and tiny vases – each of them lovingly created from solid gold.

"I can't believe it," he whispered as he became woozy and felt his legs giving way. He found himself in a pose of reverence, kneeling on the dirt floor with his head bowed, gasping for breath. He was in the prayer posture, a position that somehow seemed natural in this place.

Abdel stood behind him, unable to understand the reverence Brian was experiencing.

"Didn't I say it was unbelievable?" he said at last.

"There are no words that could have prepared me for this," he responded, slowly rising to his feet. "This is the most breathtaking sight I have ever beheld. There are more wonderful things in this cavern than in all the museums in Israel. I feel as though God is here in this room, surrounded by the treasures of His people."

Now Abdel understood. He had been here many times in the past. He always remembered his own first time and how awed he had been at the sight. He explained how his own feelings had overwhelmed him. Every time he laid eyes on this place, it was truly spectacular, even if he believed that Brian's statement about the Israelites being God's chosen people was untrue.

Grinning like a schoolboy in love, Brian walked around the massive room, taking in one pile of relics after another. Deciding the glow of his headlamp wasn't sufficient, he took out his phone and turned on the flashlight.

"No!" Abdel shouted when he saw the bright light. "No pictures!"

"That wasn't what I was doing," Brian shot back in surprise. "I was using it to see better. Is that okay?"

Abdel nodded and Brian asked why he couldn't shoot photos.

"For the moment, this discovery is mine alone. If you and I reach an agreement on how you might be involved in it, then by all means we can discuss photos ... perhaps even a documentary on television."

Those words echoed Brian's own thoughts. He was content to be an observer if there was a chance he could reveal this extraordinary discovery to the world. Since there would be no pictures to document exactly where the items lay, Brian insisted on one thing, declaring that they shouldn't move anything because everything in the room eventually must be photographed and cataloged in situ for archaeological preservation and documentation. Only after the experts were done could anything be moved. Abdel was more dealer than archaeologist, but he agreed. He'd been guilty of taking artifacts now and then in the past, but this discovery was something entirely different. The bulk of the objects lay where they had been placed two thousand years before and they were truly unique.

Many years ago, long before Brian grew up and became a real archaeological adventurer, he'd dreamed of hidden caches of treasure and read everything he could get his hands on about amazing discoveries. One surprising place he learned about buried secrets was at church in Longview, Texas. His parents never missed a service, and as a child in Sunday school, he'd heard the words of Ezra, a minor prophet whose book in the Bible wasn't that significant to many people, but to a boy already fascinated with treasure-hunting, Ezra's descriptions were exciting. Enthralled with its story, he had read and reread the book. Ezra had accompanied a vast treasure when King Cyrus of Persia told the Israelites to bring it back to Jerusalem. He had been there and his book described the temple and the gold and silver objects it contained – the very things that lay before Brian at this moment.

Using Ezra's words as a jumping-off point, he'd researched other parts of the Bible – Second Kings, Second Chronicles and Isaiah – reading fascinating accounts of massive caches of silver and gold objects that had long since disappeared. Decades later, that child who'd been fascinated with biblical tales was standing in a cavern, seeing the real thing. He was overwhelmed by the splendor of it all and awed by the knowledge that twenty-five-hundred-year-old words from the Bible were literally true. As had happened so many times through the centuries, once again God's word was proven to be fact, not fiction.

That knowledge was the most awe-inspiring thing to Brian as he stood in the cavern. He maneuvered the room carefully, illuminating the floor with his phone to avoid stepping on anything. He sidestepped stacks of golden shields, drinking vessels, bowls and cutlery lying in disarray. He imagined how it must have been that day in AD 70 with the temple and most of Jerusalem going up in flames. The high priests and trusted servants must have pushed and shoved their ways through crowded streets, guiding donkeys pulling heavy carts. Brian visualized these priceless objects – hundreds of them – hidden under heavy cloths. Once away from the hubbub, the priests would have begun the long journey to this remote place. Maybe long ago other Israelites had used this hiding place also. Maybe this was the very cave where five hundred years before, King Cyrus had brought the Israelites to redeem treasure hidden before they were taken into captivity.

Brian imagined that night two thousand years ago when priests stood on the very spot, urging servants to hurry and unload the hoard. There was no time to lovingly arrange the sacred objects. They were tossed haphazardly about in hopes they would be safe from the Roman invaders. Someday the temple would be rebuilt and someone would come for them. Two millennia had passed; so far there was no new structure on the Temple Mount. But Brian believed what the Bible said about the Third Temple. Despite the Muslims' sacred Dome of the Rock that sat majestically atop the hill, the Jews would somehow build a new temple, fulfilling prophecy and signaling the end of days for people on Earth.

Something interesting amid a stack of golden goblets and urns brought him out of his reverie. He dropped to his knees and, without touching it, examined it closely. It was a small rectangular chest sheathed in gold and crowned by two winged cherubs, their childlike faces beaming in delight.

Abdel saw what he was doing and knelt beside him. When he got a close look, he was astounded. When he had been here before, he had never seen it. "Is it ... could that be ..."

"The Ark of the Covenant?" Brian replied, his eyes ablaze with wonder. "As amazing as that discovery would be, I'm sorry to say this isn't the Ark. The book of Exodus gives its dimensions and this one's far too small. I've done a decent amount of research on the subject. According to the Bible, the Ark was one of the treasures of the First Temple, but it disappeared. When King Cyrus freed the Jews, they got their treasure back, but the Ark wasn't part of it. This small one fascinates me, regardless. I think this was a replica for public display, smaller than the original but identical to it. We may not be looking at the Ark of the Covenant, but the man who created this beauty probably sat in front of the original Ark and copied the design. That's incredibly exciting to think about!"

Abdel nodded and Brian surprised him when he said, "Let's see if we can find another one."

He swept his light across the piles of relics and saw another exactly like the first.

"Aha! There it is!"

"How did you know there would be two?"

"From research. The public areas of the temple were laid out symmetrically. I'd bet you'll discover that lots of the objects in this cave are pairs."

They talked about how the arks and the vast array of other relics – some tall and graceful such as candlesticks, others short and stubby like drinking glasses, cups and wine goblets – must have occupied prominent spots in that sacred building, according to the scriptures.

The minutes flew by as they knelt to observe as many beautiful pieces as they could. Abdel had promised only one hour and the time was up far sooner than Brian wished. They maneuvered back up the tight, narrow passageway and stretched their backs at the cave entrance. Then they climbed the rope and stood on the edge of the cliff. Abdel handed him the hood.

"I must come back, you know," Brian said as he put it on.

"If it is Allah's will, you shall."

CHAPTER NINE

Despite what his boss believed, Abdel Malouf's young driver Mohammed understood English very well. He and five other twenty-year-olds had spent two years at an al Qaeda training camp deep in the Syrian desert. In addition to English, they were taught skills and trades to make them employable by Jews and Palestinians in Israel. Instructors taught Mohammed to drive, and now he had both an Israeli driver's license and a commercial taxi certificate. He had required only one more thing to be legitimate – a list of references. Creating one was a simple matter, and soon Mohammed appeared to have a loyal following of Israeli clients who raved about their clean-cut, polite young driver.

They furnished him a reliable Land Rover – not so new as to be conspicuous but perfectly acceptable for chauffeuring people around town. He kept it impeccably clean inside and out and always courteously turned his radio low so it wouldn't disturb his passengers ... and so he could hear their conversations. It always surprised him how openly people would talk in the backseat as though he were simply a fixture instead of a human with an iPhone in his lap that recorded every word.

He arranged to meet his handler Jamel at the usual place. The men swapped phones and Abdel said, "Tell the leader this one is special. Abdel took an American to Beth Shean yesterday to show him something. He made his passenger – a man named Brian – wear a hood part of the time so he wouldn't know where we were going. And listen to this. The American is a friend of President Harrison's. Another thing – Abdel wants to move his most valuable pieces out of the Old City before Israel shuts everything down. He asked his friend to help him do that."

"What did they do at Beth Shean?"

"I don't know because Abdel instructed me to stay with the car where I parked it on a hill above the ruins. Abdel led the man away while he was still hooded. They walked northwest and disappeared into some trees. I was afraid to follow for fear he would see me. They were gone about an hour. As we drove back, they both seemed very happy and Abdel said they had seen wonderful things of incredible value. And he said that if ISIS or al Qaeda take control of Israel, they will surely destroy not only the city but also whatever things he showed the infidel."

"You will hear from me if the leader has questions," Jamel said when Mohammed was finished. He handed over an envelope with fifty American dollars in it and dismissed him. Tariq would be very interested in the recording. Abdel had been a soldier for decades, but al Qaeda hadn't used him in a long, long time. Despite that, the organization always kept a tight rein on its operatives within Israel. In past years, the Jews had turned some of them, and it had caused significant setbacks to the jihadist cause. Today things were even more stringent. With war a distinct possibility, the leader wouldn't tolerate defectors without exacting swift and horrible retribution. Only a month ago a traitor's body had been flayed while he was still alive and hung on a cross. His wife received a video in the mail, showing the gory execution, a terrifying reminder of the brutal nature of al Qaeda's young leader.

Mohammed pocketed his new phone and the money and drove home. He was scheduled to drive Abdel again soon. Hopefully after that one his wallet would be even fatter.

CHAPTER TEN

"This is the White House switchboard. Please hold for a call from the president."

No matter how many times he heard them, those words still made Brian pause. He'd known Harry Harrison since they were roommates at Oklahoma University. He'd watched his friend become a congressman from Oklahoma, then a United States senator and finally the running mate for President John Chapman, whose mysterious death had made Harry commander-in-chief.

No matter how long you've known someone, Brian reflected, *it makes your heart jump a little when you're told that the president of the United States is calling.*

"Hello, Brian. I hear Nicole's safely home and that's good news. But how about you? Did you go to the cavern with Abdel Malouf?"

"I did. I saw the treasures. It's hard to find words to describe them. If I can turn this into a documentary, it'll bring the Old Testament to life. Some of the pieces undoubtedly date back to the First Temple – the time of King Solomon. They're fascinating. They're absolutely incredible ..." He paused, realizing how shallow his vain attempt to find the right adjectives sounded. "I have to do a little more work here before I can come home."

Despite his deep concern for Brian's welfare, his friend's excitement made Harry smile. Even volatile political instability couldn't dampen this guy's enthusiasm for adventure.

"It doesn't matter if there are assassinations or airport bombings or saber-rattling, right?"

"Come on, Harry. I don't think it's as bad as that. You're as paranoid as Nicole is!"

Harry's tone changed. "I have a little advice and you can take it or leave it. You're too flippant about all this. You're one of the smartest people I know, so it's not that you're ignorant of the danger around you. It's because you choose to focus on what you want and ignore the rest.

"You're my best friend but I'm not married to you. Don't make light of how she feels. She has a whole different investment in you since you tied the knot. You're her future, and vice versa. Every time you scared the hell out of her before, it was her boyfriend who was in trouble. Now it's her life partner – her soulmate. I'm not trying to preach to you but there's no way to sugarcoat the facts. You need to think about her as much as you do yourself, Brian. Maybe you need to slow things down a little. Indiana Jones always gets away in the end, but this isn't a movie. What's developing in Israel is downright terrifying. You're right in the thick of it. It must seem ten times worse in person. If you won't accept that danger's all around you, maybe you need a reality check."

His friend's words stung and Brian struggled to shrug off his own concern – the fear he pushed down inside himself so that he could accomplish his goals. Harry was right. So was Nicole. But he knew the tremendous potential of a documentary about this extraordinary cavern.

"I really appreciate your advice. It means a lot to me. I'm trying to convince Abdel to take me back to Beth Shean one more time. Then I'll be on the first plane home."

Beth Shean? Harry knew where Brian had been but he was surprised he knew it too. "How do you know that's where you were? I thought you said Abdel kept it a secret."

"Simple. Since we never crossed a border, I googled ancient cities in Israel. I found a few and when I saw Beth Shean, that was it. There was a picture of the city from the same hill where I stood myself."

It was time to level with Brian. "I'm going to tell you something about Abdel – something confidential that I hoped I didn't have to mention. Now that you insist on going back with him, you need to know what he may be. Malouf's been on the CIA watch list for years. He conducts himself

72

like thousands of other Arabs living in Israel, but in the past, he associated with some characters who were linked to al Qaeda. Granted, it's hard to grow up in Syria without running into jihadists. Whatever he was or still is, the Mossad's still keeping an eye on him even after all these years."

Brian was amazed. Of all people, Abdel didn't seem the type – he was a little on the meek side, someone other kids might have called a chicken when he was little.

"I can hardly believe it. I wouldn't think he could be involved in anything like that." But he also knew it could be true. You couldn't always pick out the good guys in an environment where there were so many ethnicities, religions, backgrounds and political agendas thrown together in one small piece of real estate.

"We talked in the car yesterday," Brian advised. "He said he was sorry about the assassinations and that even though he didn't like the Jews in particular, terrorism wasn't the way to deal with them. I asked him about Shigon and he said it was a poor choice – a knee-jerk reaction against the Arabs. He said Shigon's such a hawk that it'll only make things worse with the Palestinians and the countries that border Israel."

"That's interesting information and in other circumstances I'd ask you to see if he'll talk about AQS. I doubt he'd tell you anything, but his body language might be revealing. All that said, I honestly hope you *don't* see him again. I'm begging you as a friend to get the hell out of there right now. But I also know what a bullheaded guy you are and that you're going to do this your way."

"I wish you'd stop mincing words." Brian laughed, wishing he were as jubilant as he tried to appear. "If I can work out this one last trip I'll have plenty of time to talk with him in the car. After that I'll leave the country, Harry. I'm not crazy and I'm not trying to put myself in danger. I think it's important that the world sees what Abdel's shown me."

He paused a moment as he recalled something Harry had said. "I have a question. All this concern for me is purely because of the chance that war's going to break out – right?

73

You're not saying I'm in danger if I go back with him, right? Abdel's as far from a terrorist –"

"Listen to me! Who knows what Abdel really is? I certainly don't – neither do you. Nobody else in Washington or Tel Aviv does either. The Mossad has no record of any recent contact between him and al Qaeda, nor has he been back to Syria in years, but you're never a former jihadist. If you're in, you're in for life. Tariq the Hawk makes sure of that. If Abdel was AQS, he was likely a low-level operative twenty years ago. I wouldn't send you into danger on purpose, but I can't promise you anything. Is Abdel a direct threat? Our intel indicates not, but we don't rely a hundred percent on anything we hear from the Middle East. Just being in Israel today is risky. It's a hotbed of seething anger ringed by hostile neighbors."

"Point taken," Brian responded, again trying to be positive. "A minute ago, you mentioned there were two things I need to know. What's the other one?"

"I can't say much; everything's evolving as we speak and the details are top secret. Your greatest danger isn't Abdel – it's war. Israel's on the very brink – you must see evidence of it every time you step outside. Security is at the highest threat level. Its Arab neighbors – Jordan, Syria, Lebanon and Egypt – are staging troops, and Israel's countering with forces of its own. I believe Shigon's the perfect man for PM at this point. He won't back down from conflict. I really don't think he'll start something, but he'll damned sure respond if someone else does."

"I saw troop buildups the other day when we were driving near the Jordanian border. The tanks and missile launchers are everywhere on both sides."

"I'm sure you noticed more fighter jets in the skies. Those aren't just Israel's – they're also ours. Listen to me, Brian. The one thing that's critical is your safety. I urge you to leave today. I'm advising you, friend to friend and as your president, that you must get out while you can. Let the embassy arrange a driver to take you to one of the smaller airports right now. You can fly to Europe and be in London by tonight. If you insist on staying in Israel, I can't guarantee when – or even if – you'll come home. I don't want that on my conscience. With one phone call I could have you detained and deported. But I won't do it that way because you're my friend. Don't push your luck. You have no idea how close to war they are and when it could start. Just come home."

Just come home. The exact words Nicole had said when he put her in a sedan to the airport.

"Thanks, Harry. I'll be careful and I'll leave as soon as I can."

The president sighed. "Dammit, you're as stubborn as you've always been. Stay safe, my friend. Keep in touch with the embassy and give them your whereabouts. And good luck."

Harry hung up and so did Stan Kendrick, who was sitting across the desk. He had asked the CIA director to listen in and give his assessment of the conversation. He wished he could have told Brian someone else was on the line, but these were difficult times. His friend was on the fringe of a very dangerous situation. He'd tried to tell Brian that, but he knew Brian would do things his way.

"Having him followed yesterday was a smart move," Kendrick said. "I wish they could have seen exactly where he and Abdel went, but our guys were close enough to make sure he stayed out of trouble."

Two junior attachés from the embassy who were really CIA agents had followed Mohammed's Land Rover through Jericho and up to a spot near the Sea of Galilee. From a vantage point a half mile away, the men watched Mohammed enter the Beth Shean Archaeological Park and take a road that skirted the ancient city. They lost sight of the car but soon saw it again, parked on a distant hill above the ruins. Through binoculars they watched the two passengers walk away as the driver waited. Afraid of being spotted, they didn't attempt to get closer. They had stayed in place until the men returned and they could follow the driver back to Jerusalem.

CHAPTER ELEVEN

Tariq sat in his secure facility two floors below what appeared to be just one more typical bombed-out building in Edlib, Syria. His cellphone had excellent reception thanks to a booster planted on the roof, and he placed a call to one of his several al Qaeda operatives who were deep-cover moles inside Israel.

His man Abdel was weak and untrustworthy, a person who had once been an al Qaeda leader but whose years among the infidels had given him too much peace and confidence. Tariq was certain he was one of them now. He should have been eliminated already, but he might still be of value. He was such a part of the Israeli fabric now that he wasn't on the government's radar. And he would do what Tariq ordered. Once al Qaeda, always al Qaeda. Every recruit learned that lesson well, and fear was a great motivator.

When his cellphone rang, the caller's cold voice sent an involuntary shiver up Abdel's spine, even though he hadn't spoken with the man in years.

"Yes, sir?" he said in his language. As they talked, the antiquities dealer tried unsuccessfully to mask his terror. His voice had shaken from the moment he answered Tariq's call. Now he sputtered responses to one staccato question after another. He was such a poor liar it was pathetic, and Tariq promised himself to deal with Abdel once and for all as soon as this issue with Brian Sadler and the treasure was wrapped up.

"I hear you have a new friend. An American."

"I ... I'm not sure what you mean." Abdel held the phone between his ear and shoulder so he could light a cigarette. He fumbled with the match, dropped it on the carpet, stamped it out, struck another, lit his smoke and took a deep puff. It helped to calm him a little.

"You don't know what I mean?"

Abdel shivered again at the man's evil voice.

"You will answer me! Who's the man you were with yesterday?"

"It was a dealer, Leader. Brian Sadler is his name. I outbid him in an auction the other day – the day of the bombing, in fact. He's from Texas –"

"I know who he is, Abdel," the man interrupted. "Where did you go?"

He was cautious because he wasn't sure what Tariq already knew. He might have been followed or maybe his driver had been paid off. It was dangerous to play games with this man; Abdel had seen the awful fate of some who tried.

"Sir, I took him to see the ruins of an ancient city in the north."

"In Israel?"

"Yes, Leader, at Beth Shean. It's one of the oldest cities in the region. It dates back –"

"Thank you for the history lesson. Why did you take him there?" he spat in sarcastic, venomous words.

This wasn't going well. Abdel had plans for Brian Sadler and he didn't understand why Tariq seemed so interested in him. Taking a moment to collect his thoughts, he took another long drag and exhaled a slow stream of smoke.

"Am I making you nervous?" the voice hissed. "I am beginning to think you are hiding something from me. Are you hiding something, Abdel?"

He stammered a response. "Of course not, Leader. It will ... it will be good for my business to have Brian Sadler as a colleague. I thought it wise to get to know him better while he is in my country. He is famous and he knows influential people around the world."

"Including the American president. And Israel is not 'your country,'" he shot back. "You are an Arab, but I think maybe you have lived so long among the infidels that you are becoming soft."

Tariq stopped talking and Abdel said nothing because he could think of nothing to say.

"Where else did you and Mr. Sadler go?"

He knows some of it, but he doesn't know exactly what we did, Abdel realized. *If he had, he would have asked about the cave. All he knows is that we went on a trip.*

"We went nowhere else, Leader. I picked him up at his hotel, took him to Beth Shean and brought him back a few hours later."

"Do you have plans to see him again before he leaves Israel?"

"No," Abdel lied, his hands shaking so hard he was barely able to hold the phone. "He was supposed to leave already, but until the airport reopens, he must stay here. I don't expect to see him again."

That was another lie. Tariq knew they were meeting tonight at Abdel's gallery. But he would deal with his deceit later.

"How intelligent of you to extend the gesture of friendship to Mr. Sadler," Tariq spat, barely able to contain his contempt for a man who had gotten so cushy with the wretched infidels. "I have a job for you. You have not been required to help the cause for many years, but now you will serve al Qaeda once again. Your cozy relationship with your new friend will also be helpful to our cause."

Abdel gulped. He didn't want to help al Qaeda and he didn't want Brian to end up in the middle of all this.

"Who is the Zulqarnayn?"

"The ... uh ... who, Leader?"

Carrot first, stick later. "Ah, you ask who, not what, so you know something. The name is familiar to you – I can sense it in your hesitation. The Zulqarnayn is the legendary protector of the people against the wrath of the evil gods. He guards a vast hidden treasure."

There was a long pause. "I don't believe I have heard of him, sir."

Liar! Allah, curse this man!

Tariq remained calm. "You're an intelligent person, Abdel. Surely you have heard of the Zulqarnayn; perhaps you have forgotten. I want to know who the present Zulqarnayn is. Find that out for me. You have twenty-four hours. I will call you tomorrow and you will tell me his name."

Abdel was becoming more afraid and his trembling voice relayed his fear to Tariq. "Why does that legendary person even matter, Leader?" Abdel fervently hoped there was a reason besides the one that haunted his thoughts.

"The world is aware how successfully ISIS has eradicated pagan sites such as Palmyra, Aleppo and Nimrud. I am going to strike a blow against the Jews in their homeland – a land they wrongfully claim was given to them by their God. Allah is the only God, may he be praised! I will destroy the ruins of Beth Shean right under their noses. It will be a stunning victory for ISIS and a shameful loss for the infidels. We will infiltrate under cover of darkness, detonate explosives and eradicate the ancient city just as we have done in Syria and Iraq. Why do I want the Zulqarnayn? Because he is the guardian of a vast treasure. I know where that cache is, Abdel, and the Zulqarnayn's last act will be to reveal it to me just before I execute him."

Abdel felt as if there were a cyclone spinning inside his mind, a dizzying, terrifying blizzard of thoughts. He had no idea how a Syrian terrorist could get into Israel with enough explosives to destroy Beth Shean, but he also knew if anyone could do it, this clever man could. With the threat of war looming, Tariq might arrange a firefight or an incursion somewhere else that would divert Israeli troops and allow him to complete his mission.

He said he knows where the treasure is! How could that be? Surely that was a bluff. But maybe it wasn't. What if the man who had showed the cave to Abdel was a jihadist himself? If Tariq really did know where the cavern was located, there was no time to lose.

"Your silence explains much to me," Tariq taunted. "Twenty-four hours. You will give me the name in twenty-four hours."

80

The call ended and Abdel pulled hard on his third cigarette. His body shook with nervous tremors and his stomach convulsed so tightly he barely made it to the toilet. He must compose himself. Everything would be fine if he just stayed calm. He could accomplish his own goal and give the leader enough to keep him at bay.

The plans he had for Brian Sadler would have to change now. *I must achieve my own goals, not those of others,* he told himself. It was regretful that he would have to betray a friend, but he had always known that someday he would be told to perform a service for Allah that would be difficult. Not that ISIS was under Allah's wing, he thought bitterly. Once, perhaps, but not today. It made no difference; Abdel had made a pledge long ago, a declaration of loyalty that would only end when he was dead.

Abdel had taken the easy road as a youth, aligning himself with others who could make life exciting and profitable for a dirt-poor Arab boy. He had been taught how to serve the cause of jihadism not as a soldier but as an infiltrator – an undercover operative hiding in the light of day. Little had been asked of him during the years he established himself as a reputable antiquities dealer in the Old City. He passed along information, did minor tasks his handler assigned him, and grew complacent when the requests for help ended. Al Qaeda wasn't a dangerous group then – at least in Abdel's opinion. It waged war against infidels, including Jews who had become Abdel's friends, but it battled even more with other Arab groups.

He had a problem. He knew a great secret, the location of the long-lost treasure trove of the Israelites. If Tariq really knew where it was, he would surely steal the objects and melt them down into gold ingots. It was only a matter of time until they would all would be gone forever. The world would never see the things that could bring Abdel great fame and fortune.

What was equally disturbing was Tariq's threat to destroy Beth Shean. If Syria invaded northern Israel and ISIS came in with the troops, the entire city would be razed. ISIS soldiers were masters at obliterating historic ruins wherever they invaded. As Tariq had pointed out, ISIS had plundered and destroyed many sites, some dating to the Bronze Age nearly five thousand years ago. It sickened Abdel to think what these two closely aligned jihadist groups might do at Beth Shean.

Years ago, he had considered himself a jihadist too, when jihadists were different. Now he'd lived in the relative safety and comfort of Jerusalem for so long that terrorism was the last thing he thought about. Regardless, he owed a debt to the leader – one that could cost him his life.

As frightening as the call had been, it had also motivated him to action. He couldn't let Tariq destroy the city and steal the treasure. Stopping him wouldn't be easy, but Abdel had always considered himself a shrewd and resourceful man. He must figure out a way to accomplish both his goals and the leader's, while staying alive in the process. That last part was the most important.

CHAPTER TWELVE

Israel's smaller airports were flooded with massive numbers of people, far more than could be accommodated in a day or even a week. Everyone was desperate to get out of this volatile country. Ben Gurion Airport in Tel Aviv had been the country's largest. Now that it was closed, the ones at Haifa and Eilat simply couldn't handle either the human traffic or the numbers of planes needed to fly people to safety.

Although Israel's second largest in terms of passengers, Eilat Airport was much smaller than Ben Gurion. Only two large planes at a time could dock at the terminal building, and a 757 on the taxiway couldn't maneuver around another plane parked at its gate. The airport was four hours' drive from either Jerusalem or Tel Aviv, but tourists eager to go home endured highways crammed with taxis, check-in lines that extended onto the sidewalk, and three to four hours going through security. Thousands had camped out there, afraid to miss the chance for a seat on any airline to any destination. But only a few hundred lucky ones left each day and the terminal buildings were a melee of hungry, frustrated, angry people chaperoned by squads of tired, irritable soldiers.

Brian assured himself he couldn't get out now, even though he knew it wasn't true. One word from Harry would put him at the front of the queue holding a ticket for the next flight to anywhere. He could also do what he often did – charter a private jet. But he was intent on seeing this through. He was on a mission to reveal it to the world.

During his call to Nicole last night, he told her part of what had happened on his trip with Abdel. He told her that the main airport was still closed but she knew as resourceful as her husband was, he could already have been home by now. But she said nothing. It was upsetting enough to lie in bed by herself and wonder if he'd come home. There was no need to continue bickering with a man who'd made up his mind.

After the call, he checked in with the embassy. His contact said that the major American and Western European airlines had added several flights to Athens in response to the closure of the Tel Aviv airport. The Greek capital was just two hours away by plane and it was a connecting point to the rest of the world. The embassy official advised that the American airline companies were holding one or two seats on each flight for governmental officials or dignitaries who needed to leave quickly. She offered one to Brian, but he passed for now, saying he had a day or two of business left to finish. She cautioned that the State Department was warning Americans to leave Israel, citing the increasing danger of war. He assured her he was leaving as soon as he could. She confirmed that he was still at the David Citadel Hotel and double-checked his correct phone number and email address.

"Stay safe," were her parting words.

"I intend to." It seemed that everyone he talked to was unusually concerned for his well-being. It wasn't a particularly calming thought.

Abdel was in a dilemma. This evening Brian would come to his gallery for another meeting. He had offered to arrange shipment of the Arab's most valuable pieces out of Israel. In exchange, he wanted to know everything about the cavern and the objects. He also wanted to see it again. Those were reasonable requests, but as desperately as he required Brian's help, he refused to tell him anything else right now.

During the return trip from the site yesterday, Abdel had refused to answer question after question. He would say nothing about how or when he had found the place, who had discovered it or why he believed this trove was the same "hidden treasure" that Isaiah spoke about in the Bible. He knew Brian had been frustrated, but the time to reveal more was after he and the American had an agreement.

Abdel had admitted taking a huge risk in showing Brian the cave. "I think at this moment it remains a secret, but others will quickly learn of its existence. Once they know what is there, they will do anything – including murdering anyone who stands in their way – to keep it for themselves. And there is a third issue. Now that we are about to go to war, Syria could gain control of northern Israel. If so, the ancient city you saw will be destroyed just as ISIS did in Palmyra. The cavern too – I have no doubt if al Qaeda – or even worse, ISIS – finds it, the priceless relics will never be seen again."

He had stopped, almost having said too much. His problem after all these years boiled down to one thing. He'd understood al Qaeda once, when he was young, poor and full of lofty goals about freeing the oppressed. But everything had changed in the last few years. Al Qaeda in Syria – AQS – had morphed into a band of ruthless murderers and ISIS – the offshoot of it – was a thousand times more bloodthirsty and dangerous. He also had changed in those years. He had a real life now, along with a reputation and standing in the community. The rebel he once had been now wanted to be a protector, guarding the monuments of bygone civilizations and the treasure of the Israelites – a nation his own people considered infidels.

"Let me help you safeguard the things in the cavern," Brian had told him. "I have resources and we can get the Antiquities Authority involved. They will send soldiers."

Abdel had steadfastly refused to consider it and Brian had backed off, saying, "You simply have to let me go back once more. If I may never see it again, I'd like to at least spend some time among the artifacts. Please, Abdel."

"I doubt it is possible, but I will try because you have promised to help me." They agreed to meet at Abdel's shop the next day.

Brian spent most of his day in the hotel, catching up on emails and watching the news. He had lunch on the patio and watched US F-35 fighter jets scream overhead, heading northeast. Was this activity in response to provocation or merely a show of force? He searched his phone for news and

BILL THOMPSON

saw that Syrian tanks and missile launchers had been moved to the border in the Golan Heights. It was a face-to-face standoff all along Israel's borders and Brian figured the US warplanes were demonstrating that America wouldn't tolerate aggression against its ally.

He wanted to call Nicole, but it was nighttime in Dallas. He'd touch base with her before he left for his appointment with Abdel at six.

He spent the afternoon doing research. He learned about Cyrus, the king of Persia to whom God was speaking in Isaiah 45:3 when he promised to give him "treasures of darkness and hidden wealth of secret places." His was an interesting story with a fascinating twist. Although Isaiah had called Cyrus by name and prophesied that he would help the Jews escape from Babylonian captivity, Isaiah couldn't have known Cyrus because the king was born one hundred and fifty years after Isaiah's predictions were written.

Bizarre! Brian thought, but he knew from Sunday school decades ago that the biblical prophets had done a lot of prognosticating that turned out to be one hundred percent accurate.

Once the Persian king arrived on the scene, his actions were exactly as Isaiah had written. He issued a decree freeing the Israelites and supported the rebuilding of God's house in Jerusalem by providing money from his treasury. He also returned the temple objects, which King Nebuchadnezzar allegedly brought to Babylon.

Now we're getting somewhere. Brian excitedly read more about the Persian king who actively helped "God's people" – the Israelites – build a temple here in Jerusalem in the sixth century BC. There had undoubtedly been treasure and lots of it, given how many times it was described in the Bible. There had been artifacts from the temple, utensils and even "golden vessels dedicated by King Solomon."

He searched for something else. He googled ancient sites fifty to a hundred miles north of Jerusalem. He found several and narrowed his search to Canaanite sites with Egyptian influence, and a view inside Beth Shean Archaeological National Park nailed it. A panoramic video

86

of the ancient city, taken from the same hill, showing the same towering Roman columns Brian had seen in person, proved that this was where Abdel had taken him.

He read about caves and unexcavated ruins throughout the area, and he grew more excited with each word he saw. He caught himself daydreaming about the trove of artifacts he'd barely gotten a glimpse of. Now he absolutely had to see them again. *This documentary would be my greatest achievement yet,* he thought. *The Hidden Treasure of Isaiah. The Lost Treasure of the Temple. The Treasures of the Israelites.*

He forced himself to slow down. *I'm already naming the program and I don't even know if I'll ever see the place again.*

The ring of his phone startled him back into reality. He shook his head to clear the cobwebs. Had he fallen asleep? He wasn't sure. He glanced at his watch – it was already after five and he was supposed to be in the Old City with Abdel at six. He answered.

"Hi, sweetie!"

"Hi, Brian. Please tell me you're sitting at an airport somewhere on your way home."

"It won't be much longer, I can tell you that. I have a meeting with Abdel in a few minutes. I'm going to get him to take me back to the cave one more time before I leave. I may never get to see it again ..."

There was a silence that lasted so long Brian thought the connection had been broken.

"Are you there, Nicole?"

"I'm here. I've been waiting to see if you'll come to your senses. I spoke with Harry, Brian. You can leave if you want to but you turned down a seat on the next plane. I'm going to tell you something I asked Harry to do for me. I asked him to revoke your passport."

"You did what?" he shouted into the phone, aghast. He only needed a day or two and this could ruin everything!

"Don't worry, my darling," she replied sarcastically. "You're safe to continue your crazy mission. He said that things didn't work that way. They'd have to arrest you and treat you like a prisoner and Harry absolutely refused to do it. He said something I still want to believe myself. He said you're an intelligent man and a caring husband. He said you're not a man who'd carelessly create anguish and worry for someone you love."

"I won't —"

She exploded. "But you *are*! Don't you understand anything? The only person who isn't concerned about your welfare is *you*. How crazy is that? Why should I care when you don't? Why should Harry care? Because we love you, that's why. I've hung in with you for years and I'm getting tired."

"You're right and I know it. It's just that I'm already here, halfway around the world, and I want to finish what I started. Two days. That's all, I promise."

He waited for a moment, but there was nothing. He looked at the screen and saw that the call was disconnected. She had hung up.

I'll be home in two days, he promised himself. *Just forty-eight hours.*

CHAPTER THIRTEEN

Abdel faced some challenges. He respected Brian as a colleague, he admired his stature as an authority in his field, and he envied the fame and fortune that had come with the man's worldwide television broadcasts. Those documentaries had made Brian's name and face familiar to millions; in his gut, Abdel wanted that same thing for himself.

His first dilemma was that war was inevitable. As much as Beth Shean and the temple treasures weighed upon his conscience, there was something even more valuable to him. Over two decades he had built a showroom filled with unique, valuable objects that would surely be stolen if the Israelis shut down the Old City. Brian could help him get the pieces to safety, but the quid pro quo was his next dilemma. He couldn't give Brian what he wanted in return unless he somehow broke free from what he once had been.

Abdel was trapped between the choices of his past and his dreams for the future. *I've been in the business far longer than Brian,* he justified, allowing himself another cigarette and a daydream as he waited for Brian's arrival. *I've dealt with relics equally as impressive as the ones that made him famous. I deserve recognition as much – no, even more than he does! And I hold a key that can make it happen. I know about the cavern and the treasures Isaiah mentioned in the Quran and the Bible. I too can be a man whose face is known to the world through television documentaries. Think of it!* Discovering Secret Treasures of the Bible – *a two-hour documentary starring Abdel Malouf and Brian Sadler, two noted experts about ancient relics. We would be there together, leading the camera crew down into the cave as millions of would-be adventurers around the world were glued to their televisions. I would be famous – as famous as Brian Sadler! I am already wealthy, but after this I will have much more. I will buy that house in the south of France, where I will sit on my veranda and gaze at the peaceful waters of the Mediterranean Sea.*

Brian Sadler is my key. I can make all this happen. All that I must do ...

All that I must do, he admitted ruefully to himself, *is pull off a miracle. All that I must do is eliminate one of the most dangerous and ruthless individuals on the planet.*

He dismissed that negative, impossible thought and went back to the pleasure of daydreaming.

The first thing that caught Brian's eye – and his nose – when he walked through the narrow front door of Abdel's gallery was the thick cloud of smoke that hung like smog from the ceiling. He saw the Arab rise from a desk in the back and stub out a cigarette. Brian wondered how many it had taken to create that nasty fog.

"My friend, please join me here," Abdel gushed. "Tea and dates?" He motioned to a chair next to a table with a plate and kettle on it, poured two cups of steaming black tea and asked him how his day had been. Before Brian could reply, Abdel asked him another simple question, then another. Brian noticed the total transformation from the man's reserved demeanor on the road trip yesterday. Now he could hardly stop talking and the words were cascading from his mouth like a waterfall. He wondered if the man might be high on something.

"What have you been doing today?" Abdel chattered.

Remembering Harry's warning about al Qaeda, Brian reminded himself to be wary.

"I caught up on work. How about you? How was your day?"

"It was good. I spent most of it doing an inventory of the things I want to ship to London. Again, I deeply appreciate your offer."

Brian replied that he was glad to help. Then he asked again about going to the cave.

"We can go there again," Abdel replied, his hands trembling so hard that he spilled his tea. He giggled nervously. "I will show you the treasure once more."

That is surprising news! "When?"

"Tomorrow morning, same time as before. Mohammed and I will be there at 6 a.m."

Brian was ecstatic. "Thank you so much! It means a great deal to me and you are very kind."

"No! No!" Abdel burst out, waving his hands in the air. Something was clearly wrong; he was becoming more agitated by the minute. "I am not kind at all. I need your help, that's all. Please, let us now talk about shipping my objects to your gallery."

Brian had found the solution for Abdel's problem, but now he was getting worried. To call Abdel uneasy would have been an understatement. Ever since he arrived, something hadn't felt right about all this.

"What is it, Abdel? What's wrong?"

"I am fine," Abdel said unconvincingly, making up an excuse on the fly. "I have a meeting with an important client later this week and I am anxious about it. If you can help me, then I will show you the cavern again if you wish. But you must understand that it is dangerous to go there."

"Because of the threat of war. Yes, I know that, but I'm willing to take a chance."

His thoughts filled with remorse, Abdel said nothing. The threat of war wasn't what he was talking about at all. Brian couldn't possibly know what the real danger was and Abdel couldn't tell him.

Brian continued, "I've been on the phone this afternoon with some friends of mine and I've hired a private security firm to handle your artifacts." He explained that Abdel should prepare the goods for shipment. When they were ready, a truck would take the crates to Eilat airport to be loaded on a cargo plane to London. From there the boxes would be stored in one of the high-security locations Bijan Rarities maintained.

Instead of reacting with exuberance at the news, Abdel hung his head and shook it. "No. No. You are being too good to me. I don't want all that help. I can do it myself."

What? What is the man thinking? I'm offering exactly the solution he wanted!

"Okay, Abdel. What's going on here? What I worked out is exactly what you asked for –"

"There is nothing going on here!" Abdel shouted. "I should never have involved you!" He paused and stammered, "I mean, I should never have asked for so much."

"Is it because I arranged everything without consulting you first? I thought you would appreciate it. I thought it was the safest way to transport your things to London."

"Forget about my needs." He sighed. "It is too late for that."

Brian was alarmed. He had only known Abdel a few days, and his behavior today was very unusual. The man was clearly upset about something.

"What do you mean it's too late? Are you saying that Israel is about to go to war? What about our trip to the cavern?"

"I know nothing more about when or if war will come than you, Brian." That was the first time, Brian would reflect later, that Abdel called him by his first name. "And if you insist on going to the cave again, then I will take you there, as I already said. Mohammed and I will be at the hotel at 6 a.m."

He stood abruptly and ushered Brian to the door, which he locked once Brian was on the sidewalk. He sat in the dark for over an hour, smoking one cigarette after another and wondering how all this would work.

Brian was completely baffled. After that peculiar meeting, he needed to clear his head. As he had done before on this trip, he walked along the Via Dolorosa – the Way of Suffering – once again humbled that he stood on the very stones that Jesus walked on His way to Calvary. Tonight, he paused to reflect at each station of the cross. Soon he reached the end of the Muslim Quarter, where he would pass into the Christian Quarter and exit via the New Gate.

As he neared the intersection where the quarter ended, he began to hear shouts. A few people anxiously approached and pushed past him, and at the end of the street there was a throng of people yelling and shaking their fists at Israeli soldiers.

All the shouting was in Hebrew, but Brian saw the issue. The soldiers were blocking the entrance to the Christian Quarter and refusing to let anyone pass. A man and woman in front of Brian asked one of the soldiers in English, "Why is this way closed?"

"For your protection," she snapped. "There are new threats against the government. Until they are searched and questioned, no one may pass from one quarter to another or leave the Old City."

Brian knew what a mess this was going to create. There had to be thousands of people in the Old City right now – tourists, vendors, shop owners, residents, deliverymen and every other imaginable player in the day-to-day economic life of a place like this. For now, everyone inside was a prisoner within the walled city. He thought a moment and resigned himself to the inevitable. He joined a long line to wait until his turn to present his papers to the guards.

From somewhere close a shot rang out, then another. The crowd around Brian rushed the soldiers in a desperate attempt to run from danger. The guards prepared to defend themselves, but wisely they held their rifles across their breasts instead of pointing them at the mob. Mostly tourists in shorts and T-shirts, they didn't pose a real threat, and within seconds it was clear no one was going to push the issue.

Whatever the shooting had been about, Brian was sure the security at the exit gates would be far heavier now than before it had happened. He ran back to Abdel's store, knocked several times and was about to give up when the door opened.

"What do you want? Why are you still here?"

Brian told him about the lockdown. "I'm going to call the embassy," he explained. "I'm not sure what they can do, but if they can get me out, I'll ask them to take you too."

Abdel shook his head. "Not me. If the Jews are locking down the Old City, I'm going to stay here and defend my property. I'm fully stocked with provisions – my living quarters are upstairs – so don't worry about me. Come in; you're safe here and you can call the embassy. If they won't help, you may spend the night here." His more cordial demeanor surprised Brian.

Thirty minutes later an aide knocked on the door to Prime Minister Daniel Shigon's office and informed him that the American embassy was asking permission to remove one of their citizens from the Muslim Quarter through Herod's Gate.

Shigon had bigger things to deal with than this, but he'd also instructed the soldiers that no one – absolutely no one – was permitted to leave until he or she was questioned at one of the checkpoints. He was aware of the bottleneck this would create, given the tourists and others who would be angry that they didn't get to afternoon tea or a tavern on time. Arabs would see it as an aggressive move, but none of that mattered to the prime minister. The lockdown was merely a demonstration of who was in charge. Despite the Temple Mount's being under Arab control, it would be the Jews who would decide who entered the Old City, and everyone else could be inconvenienced – or go to hell, for that matter. His country was on the verge of war and he was determined to be steadfast and strong.

"Who's the American, and why the hell is the embassy involved?" he snapped, irritated at the interruption.

"Sir, it's the famous antiquities dealer Brian Sadler."

That revelation infuriated Shigon even more. *What is this all about?* he wondered. *What's this guy doing in Israel, and why is the embassy asking for special favors?* He knew who Sadler was, of course. He was interested in history and Sadler's TV specials provided fascinating trips into the past. He also knew the man had occasionally helped the American government, acting as an informant or a go-between on sensitive international issues. Now he was in Jerusalem, caught up in the lockdown, and he was pulling strings to get free. Given what was going on, the request pissed off Shigon much more than it might have at another time. There were strategic meetings every few hours, Israel's military was on full alert, and he had a war to plan. Instead, he was being interrupted to get some celebrity out of a jam.

Shigon had deliberately left the United States out of discussions about the current Arab conflict. He had refused to take the president's calls because for once Israel was going to do what was best for Israel, period. He knew that America would be there in a crisis, but he wasn't going to beg for help only to find his request tossed from committee to committee in the American Congress and endlessly debated in the media. Israel was strong. God was on Israel's side. The Muslims believed the same thing about their cause, but Shigon knew his people's destiny. Their God would protect them until the end of time.

"Get me the ambassador!" Shigon bellowed. Cowering, the aide rushed out and moments later the PM's phone rang. He snatched it from its cradle.

"Why the hell does Brian Sadler warrant special treatment?" he roared.

"And good morning to you, Mr. Prime Minister," the ambassador replied cordially. He'd been here five years and knew Shigon socially. He also had heard of the man's domineering, oppressive demeanor. "Brian Sadler is an American antiquities dealer. You may have heard of him; he's quite well-known."

"Everyone knows who he is! I want to know exactly what he's doing in my country that affords him special treatment."

The ambassador remained calm and kept his voice even. "There's nothing going on, I assure you. He's somewhat of a celebrity and that makes him more of a target in an unstable situation. I'd appreciate your cooperation in allowing him to return to his hotel, where he can be better protected."

The prime minister asked where Brian was staying and what day he was leaving Israel. When he was told Brian had no firm departure plans, he bellowed, "What exactly is he doing here, Mr. Ambassador? I asked you this before and now I want an answer. Is he still sightseeing, even though the entire country is on full military alert and the airport's been bombed? Israel isn't exactly the French Riviera these days. What's going on here, and who asked you to get him out of the Old City?"

The ambassador couldn't explain why Brian was still here because he didn't know. He told the prime minister it was Brian himself who had called and requested help in getting back to his hotel.

Shigon was furious. "You're telling me some American celebrity who rings up his embassy can demand that you call the prime minister? Do you think I'm an idiot? Answer my question! Who's this guy Sadler, and what's he up to?"

"He knows people in high places," the ambassador replied testily. He was getting tired of being berated. Either the PM was going to help or he wasn't. It was time, as Americans would say, to fish or cut bait. "I know you're busy, Mr. Prime Minister," he continued. "Are you going to honor my government's request or not?"

"Who does he know in high places?"

"President Harrison," the ambassador disclosed at last.

"How does he know him?"

"They were college roommates. They're best friends."

Shigon paused. He didn't want to appear weak, but now he had no choice. "Where is he?"

"He's in a gallery off the Via Dolorosa. It's owned by an Arab named Abdel Malouf."

Shigon knew the name. The man dealt in high-quality pieces and had a stellar reputation, just as Sadler did.

"Send your people to the Lion's Gate in twenty minutes," Shigon commanded. "The soldiers will allow him to pass through without interference. This is a major inconvenience, Ambassador, and I do not appreciate it. I have better things to do than babysit your president's friends. I am diverting soldiers from critical duties to accommodate you, and you will in turn do the same. I want this man out of Israel in twenty-four hours. If he does not leave voluntarily by the deadline, he will be arrested and detained until he can be deported. One more thing – if you're thinking of granting him asylum in the embassy, you should think again. I would consider that an act of aggression against our country and me personally, since I am the one ordering him to leave. Do not trifle with me, Ambassador Sheller. I am in no mood to play games. I have a country to run and a war to fight."

He slammed the phone down, lit a cigar and yelled for his aide-de-camp.

CHAPTER FOURTEEN

The handoff occurred without incident. Two Israeli soldiers, each holding one of Brian's arms, guided him to the front of a two-block-long line of people waiting to get out through the Lion's Gate. Just outside, a man in a coat and tie showed his diplomatic credentials to the officer in charge, and Brian was ushered through the checkpoint.

When they were in a sedan on the way to the hotel, the man dialed a number and handed Brian the phone, saying, "The ambassador wants to speak to you, sir."

Ambassador Sheller had never met Brian, but now wasn't the time to mince words. He told him about the call with the prime minister and explained that Shigon was livid. "You have twenty-four hours to leave Israel or face arrest," he continued. "My assistant is making your arrangements. She'll email an itinerary later today. You'll go from Haifa Airport to whichever destination in Europe she can book. You'll be responsible for paying the fare and booking your next flight from there."

"I'm not sure I can finish up that quickly —"

The ambassador interrupted. "Perhaps I didn't make myself completely clear. I don't know what you're doing here, Mr. Sadler. It's none of my business, but I can assure you that the prime minister is beginning to believe President Harrison sent you to Israel on some type of mission. You *will* finish up, sir, and you *will* be on a plane tomorrow evening. If not, you'll be detained and it will create an incident neither you, I nor President Harrison wants. This is not a request. Am I clear?"

"Absolutely."

The next morning it was raining lightly as Brian, Abdel and his driver, Mohammed, left the hotel. The early-morning traffic was light, just as they'd experienced three days earlier. Mohammed made a sharp right turn, his tires squealing as he swerved and then regained control. He spoke quietly to Abdel and then pulled to the curb. He waited a moment, screeched back into traffic and ran a red light at the next intersection, which created a firestorm of honking from drivers who'd barely avoided hitting his car.

"What's going on?" Brian asked. "Why's he driving like this?"

"He thinks he was being followed," Abdel answered. "He's just making sure everything is all right."

Alarmed, Brian asked why someone would be following him.

Abdel didn't reply.

"Abdel, tell me what's going on."

The Arab spoke to his driver, got a response and said, "Nothing is going on, Brian. It's not our problem. It has to do with his wife. They're getting a divorce and her parents are angry with him. His father-in-law is an influential man, he tells me. At any rate, everything is fine now. If there was someone following, he has managed to lose them."

From that point on, Mohammed drove normally, although Brian caught him checking his rearview mirror every few minutes. Once they were out of Jerusalem, he took the same route as the last time, turning north in Jericho on the border highway. This time he saw many more tanks and soldiers on both sides of the fence separating Israel from Jordan. The troops seemed calm, but it was clear that everyone was preparing for conflict.

Shaken by the driver's evasive driving earlier, Brian tried to settle back and relax. He was booked on a 6:15 p.m. flight to Istanbul, according to the email Ambassador Sheller's assistant had sent last evening. Since he was required to check in by four, an embassy driver would pick him up at the hotel at 2:30. If today's visit to the cave went as planned, he would be back in plenty of time to grab a bite of lunch before he left.

"How does al Qaeda fit into the struggle between Israel and the Arab nations?" Brian asked Abdel casually.

The rather simple question appeared to startle Abdel. He twitched, turned to face Brian and replied, "I'm not sure what you're asking. From what I hear on the news, al Qaeda is more interested in overthrowing the president of Syria than fighting the Jews. Why do you ask?"

"Everyone knows al Qaeda and ISIS are constantly waging war against someone. Since you're both an Arab and an Israeli citizen, I wondered if you had thoughts about whether they were involved in what's happening now."

"Al Qaeda hasn't the resources to mount a full-scale battle on its own and neither does ISIS," he responded, knowing that statement likely wasn't true. "Furthermore, neither group would be invited to join any aggressive move against Israel. They're terrorist organizations, pure and simple. This impending conflict is about disputed territory and the rights of Palestinians to free movement and land to build settlements. The Jews have been a thorn in the flesh of Syria, Iraq and Iran for years. Jordan and Egypt too, although the leaders of those nations put on a false face for appearance's sake." He hesitated and then concluded a bit too casually, "All that is simply my opinion. Who am I to know what al Qaeda really is after? Why should I care? It means nothing to me."

Abdel fidgeted for a moment, wondering if now was the time to reveal his real concerns. He decided there was nothing to lose.

"As noble as AQS and ISIS may consider their goals, they have destroyed ancient monuments that have withstood everything that the centuries have tossed at them. It is appalling to watch them loot museums, bulldoze majestic ancient buildings and blow up mosques. Those acts are not Allah's will and I must stop them from stealing the treasure ..." He paused and glanced at his driver, who seemed to be listening intently.

Shaking his head, Abdel blurted, "I've said too much."

Brian processed the very telling comments as Mohammed contentedly kept his eyes on the road.

The rain had stopped and the sun was peeking from the clouds when Abdel at last passed the hood to the backseat. Brian put it on and rode in silence for considerably longer than the last time. It was hard to hear under the heavy cloth bag, but he could make out words as Mohammed and Abdel spoke now and then.

There were turns and more turns, some of which he took very quickly. It felt as though the driver was again making evasive moves. He drove onto a bumpy surface. After a few miles, he decelerated and stopped. As before, the driver rolled down his window and spoke in rapid Arabic. Moments later the car began moving again and Brian braced himself for the rough stones they would encounter in a moment.

But they didn't. For more than ten minutes the car drove on the same unpaved surface.

"Abdel, are we on a different road?" His voice was muffled under the hood and he didn't hear a response. He raised the hood slightly so he could speak. "Abdel?"

The hood was jerked roughly down. "Quiet!" a voice said – Mohammed's voice. And the word was in English.

What the hell's going on? Worried, he began to perspire under the hood and he sucked in gasps of stale air. Determined not to hyperventilate, he forced himself to calm down and not think about what might be happening. He sat with his hands folded in his lap for ten more minutes until the car stopped and the driver's door opened. No one spoke to him, so Brian took off the hood.

They were parked on the shoulder of a two-lane road. The terrain here was nothing like where they'd been before. The ruins of Beth Shean were nowhere in sight. Instead there were rocky, dusty fields on both sides of the road, mountains in the distance, and a highway sign ten feet away. Ominously, the words on it were in Arabic. Mohammed was urinating on the front wheel of the car and smoking a cigarette. Abdel sat in the front seat, a look of miserable resignation on his face.

"Abdel," he whispered, "where are we?"

"I'm sorry, Brian. The driver thought his father-in-law was following again. He said he had to get away. I'm sorry."

"Sorry? Sorry for what? Where are we?" Whatever was going on, Brian realized that Abdel was part of it. For an instant he considered running, but he had no idea where he was, and there was no place to hide. There wasn't even a grove of trees – just low desert scrub and dusty fields full of rocks extending for miles in every direction.

He got out of the car as Mohammed turned around, zipping his pants.

"You speak English, don't you? Where are we?"

Without answering, the driver looked down the road behind Brian, watching as an old Willys Jeep skidded to a stop across the road, throwing rocks everywhere. Two young Arabs got out, lifted automatic rifles from the backseat and slung them over their shoulders. One of them stuck a wad of bills in Mohammed's hand, patted him on the back and said something. The other man walked to Abdel's side of the car, opened the door and motioned him out. Mohammed started the Land Rover, made a U-turn and drove back the way they had come. He was anxious to connect with Jamel, his handler, and turn over the cellphone from this trip. This one was worth a lot more dollars.

One of the men turned to Brian. He appeared to be in his thirties, dark-complected with unruly black hair and a scruffy beard. He was dressed in dirty fatigues. Except for the AK-47 by his side, he looked like just another Arab student on an American or European university campus, and so did his driver.

"What is this?" Brian asked in as calm a voice as he could muster. He hoped this was something random – maybe a robbery by some guy who wanted money and who had gotten lucky nabbing an American. But it felt more ominous somehow. Whatever was happening here, it wasn't good, and he was getting more concerned by the minute.

"You insisted on seeing the treasure again, Mr. Sadler. That was fortunate for me, as I wanted to have a private conversation with you. I persuaded Abdel to let me have a few minutes." The man spoke decent English with a British accent, as did many Middle Easterners who had been educated in the United Kingdom.

He knows my name! "Where am I?"

"You are in Jordan. I know you are thinking of how to escape, but I don't recommend it. As much as you may regret being my guest, the alternative is far riskier. It would be very dangerous for an American to be here alone with everything going on just across the border. A war with the Jews is imminent and your impotent president is not respected by the Arab nations, as I'm sure you've heard. He may even have told you that himself. You and he are very close friends, is that not correct?"

This was not going well! He willed himself to remain composed and not show fear. He'd been in jams like this before. He'd even been kidnapped once. But this was something else. There was much more going on here. The man knew he and Harry were friends. And how could they be in Jordan? They had driven by the border crossings last Friday; he saw formal checkpoints with guards and gates on both sides. Even wearing the hood, he could tell there had been nothing but a brief stop, a short talk between the driver and someone, and more driving. They hadn't passed through a formal border crossing, that much was certain.

"What do you want?" he asked, trying to control the high-pitched tremor that wanted to creep into his voice.

"I told you already, Mr. Sadler. I want to talk to you. But we haven't been properly introduced. My name is Tariq. Some people call me the Hawk. It is what you Americans call ... a nickname. Correct? Do you know who I am?"

Brian nodded. He knew all too well. He and Harry had had many discussions about this man since the time a couple of years back when Tariq unsuccessfully attempted to assassinate the president and Vice President Marty Taylor. Since Tariq never allowed himself to be photographed, Brian wouldn't have recognized him.

"I know who you are. Everyone knows," Brian replied at last. That made Tariq break out in a wicked grin.

Tariq the Hawk was a carefully engineered killing machine created by Mohammad al-Joulani, a Syrian who had been head of the al Nusra Front. Many other youths in training were destined for suicide missions in the name of Allah, but not this one. Joulani took a personal interest in the boy, observing how dedicated and driven he was. He twisted and turned the boy's mind until Tariq was beholden to no one and loyal only to Joulani himself. He was a machine – a robot controlled by his mentor.

Tariq had a natural talent for bringing sympathizers to the cause of jihadism, and he had raised millions of dollars for al Qaeda and ISIS in only a few short years. With Joulani's blessing he established the Falcons of Islam, a subset of al Nusra that CNN termed "terrorism on steroids." Tariq's new organization wasn't simply into jihadism; his killers took contract jobs – assassinations, coups, suicide bombings and the like – working for anyone who could afford their exorbitant fees.

He forced his jihadists to follow him blindly: those who didn't faced the sword. As he grew in power and notoriety, Tariq's loyalty to Joulani ended. His mentor realized that when Tariq diverted fifty million dollars intended for al Nusra to his own account. Furious, Joulani ordered him killed. But it was too late. Like Frankenstein's monster, the killing machine he had created turned against its maker. Tariq repaid the years Joulani had invested in his development by executing him. Afterwards he combined al Nusra with al Qaeda in Syria, seized control of the even more powerful terror organization, and became the poster child for jihadism.

Before Brian realized what was happening, Tariq gave a quick nod and the other man – the one who'd been Tariq's driver – came up from behind, grabbing Brian's neck roughly and clamping a rag over his mouth and nose. He struggled vainly, choking as he tried to suck in air. He became light-headed and dizzy and felt his knees give way. Through the fog, he noticed Abdel was doing nothing to help him.

As he slumped to the ground, misty thoughts of regret wafted through his brain like smoky tendrils. He'd let his greed, his lust for treasure and his reckless pursuit of adventure push away sensibility once again. But it had never been like this. He was in the hands of one of the world's most wanted men on the wrong side of the border in a country on the brink of war with Israel.

Those thoughts faded as a shroud of blackness swept over him.

CHAPTER FIFTEEN

Through the haze in his mind he heard a familiar voice. Someone was jostling him, asking him to wake up. He opened first one eye, then the other. He was lying on a floor in a dark, empty room. A window high on one wall was so filthy that only a little light seeped through. Abdel was sitting cross-legged next to him. It took a moment to orient himself, but then he began to recall what had happened. He patted his pocket for his phone, but it was gone.

"Where are we? What happened back there?"

Abdel spoke in a whisper. "We're at an al Qaeda safe house in Dayr Abu Sa'id, Jordan. Mohammed took a back road to cross the border. We're only twenty miles from Beth Shean. That's the ancient city where I took you to see the treasure. I am sorry, Brian. I am sorry for betraying you. I truly wanted to help you, to show you the treasure and to produce a television show with you. And I needed your help to get my pieces out of Israel. You were my friend and you agreed. But instead of being a friend myself, I succumbed to fear. I'm afraid of the leader ..."

Brian knew that Harry was right. Angry over Abdel's betrayal, he shot back, "The leader? Is that what he is to you? He'll kill me and you know it, but you handed me over. You're no friend; you're one of them. I trusted you and I offered to help you, and this is what you give me in return. You're a spineless, pathetic wretch with no conscience."

"You are wrong about what you think," he answered quietly. "Yes, I once was part of al Qaeda, but I was never a terrorist. I was a mole in Israel and I passed along information."

Brian interrupted him harshly. "And that doesn't make you a terrorist? Seriously? How many people died because of information you passed along?"

"Please let me finish. As I became a prominent antiquities dealer, I met important people and had access others did not. But I hated what I was doing to the very people who had helped me. No one ever died from what I revealed, I pray to Allah. And years went by without any contact from al Qaeda. I began to think they were finished with me. But I knew better. No one leaves al Qaeda except in a body bag."

As Brian snorted derisively, Abdel wiped away a tear. "I was a spy in the country that gave me freedom and a real life. I felt sorry for anyone who might have suffered because of my actions. I never killed anyone myself, but my information may have harmed Israel. I will go to my grave regretting what I did."

Abdel's confession meant one thing to Brian – he was in grave danger. Once again, he'd ignored his wife and her heartfelt attempts to reason with him. In his usual dismissive way, he'd put himself into a precarious situation purely for the thrill of one more adventure. He could have been home with her, but instead he was a prisoner in Jordan. And he'd trusted a man whom he now realized was everything Harry had thought he might be. He was one of Tariq's men.

"I don't believe all that bullshit about how sorry you are," he snarled. "If you're al Qaeda, you're a terrorist. You're so sorry about how you treated your friends, but supposedly I was your friend, and thanks to you I'm a prisoner. You and Tariq planned this all along and I blindly trusted you!"

"I'm telling the truth! I didn't plan this; Tariq called me. He told me he was going to destroy the ancient city and steal the treasure. That's why I'm a prisoner here too. I'm locked in this room just as you are."

"Do you think I'm stupid? You're no prisoner. You know exactly where we are and exactly what's going on. Is that the plan? You pretend to be a captive too and get me to do whatever it is you brought me here for?"

"No, no! You must believe me! I want to save Beth Shean and the treasure. I am not on their side any more, even though Tariq forced me to help him today. You are in no danger. He promised me that he only wants to talk to you. You should not be afraid. He will let you go soon."

Brian stared at him in disbelief. "For God's sake, he killed Vice President Case and the Israeli prime minister! He's a madman! Do you think he kidnapped me so we could have a little chat? Are you insane? He's going to kill me, and you won't do anything to stop him."

Abdel spoke more calmly, hoping Brian wasn't right. "That's not true. He brought you here because he wants a commitment from America to make the Jews be reasonable. Your president should not have moved the embassy to Jerusalem –"

"I'm a prisoner and you're lecturing me about the embassy? Abdel, this guy's a lunatic. How many people has he personally murdered? Hundreds? Thousands? He's not interested in peace. He's interested in something else. It's the treasure – you said it earlier. And you're going to help him steal it. I get it now."

As Abdel shook his head, they heard footsteps approaching. A swarthy man in fatigues opened the door and spoke to Abdel, who pushed himself up.

"Come on," he said. "It's time."

The guard ushered them down a narrow low-ceilinged hallway and Brian's heart began palpitating wildly at the thought of what might be about to happen. He glanced at his watch. 4:15 p.m. His flight to Istanbul was departing in just two hours. He wondered if he'd ever see home again.

They entered a dingy ten-by-twelve room. It had been a living room once, but now there were just two wooden desks and a few rickety folding chairs. Tariq sat behind one of the desks. A guard with a Kalashnikov stood beside him and another sat by a door across the room that led outdoors. Brian glanced at Abdel; the man's face was contorted in terror. But was Abdel really a prisoner? It took only a moment to learn the answer.

"Sit," Tariq ordered. They took chairs facing the desk, but the terrorist said, "Not there, Abdel, you may sit here." He patted an empty chair beside his. "Only the infidel will sit across from me. You will be seated at my right hand, as a loyal follower of al Qaeda should be. You are my brother."

Abdel looked meekly at Brian, hung his head and sat next to Tariq. Brian thought he could see a slight shake of Abdel's head – perhaps a sign that everything wasn't as it seemed – but the time for putting his trust in the man he'd thought was a friend was over. It was time for praying that he'd make it out of here alive.

Tariq's eyes glimmered with excitement as he began to speak quietly. His body language displayed the self-assurance, the sheer arrogance of a man accustomed to gaining respect through intimidation and fear.

"I want to get your president's attention. I have debated the best way to do that. In the movies, the aggressor sends a souvenir from his captive – a finger perhaps, or an ear – but that seems so passé, don't you think? Can you help me decide a better way? Or you, Abdel? Can you offer a suggestion?"

Dread crept over Brian like an engulfing blanket. He struggled to maintain his composure and dug his fingernails into his palms to stop his hands from trembling while Abdel sat next to Tariq, staring ahead and saying nothing.

"I asked you a question, Mr. Sadler. It would be impolite for you not to answer me."

"You don't have to do that," Brian spluttered. "I can get his attention without your doing anything to me."

"You can indeed, and that is why we are together now. But I want him to know how serious I am. President Harrison is only alive today because that idiot Chambliss Parkes failed me. I made him president of the United States, Mr. Sadler, but all too briefly. Surely you recall all of that."

Brian nodded.

"I want to make a statement to your friend. I have been told I have a – how do you say it in English? – a flair for the dramatic, and I want to do something the president

110

will never forget, something that will make him listen. If it's not to be your ear or your finger, what should I do?"

"I'll tell him whatever you ask. He'll listen – I'll convince him."

Tariq smiled. "I have an idea. What if I kill your wife? Would that help convince him – and perhaps yourself as well – that I am someone to take seriously?"

Brian flew out of his chair toward the killer. One of the soldiers rushed across the room, grabbed him by the arms and forced him back into the chair.

"Leave her out of this! I've told you I'll help, you crazy bastard! This isn't her fight!"

The terrorist laughed mirthlessly. "Have I struck a nerve? I can see that she is my best course of action. In fact, I have already asked some of my associates in Dallas, Texas, to occupy her for a few days until you and the president can sort things out. Now that I have your attention, I will tell you what I require."

Tariq handed Brian a pad of paper and a pen; then he enumerated several demands. When he was finished, he barked an order and Brian was pulled from his chair and taken back to the room where they'd been held earlier. Five minutes later the door opened and Abdel walked in, visibly shaken and vainly attempting to pull himself together.

"Did you and your friend get everything worked out?" Brian snapped. "Are you still going to pretend you don't know what's going on here?"

Abdel said nothing. He merely glanced up now and then at a camera mounted near the ceiling, its faint red light indicating it was functional.

"He's kidnapped my wife! Do you care about that, you bastard? You're just like he is – a lying coward who pretends to be something he isn't. Tariq's a lunatic, but you're just as bad. You betray your friends. You double-cross people who offer to help you. If my wife ..." He paused, choking up. "If something happens to her, it's *your* fault. And you'll pay. I'll make you pay."

The Arab sat on the floor with his head hung low until some men came for them.

Two hours later Brian and Abdel arrived back at the primitive Sheikh Hussein border crossing. They had made the trip in silence. Furious, Brian wanted to force Abdel to reveal what was really going on, but with Tariq's goons in the front seat, he had to wait. Regardless, his most pressing priority was Nicole. He was terrified – desperate to hear her voice, to learn that Tariq's words had been merely threats and that she was safe. It was all he could do to remain calm until he could get to a phone.

At the border his captors handed back everything he and Abdel had come with – passports, cellphones, credit cards and cash. Night had fallen and floodlights bathed the ten-foot fence between the countries in an eerie yellow glow. Tariq had given them safe-passage documents to present to the Jordanian guards, and they moved easily through the checkpoint. The Israeli side was a different story. Six soldiers raised their rifles and ordered them to drop to the ground with arms and legs outstretched. They were searched and their passports were seized.

A few minutes later a captain arrived, handed back their documents and apologized that they had been ordered to the ground. It was because they had walked across, he explained. The customary way to come from Jordan was on a shuttle bus and two men walking had caused alarm.

Once Brian had missed his deadline for leaving the country, the prime minister's office circulated a flyer via email to police stations and army checkpoints throughout Israel. If Brian was sighted, he should be detained, treated with the courtesy afforded diplomatic personnel, and transferred to the American embassy for deportation.

"I've already called your embassy," the captain advised. They're sending a car from Tiberias. It should take less than an hour. In the meantime, please relax here in my office. May I offer you some tea and something to eat?"

"I have to make a call. May I have privacy?" he asked.

"Of course, but I must inform you that you are being officially detained. You are not under arrest, but you also are not free to leave. Please do not attempt anything foolish." He

112

stepped out of the room, positioning guards outside the door and windows. If Brian had intended to run, it would have been impossible.

Now it was just him and Abdel in the tiny office. "Get out of here!" he said curtly. "Wait outside until I'm finished." After today, the less the Arab knew about his personal life, the better.

"I'm sorry," Abdel mumbled as he walked out.

"Sure you are. Screw you."

He called Nicole's cellphone, but it went immediately to voicemail. "Call me when you get this," he said, desperate to hear from her. "It's urgent."

He called the concierge in the lobby of their condominium building. Nicole had left a couple of hours ago with two men, he advised. Fear and anger swept over Brian once again as the concierge explained, "She seemed in good spirits when they drove away. Is everything okay? Is there something I can do to help?"

"No, it's fine," he said, wishing it was. Calling the police wasn't an option. He had nothing to tell them. There was only one person he could reach out to. Frantically he placed a call to Cynthia Beal at the White House. When she picked up, he literally screamed into the phone.

"I need Harry! I need to talk to him now!"

His panic-stricken, gasping words startled her. "The president's in a meeting, but he left specific instructions to interrupt if you called. Are you all right, Brian? Can you hold a moment while I get him on the line?"

He said he was all right but to hurry. He held everything together until he heard Harry's voice, but when that happened, he lost control.

"Nicole's been kidnapped!" Brian blurted in a moan of anguish.

"She's okay. Don't worry."

"No, she isn't! You don't know what I'm talking about! Tariq kidnapped her! He told me he has her!"

"Easy, Brian. Everything's okay. He lied to you. He may have wanted to kidnap her, but she's safe – *we* have her. The ambassador called me three hours ago and told me you didn't show up at the airport. It was clear you were going to miss your deadline and the PM was going to issue an arrest warrant. I didn't know what you were doing, but I knew that you wouldn't simply ignore his order. I asked the FBI to take Nicole to a safe place until I heard from you."

"Where is she? I want to talk to her!"

Harry tried to soothe his desperate friend. "I understand, and I'm going to work that out. I don't know exactly where she is because I didn't ask. Her phone is turned off, but I'll call the FBI director when we hang up. I promise she'll call you soon. But what about you? You said Tariq kidnapped you? Where are you now? Are you safe?"

"He took me to Jordan and gave me a message for you. Then he let me go. I'm at an Israeli checkpoint, waiting for someone from the embassy to pick me up. Abdel's with me, but I'm not going into all this right now. I want to talk to Nicole first. I hope you understand. After I speak with her, I'll tell you everything."

"No, Brian! This is critical! I need to know what Tariq wanted."

"I get it, Harry, but it'll have to wait until Nicole calls me. Once I hear her voice, I'll tell you everything. There's nothing that can't wait and she comes first." He hung up, thinking that he'd never spoken to the president so harshly. But Harry would understand.

He sat in the cramped office and fidgeted for twenty minutes, unable to concentrate on anything but her. At last his phone rang and Nicole sobbed, "Honey, are you all right? FBI agents came to our building. They said you failed to show up for a flight and they made me leave the house on five minutes' notice! I'm in a safe house, but I can't tell anyone where it is. There's an agent here in the room with me right now. I'm scared, Brian. Where are you? Are you under arrest? Why didn't you tell me you were leaving Israel tonight?"

"I'm fine," he assured her, breathing deeply as relief swept over him. He didn't tell her much of his saga because there was no need to give her more reason to worry. "It's a long story and I'll fill you in later. I'm at a border crossing point in northern Israel and I'm waiting for someone from the embassy to pick me up. I was taken to Jordan and given a message for Harry. I wasn't harmed at all and I'm safe, so everything's good except I missed my flight. I didn't tell you because ..." He paused, trying to put a positive spin on the prime minister's twenty-four-hour eviction notice. "I ... I wanted to surprise you. I was going to Istanbul. I think I would have spent the night there and then flown to the States tomorrow. I hadn't worked it all out."

She could tell from his hesitation that he was holding something back. "What is it, Brian? Since I've known you, I've never heard you say you hadn't worked out a flight itinerary the minute you knew you were going. What are you not telling me? Do you promise you're safe?"

"I'm as safe as I can be sitting at the border a hundred feet from Jordan with people on both sides itching to start a war. You're right, Nicole. You're right about the danger here. There are tanks and soldiers all over the place, but I'm in Israel so, yes, I think I'm safe for now. And I'll tell you the real reason I was leaving Israel tonight." He told Nicole that he had been caught yesterday afternoon in the Muslim Quarter during a lockdown. He'd called the embassy for help but hadn't expected the ambassador himself to intervene. Tempers had flared, feathers had been ruffled, and the prime minister gave him twenty-four hours to leave. He missed the deadline because he was "meeting" – he sugarcoated the kidnapping part for now – with a member of al Qaeda who wanted Brian to pass a message to Harry.

"Have you talked to Harry?"

"Yes. I called him after I couldn't reach you a few minutes ago. He had them take you away because I went missing for a few hours and Harry was concerned for your safety." Brian didn't mention Tariq's terrifying claim to have kidnapped her.

"I'm sorry I've been such a jerk," he said earnestly. "I'm out of here as soon as I can make it happen."

They agreed she'd call him again a few hours from now, around 11 p.m. in Jerusalem. By then he should be back at the hotel.

He opened the door of the captain's office and saw a Mercedes sedan with diplomatic plates swing into the parking lot. Two men ushered Abdel and Brian into the backseat and they began the drive to Jerusalem. The man in the passenger seat made a call, spoke for a moment and handed the phone to Brian.

"The ambassador would like a word," he advised.

There was no small talk and no expression of relief that Brian was back on Israeli soil. The diplomat's words were terse and devoid of emotion. Given that he only missed his deadline because he'd been kidnapped, the prime minister had given Brian a twenty-four-hour reprieve. The same flight – Haifa to Istanbul – was arranged for tomorrow. A car would pick him up at the David Citadel at two.

"Be in that car," the ambassador warned. "The prime minister is at the end of his rope. He promised you'll find yourself in jail if you miss the deadline again, no matter what excuses you come up with. You're out of time, Mr. Sadler. Is there anything about what I am saying that you don't understand?"

Brian understood. His mind raced to figure out exactly how he could do what he needed in the short time left.

"How long a drive is it from Haifa to Beth Shean?" he asked the driver.

"Maybe an hour," the man replied. "But my instructions are to deliver you to the David Citadel Hotel, sir."

"Right. I'm just asking."

Brian texted Cynthia Beal and told her he should be at the hotel in ninety minutes and could talk with Harry then if the president was available.

He turned to Abdel, who was sitting next to him, looking straight ahead. The dealer had been part of Brian's plan to produce the greatest television documentary of his career, but that dream was gone now. Abdel wasn't a colleague any more. He was as much a terrorist as his boss.

"I was a fool to trust you. You're a damned liar."

116

"No! I told you the truth!" Abdel whined. "I admitted I was once involved with al Qaeda, but that was before Tariq's time. I detest him and everything he stands for. I am not his brother – I never have been. That was his ruse to make you distrust me. You must believe me. Everything I told you is the truth. We must protect the treasure immediately!"

"That's not what you want at all! He kept you with him when I was taken back to the cell. What did you talk about? Did he give you instructions on how to steal the treasure?"

"No! No, that is not true! He wants me to do a job for al Qaeda. He wants me to find out who the Zulqarnayn is. It's a legendary figure – a person who guards a treasure and who protects the world against evil, false gods. I told him I don't know who it is and I can't find out."

"You expect me to believe that a terrorist asked you – his follower – to tell him about some legendary creature?"

"It's not a creature. It's a man. It's a position that's been passed down for centuries. Some people believe Cyrus the First was a Zulqarnayn. Do you see why they might think that? It was he who allowed the Jews to leave Babylon and recover the temple treasures. Tariq wants the treasure for himself. That's what that is all about."

Brian refused to believe anything the man said now. He needed Abdel for just one more thing. Then it would all be over. There would be no help from him to move Abdel's precious objects to London. They wouldn't create a documentary together. Brian would cut the cord after just one last mission.

He leaned toward the front seat and asked, "I'm not a prisoner, correct?"

"No, sir," the agent replied.

"Then please turn on your radio. I want to speak to my colleague in private."

The man complied, selecting a station with American pop music and turning it up enough to mask a conversation in the back.

Brian whispered, "If you want me to believe you, then take me back to Beth Shean. How early can we get inside the park and go back to the cave?"

Abdel raised his eyebrows. After all this, why did he want to go back? The experience with Tariq had terrified Abdel. He could only imagine how scared Brian must have been, yet he wanted to go to the cavern again.

The man's delusional, he thought to himself. But Brian's request gave him hope. *As much as he distrusts me now, he still needs me to show him where the cave is. He still wants to do a documentary. If I am to be part of it, I must regain his trust.*

"Certainly, I will take you," he murmured eagerly. "We could leave at four in the morning, be there by six, spend two hours and be back at your hotel by noon. But it may be dangerous."

"Tariq won't do anything to me for now, because I'm his messenger boy," Brian replied, hoping that was true.

"It's not Tariq I'm concerned about. War could break out at any moment. I'm not sure how safe it is to travel anywhere in Israel."

"I'll take my chances and I'm arranging the driver this time. I don't trust Mohammed or you, and maybe it'll be less dangerous if we do things my way. Leave the hood at home. There are no more secrets after what you put me through today."

Abdel apologized again. Even after everything, part of Brian wanted to believe that his trust had not been misplaced – that he wasn't as bad a judge of character as he'd been on other occasions in the past. But none of that mattered. At 6:15 p.m. tomorrow Brian would be on a flight to Turkey and this part would be over.

Brian hadn't been in his hotel room five minutes when his cellphone rang. He took a split of white wine from the minibar, poured a glass and lay back on the bed, ready to explain everything to Harry.

CHAPTER SIXTEEN

Five men sat around the president's desk in the Oval Office. Besides Harry, there were Stan Kendrick, the CIA director; Clark Vernon, Secretary of Defense; Ken Upton, NSA director; and Bob Cruickshank, head of the CIA's Mossad desk.

The president's advisers had been brought up to speed on where things stood. They knew that the two CIA agents assigned to follow Brian yesterday had been forced to drop the tail when the driver became aware he was being followed. They were far more skilled at this than the driver was, but with so little traffic at that time of day, there was no way to stay out of sight. Instead they had headed to the toll road and driven as quickly as possible to Beth Shean, knowing that Brian was supposed to be returning to the site that morning. But the driver and his passengers hadn't shown up.

CIA agents at the American embassy tracked Brian's phone as he'd been driven to the border town of Hamat Gader, Israel. The agents who had gone to Beth Shean were redirected to the area, where they found a long-abandoned dirt road with fresh tire tracks. The tracks ran directly to the border, where from a distance they watched Jordanian soldiers guarding a hole in the fence – one large enough for a car to pass through.

A few minutes later Brian's phone had stopped sending signals. The CIA agents waited until they saw Brian's driver driving back along the abandoned road, alone. The soldiers waved him through the fence into Israel and then began to repair it.

The agents had been told to follow without intercepting, and they successfully tailed him back to

Jerusalem without his realizing it. He went directly to his house and parked the Land Rover outside it. They returned to the embassy, but if they'd watched his house for another hour, they'd have seen him leave to meet his handler.

They'd lost track of Brian for several hours, but his cellphone came back online at the Sheikh Hussein border crossing, twenty miles south of where he had entered Jordan. Minutes later he had called Cynthia Beal and spoken with the president.

"I'm going to try Brian's phone now," Harry said when the background discussion was concluded. The call went through, and he told Brian he was on speaker and announced who the others in the room were. His first words expressed his relief that Brian was safely back in Israel.

Brian told them everything that had happened after he donned the hood when they were on the road to Beth Shean. He described the kidnapping and Abdel's apparent fear of Tariq. He said that the terrorist had seated Abdel next to him and called him a brother. After the experience, he had no idea if Abdel was friend or foe. He revealed the terror he'd felt when Tariq told him Nicole had been taken captive, and his relief when he learned that wasn't true.

"Please keep an eye on her," he implored. "I'm certain Tariq's men would have kidnapped her today if the FBI hadn't gotten there first."

"I agree," Secretary Vernon interjected. "That failure must have really pissed him off, like poking a rattlesnake with a stick."

"Is there any way she could safely meet me in London? I'm planning on flying there tomorrow and I was hoping she could be there too."

"Throw enough money at a problem and you can make anything happen," Harry kidded. "It's a good thing you're a wealthy adventurer!"

"Whatever it takes is fine. I'd appreciate it if your people could check into it. If she wants to, that is."

Harry promised to speak with her.

"Now to the real issue here. What message does Tariq have for America?"

"He made me write it down. I'll shoot a picture of my notes and send them when we're done. He has three demands, each one with its own consequence should you fail to act. The first one's about the embassy. You have seventy-two hours to announce that you will move the embassy back to Tel Aviv within thirty days. If you refuse, he will inflict terrible casualties on the Americans who work there.

"Next, he wants US involvement in the Syrian civil war to end within three months. If that doesn't happen, he promises to rain down terror from the skies on what he calls the Hebrew infidels."

"That son of a bitch!" the CIA director blurted. "Mr. President, you know what he's capable of. How can we respond –"

"Hang on, Stan. There's one more demand."

"Right. The last one is that all fourteen members of al Qaeda who are prisoners in Guantanamo must be released within sixty days. If you refuse, beginning on day sixty-one he will kidnap and publicly execute one American per day until the demand is met."

Harry thanked Brian for the information and expressed his regret for the danger Brian had gotten himself into. "Get out of there safely," he urged. "We all want you back."

"Tomorrow," Brian promised. "Istanbul tomorrow, London the next day. I can't wait."

He had one thing left to do – one last visit to Beth Shean.

Once Brian was off the call, the men in the Oval Office sat in silence. They'd heard bluster from one wannabe terrorist after another, but this was different. Tariq was a known quantity. He had no compassion or scruples. Moreover, each of them knew this wasn't about justice for al Qaeda.

"Bob, give us your take on what he's up to," the president said.

"Sir, Tariq's not in this for the noble gesture of helping his people," Cruickshank replied. "This is about humiliating America. He's been furious ever since he found out you and Vice President Taylor didn't really die a couple of years ago. He was tricked and he's fumed about it ever since. What he wants is to force America to comply with his demands, giving him stature and credibility as someone we're afraid of."

"That's right," Secretary Vernon interjected. "He's a classic bully who didn't get his way. The problem for us is that he has the power to do everything he's threatening. We have only one course of action – take him out and do it quickly."

"Let's stay on this subject for now and we'll get to that one later. Any suggestions on how we deal with his demands?"

Upton said, "Mr. President, there's only one of that bastard's demands that we have to deal with immediately. Everything but the first one is months out. Let's cut to the chase. Do you have any intention of moving the embassy back to Tel Aviv?"

"Absolutely not."

"I figured as much, and I agree wholeheartedly. But Tariq only gave us seventy-two hours to comply. If you don't make a statement in three days, he says he'll inflict casualties on the people there. Can he do it? Who the hell knows, but the clock's ticking and we don't know exactly when he started the timer. Since we're not going to give him what he wants, I think we need to get our people out of harm's way immediately."

"What kind of safe rooms do they have in the compound?" Harry asked.

"Nothing like what an embassy would typically have. As you know, they're occupying temporary space in the consulate general's office. It's a grouping of buildings with perimeter security and there are rooms below ground level, but they're meant for classified briefings, not protection."

"Get the ambassador's assessment," the president ordered. "I want his people out of there if there's the slightest risk of harm to them. They can go right back to the compound in Tel Aviv. It'll be inconvenient, but safety's all that matters. Get back with me as quickly as you can. We'll meet again tomorrow morning."

———

Thirty minutes after his conversation with Harry, Brian lounged in the bathtub, savoring the second martini from a pitcher room service had delivered, and recalling his frightening day. It all seemed surreal now that he was back in civilization. This time he'd gone too far, Brian had to admit. He'd been terrified during the ordeal, but now he felt confident that he could make one final trip without putting himself in danger. He had an amazing, irrational ability to cast off negativity when he wasn't in trouble, and he was aware of it. Now he allowed the martinis to do the talking, presenting a convincing case for a quick trip up to the cavern and back before anything bad happened.

The ring of his cellphone pierced the reverie and the rational argument the martinis were making.

The caller's words were curt. "Mr. Sadler, this is John Sheller. I hear you plan to go to Beth Shean again before you leave tomorrow."

"You know, Ambassador, that pisses me off. I asked for a conversation in private. What did they do, record it? With all due respect, my only requirement is to be on a plane at 6 p.m. tomorrow. Unless you're placing me under arrest, I'm free to do anything I wish until then. Am I correct about that, or am I missing something?"

The ambassador was almost out of patience. "I'm being as tolerant of the situation as possible only because of your relationship with President Harrison," he snapped. "To be perfectly frank, I can see why the prime minister is fed up with all this. We're in a crisis here and more than enough time has been wasted on one American visitor. I've offered you protection, but you refused. You're pissed, Mr. Sadler, but so am I. I've informed the president that if you're not out of Israel by tomorrow's deadline, I refuse to help you further. He agreed with me. We can only do so much. It's up to you to cooperate."

"Understood," Brian replied, a little remorseful at how he'd treated the man who had helped him out of trouble more than once. Brian truly did understand. He hadn't wanted the problems he'd encountered, and he had undoubtedly created his own perils. Even now his quest for the treasure of Isaiah was causing him to make plans that might be dangerous. The smart thing to do was to go to the embassy and stay until a chauffeur took him to the airport tomorrow afternoon. He'd be safe and he'd get out of the country without a hitch. But instead of cooperating, he was throwing curveballs. And here came another one.

"You're correct that I'm going to Beth Shean tomorrow morning," he continued. "My driver will drop me at the airport by four. That's two hours before my flight, so I won't need your people to pick me up in Jerusalem."

"Have it your way," Sheller replied. "There's just one last thing. The prime minister is sending a man from the Mossad over to the hotel to interview you about what happened to you and Abdel Malouf today. He'll be in the lobby in a few minutes."

"I've had a long day –"

"And it's about to get even longer," the ambassador replied testily. "You have no choice, sir. You're in Shigon's country and you'll do what he requires."

It was after ten when he walked downstairs, found the Mossad agent and told him their conversation was going to be over dinner. Brian hadn't eaten all day and he was famished. He spent an hour with the man, giving him every detail about the kidnapping, Abdel's involvement and why Tariq had brought him to Jordan.

"What message did he want to give to your president?" the agent asked.

"I can't tell you that. The information was for President Harrison and it's not my place to say what it was. If my government wants to share it, that's a decision for someone in a higher pay grade than mine."

His phone rang from the same blocked number Nicole had used earlier. "I have to take this," he said. "Give me some privacy, please."

The agent walked across the room and waited by the entryway, his eyes never leaving Brian's table.

"Hey, baby. I'm being interviewed by the Mossad, so we need to make this quick."

"Where are you?"

"In the dining room at the David Citadel. Everything's fine and I'll be in Istanbul tomorrow night. Why don't you fly to London and I'll meet you at the flat the day after tomorrow?"

She said she'd think about it and he explained that he had to get some sleep tonight for an early wake-up call. He was making a last trip to Beth Shean to video the treasure in hopes of making a documentary, and he asked that she call him again after 8 p.m. Dallas time. They would be on the road to Beth Shean by then.

Dear God, she thought to herself. *After all this he wants to go back.*

"This time nothing's going to happen because they've asked me to communicate with Harry. I'll explain everything once we're together. I have to get some sleep. Call me later, sweetie."

He motioned the agent back to his table. After more questioning Brian went to his room, grateful to be alone at last. He packed his gear, crawled into bed and fell into a dark, dreamless void that only ended with the shrill sound of his phone's alarm at 3:30 a.m.

CHAPTER SEVENTEEN

Brian checked out and the concierge directed Abdel and him to a black sedan. The driver stowed Brian's luggage in the trunk and asked where they were going.

"Beth Shean National Park," Abdel instructed and moments later they were speeding through empty streets that would be jammed with traffic in a few hours. He asked the driver to use Highway 90 through Jericho, the shorter route that Mohammed had taken, but the driver said it wasn't possible.

"They closed parts of the highway last night because of the troop buildups along the border. We have to take the toll road, but it should be a quick trip this time of the morning."

"What have you learned about your wife?" Abdel asked anxiously, having heard Tariq's claim to have kidnapped her in Dallas.

Brian was conflicted. He had trusted Abdel once and the Arab was his key to seeing the cavern again, but naively trusting people was a fault of his. Warning signs about Abdel were everywhere. Was he an al Qaeda operative after all? Brian couldn't afford to be naive again. He wouldn't tell Abdel about Nicole.

"Tariq was bluffing," he said as his phone rang. It was Nicole; he told her that he was in a car with two other people and she understood that he wouldn't be saying much on his side. Exuberantly she advised him that she was taking the overnight flight to London this evening.

"Did Harry call you?" he asked.

"Yes, and Brian, if you'll just meet me tomorrow I'll forgive you for being such an ass. I feel like all I've done is nag at you but I really don't think you understand how what you do makes me feel."

"I've been a fool," he admitted. "I've been selfish about all this. I can't talk now but I promise things will be different."

He changed the subject. Since he knew she'd been in federal protection, he asked her how Harry had arranged for her safety during the flight.

"He said it's not going to be cheap, but I told him you were good for whatever it took. I hope I'm right about that!"

She explained that an armed federal marshal would take her from the safe house to the airport. He'd fly to London in the seat next to her. Upon arrival, she would be handed over to agents from a London security firm Brian had used in the past. There would be a guard inside their apartment and two more outside, twenty-four hours a day. It all sounded fine to Brian and he told her how glad he was too.

"Please tell me this time you're really coming back to me," she said. He could sense the hesitancy in her voice, the desperate hope that he was still coming.

"Yes! You can count on it!" He'd be in Istanbul tonight and on a British Airways flight to London tomorrow morning. By evening they'd be together. She told him how happy that made her, and as always, she urged him to be careful. He promised to check in with her later.

"That was your wife?" Abdel asked.

Brian nodded and changed the subject. He wondered if Abdel had been questioned by the Mossad last evening, but he decided not to ask. Instead he mentioned the growing likelihood that someone with an itchy trigger finger would start a war. Abdel expressed hope that conflict could be avoided and he apologized again for selfishly wanting to get his antiquities out of the country as soon as possible.

"I have worked a lifetime in this city, building a business and a reputation of which I am proud, and it would be devastating to see everything go away on a moment's notice. After everything that has happened, I am grateful you are still willing to help me."

This moment – when Abdel was leading him back to the treasure – wasn't the time to tell him the offer was off the table. Instead Brian pointed out how many times people in similar situations to Abdel's – doctors or dentists in Cuba, scientists and teachers from Vietnam and so many others – had walked away from everything and started over. A veterinarian from Havana might be sweeping floors in a bank building in Dallas for minimum wage, but the man would be thankful that his life had been spared and that his family had gotten out with him.

"If worse comes to worst," Brian advised, "you could leave Israel and start all over. Even if you lost everything you owned, you'd still have the most important things – your contacts and your reputation."

Abdel chose his words carefully in front of the driver. One never knew who worked for the Mossad. There were spies everywhere. He should know – he'd been one himself.

"I can only pray that Allah does not intend such a fate for me," he lamented. "I have done many wrong things. I pledged allegiance to a group now run by a merciless monster. But I saw the error in that decision and I have made things right. I am a good man, Brian. My hope is for peace in Israel, a home for both Jews and Palestinians and a life for all people free from strife and worry."

Brian wasn't sure if he should believe what Abdel was saying. "As noble as it sounds, that's not realistic," he replied. The threat of military action was greater at this moment than at any time since the Six-Day War in 1967 and both knew it. It was wishful thinking to believe this could somehow go away. Both the Bible and the Quran predicted conflict between these peoples until the end times.

Around seven, just as the sun's first rays were peeking over Mount Gilead, they arrived at the archaeological park. Abdel guided the driver to the top of the hill and asked him to stay with the car until they returned.

"Ready for a hike?" he said to Brian, pointing to a trail leading into a grove of trees.

"You bet!" he replied, his adrenalin pumping.

In a few minutes, they were at the edge of the cliff where Abdel had allowed Brian to remove his hood the last time. He found the rope; they lowered themselves to the brushy ledge and crawled into the cave. They donned their headlamps and Brian found himself captivated once more by the Egyptian statues.

"Who else knows about this place?" Brian asked.

"I learned about it from its discoverer, and I trust him to keep it a secret because of something I promised him. I hope this does not offend you, but I told him he might become wealthy if he would let me show this cave to the famous American treasure hunter Brian Sadler. I let him think that you and I might collaborate on a television documentary called 'Hidden Treasures of the Bible.'"

Brian wasn't offended; he would have done the same thing in Abdel's situation. One way or another, he intended to film the cavern before anyone disturbed the treasure. This opportunity would never come again. For now, he had to pretend their agreement was still on and he would talk about his promise to Abdel later.

"I'm excited about a documentary," he replied truthfully. "But it simply won't happen unless you allow me to take videos and pictures today. The networks have made a lot of money off my work, but they're hardheaded businessmen who are motivated by one thing – profit. If I demonstrate what kind of revenue the show can generate, I'm certain they'll jump on it. There may even be network bidding wars on this one."

Abdel thought to himself that he would soon be a celebrity. He had expected Brian to want to shoot video this time, and his reasoning made perfect sense. Bubbling with excitement, he gave permission for pictures and videos but only for Brian's production people. He made him promise there would be no announcement until Abdel allowed it.

Brian shot footage of the statues and filmed their walk through the narrow passageway. At the entrance to the treasure room itself, he took a panoramic shot. He walked around the room, zeroing in on the things that had most captivated him the first time he came – the miniature arks, the candelabra and goblets, and the haphazard piles of golden relics.

Forty minutes later he pocketed his phone and stood silently.

Abdel asked if he was ready to go, but Brian shook his head.

"Another couple of minutes," he said. "This place makes me feel like I'm in church. I have a sense of peace and reverence here, as though God is nearby. Do you know what I mean?"

"Yes," Abdel confessed. "I have similar feelings, even though these objects are not a part of my religion. The prophets Isaiah and Ezra, King Cyrus of Persia and the other great men who had a hand in the story of the temple treasure – all of them are important in Islam just as they are to Christians and Jews. One cannot help but be awed by the presence of such wonders."

They sidled back up the corridor and emerged into the sunlight. Brian thought he heard someone yelling. They quickly climbed the rope, and as they entered the grove of trees, he heard it again.

"Mr. Sadler! Mr. Sadler! Can you hear me?"

"That's our driver! Hurry! Something's wrong!" As they ran, he yelled, "We're coming!"

The driver was in the front seat with the engine running. "We must leave quickly!" he cried. "There's been an attack!"

As he drove frantically toward Jerusalem, the man explained that Syria had launched a missile against Israel that had exploded before entering Israeli airspace. Early reports indicated it struck and destroyed a building on the Syrian side of the border. Regardless of its failure, the intended attack sent an ominous message that the Arabs didn't intend to sit still any longer. If the missile had worked properly – if it had entered Israeli airspace – it would have been an act of war.

Brian read the report on his phone, noting that Israel was going into full battle mode. All airports had been closed and a no-fly zone had been established across the nation.

There would be no cross-border vehicular traffic, and interior checkpoints between Jewish- and Palestinian-controlled lands were closed. Residents of the Gaza Strip, the West Bank and other areas occupied by the PLO were no longer allowed to pass into areas controlled by the Jews.

Jerusalem was a unique problem, given the tenuous coexistence between Palestinians and Jews. Definable Arab areas would be cordoned off, the news report advised, and the Old City itself would be emptied. Everyone inside would be forced to leave and the walled city would be on lockdown.

Brian read that part of the story to Abdel, who lamented that he had waited too long to act. "Everything I have worked for will be gone when I see my shop next."

"But if the authorities remove every single person from the Old City, there won't be anyone left to loot your store."

"They can't remove everyone. Forty thousand people live inside the walls. Forty thousand! The Jews aren't going to send soldiers on a house-to-house search because it would infuriate the people. They will attempt to clear out the area, but they won't find those who are determined to stay. Those people are the ones who will create problems for the rest of us. They will rob and loot and vandalize."

Brian knew he was right, and there really was nothing they could do about it now.

The trip back took much longer because of hastily erected military checkpoints along the highway. Long lines of cars waited to be searched and cleared to pass. At the first one they encountered, soldiers examined their passports, asked where they had been and were going, and looked under the car's hood and in its trunk. The next checkpoint was at the exit from the tollway to the main east-west highway between Tel Aviv and Jerusalem. The search at that one was far more thorough. This time they had to exit the vehicle and bomb dogs sniffed through its interior. With all the delays, it was mid-afternoon when they finally arrived back in Jerusalem. Brian would have been late, but it didn't matter now. Nobody was leaving the country now.

Hoping he could get his room back, Brian had called earlier and snagged the last room – a two-bedroom suite at a nightly rate three times higher than his last one. He would have paid even more for the security and comfort of the David Citadel.

They passed throngs of people marching in the streets, screaming and chanting. Police and soldiers in riot gear kept a close eye, but they also maintained a respectable distance. Although the situation was unnerving, Brian understood that unless things turned violent, it was better for soldiers to let people vent their emotions instead of inciting them further. The news flashes were popping up on his phone faster than he could read them. Brian told the driver that there were several thousand students massing outside the parliament building. Since streets all around the Knesset were shut down, the man took an alternate route.

Brian got a call from the ambassador, who pointed out sharply that Brian had successfully dodged one more attempt to force him to leave Israel. The country was virtually an island now, sealed off from the rest of the world and hunkering down for an attack. The ambassador said he'd been in touch with the prime minister's office. The whereabouts of Brian Sadler was no longer a priority for Shigon, but again Sheller strongly urged him to move to the embassy.

"I'm back at my hotel for tonight," he answered, unwilling to give up what little freedom he might still have. The embassy would be a fortress within a fortress, and once he was inside, he knew he wouldn't be allowed out again. The ambassador was neither happy nor surprised about the response. President Harrison had told him that Sadler didn't handle restrictions well, and he had asked Sheller to do what he could without curtailing Brian's movements. That was fine with him. If the president's friend deliberately put himself in danger, then that was his problem. If Sadler came calling for help, that would be another thing. He didn't intend to jeopardize American lives to save one foolhardy adventurer, although his boss – the president – could change Sheller's mind in a flash if it happened.

The David Citadel Hotel was a different place than when they'd left eight hours before. It was a stronghold with tall metal fences blocking both ends of the porte cochere that was usually packed with idling taxis and limos. The driver dropped them along the sidewalk that was teeming with people in line to enter the hotel. When it was their turn, Brian showed his passport to an armed security guard, who checked his name off a list of registered guests. Abdel presented his documents and Brian said they were together, working on a business deal. The man jotted Abdel's information on another sheet while a guard frisked him.

Once they were inside, Brian left his suitcase with the concierge and they went directly to the second-floor bar. Brian ordered a glass of wine and Abdel had a coffee. Relaxed at last, they visited the lunch buffet and chose an outside table. From this vantage point it was easy to forget what was happening just outside their five-star refuge. Guests chatted and families with kids splashed and laughed in the pool a floor below them. It was a pleasant, surreal oasis in the middle of a city on edge, tensely awaiting the next move.

Brian stepped away from the table and called Nicole. He brought her up to speed on where he was and how his day had gone. He had proof of the treasures now, something tangible to begin the process of a documentary, and he said his work here was almost done. He wanted a meeting with the director of the Antiquities Authority and he'd be out of Israel immediately afterwards.

Sitting in her office alone, Nicole thought about her husband and all the things he was experiencing in Jerusalem. Normal people would be terrified, she mused, wishing for a moment that Brian was one of those.

But there was nothing normal about him. She knew he was happier to be in the middle of chaos than to be tied down to a desk job somewhere. She knew him well after all these years, and there was one thing she knew for sure – when his time was finally up, he damned sure wouldn't die sitting in a La-Z-Boy at some retirement village.

She asked herself which way was better? She hoped they'd grow old together, strolling through Walmart on the weekly grocery run or going to dinner with friends. But there was also the realization that someday he might head out on one of his adventures and never return.

He was never happier than when he was on the trail of another discovery. She knew that better than anyone, and so she would keep on listening without complaining while her heart and her gut wrenched from the terrifying possibilities of his choices.

CHAPTER EIGHTEEN

Having nowhere to spend the night in Jerusalem, Abdel gratefully accepted Brian's offer to use his second bedroom. That offer almost didn't become reality, however. Instead of fighting the hubbub and sporadic demonstrations outside, not to mention the endless line to reenter the hotel, they decided to stay in the suite until cocktail hour. Brian shared his computer, allowing Abdel to check emails and conduct some business. That allowed the time to pass more quickly, and at five they went downstairs for Brian's nightly martini and an early dinner. Soon after they were seated, a hotel employee approached and asked when Mr. Malouf would be leaving the building. The government had put a 10 p.m. curfew in place, he advised. Brian saw through the man's question – it was clear that the hotel's security team was carefully monitoring those people who belonged in the building and those who did not.

Brian explained that he had asked his friend to stay overnight since he wasn't allowed to return to his house in the Old City. The employee excused himself to speak with the manager. When he returned, he asked Brian and his guest to stop by the front desk after dinner. There the night manager, a man with whom Brian had interacted previously, apologized for the inconvenience but said that his orders were that no one except registered guests could be on the premises after the curfew. Mr. Malouf would have to leave.

He rarely pulled strings to make things happen, but now it was required. Abdel truly had no place to go. "We'll be back in a moment," Brian said, looking at his watch and calculating the time in D.C. With the manager keeping a close eye, he and Abdel sat in the lobby as he placed a call, spoke for a moment, put it on hold and walked back to the front desk. He handed his phone to the manager, who listened as Cynthia Beal, personal assistant to the president of the United States, requested that Mr. Sadler be allowed an exception to the rule.

The manager handed his phone back and left for a few minutes, returning to say he was pleased to allow Mr. Malouf to spend the night, given his stature in Jerusalem as a prominent antiquities dealer. "But only the one night," he advised. "I'm afraid tomorrow we must enforce our policy."

Brian took the master bedroom and Abdel the other. Drained from the long day, they turned in early.

At 1:49 a.m. three bombers soared into the sky from the deck of the USS *Harry Truman*, a Nimitz-class aircraft carrier in the Mediterranean Sea. Within the hour, the Syrian base from where the dud missile had been launched lay in smoking ruins. Soon after, the White House press secretary issued a brief statement saying that there would be no further strikes unless Israel and its allies were provoked again.

They awoke around seven, turned on the news and watched the head of the Palestinian Liberation Organization offer peace in Jerusalem in exchange for a lifting of the lockdown at the Old City and the other Arab-controlled areas. By noon Shigon had agreed. Although its borders and airports remained closed, things slowly began returning to normal inside Israel.

"Will you come with me to the shop?" Abdel asked Brian. "I am apprehensive about what might have happened, and perhaps we can discuss once again how to safeguard my property." Brian said yes; he was interested to see for himself how the Old City had fared during the tumultuous night.

They encountered a gaggle of soldiers and news reporters at the Herod's Gate entrance, but pedestrians flowed in and out of the ancient passageway without impediment, Brian and Abdel among them. They'd heard that the Jaffa and New Gates had reopened for vehicular traffic, although soldiers were still screening for bombs before cars and trucks could enter.

When they turned off the Via Dolorosa and entered the narrow side street, Abdel breathed a sigh of relief. One of the store's plate-glass windows had been shattered, but iron bars behind it had kept anyone from entering. He had wisely removed everything from the windows and covered things on the showroom floor with tarps. It took only a few minutes to determine that nothing was missing. Shortly afterwards a man in a pickup truck stopped by and offered to put plywood over the hole where the window had been. Looters or hoodlums – who knew which? – had broken dozens of windows overnight while the Old City was on lockdown and the enterprising man was making good money boarding them up. It was a lucrative business, and Abdel quickly hired him.

Brian wanted to focus on the treasure, but Abdel could talk of nothing else but removing his things. He hired the man who was covering his broken window to build shipping crates. Since Brian had made up his mind what he was going to do about the situation, he decided not to stay any longer. He told Abdel he needed to get back.

As he went to the hotel, he saw couples back outdoors at cafés and wine bars, smoking cigarettes and laughing among themselves. People were strolling along the main thoroughfares, window-shopping as though everything were perfectly normal. *These people are resilient as hell,* he thought to himself. *You must give them credit for having guts.* And he longed to be with Nicole.

He called her and she said she was growing increasingly concerned about his safety. "Harry says you won't go to the embassy. Why, Brian? They're offering you a safe haven until they can get you out. Why do you insist on taking the dangerous path every time?"

Same song, second verse, he reflected, and he felt like a heel for even letting such a thought into his head.

"I'm safe at the hotel," he answered, "and I still have freedom to move around. I don't want to make you worry. I hope you understand that."

"You're right. After all, you really are stuck there for the moment, and I'm sure you couldn't be happier that for once I can't nag at you about leaving."

He told her about his second visit to the cavern and about Abdel's spending the night in his suite. He described how yesterday's fear and uncertainty among the people had been replaced by peace and calmness today.

But you know it's not going to last. Just because it's calm at this moment doesn't mean the problems in Israel are over. "I guess you heard that the USA bombed Syria last night," she continued. "I'm glad Harry did something, but I'm also glad he's not pushing too hard. I heard an interview with the Secretary of Defense. He's concerned about another strike on the Sabbath. Remember what happened last Saturday?"

"The airport was destroyed," Brian replied, realizing for the first time that Saturday – the Sabbath – had been chosen deliberately. "Let me get this straight. He thinks another attack this weekend is likely?"

"He used the word *possible* more than once, but I never heard him say *likely*. You know how it goes, though. They're always careful; they don't want to say things that make the friction even worse. Just be careful, especially Friday and Saturday. Unless, of course, you're going to follow your marriage vows – the part where you promised to love and obey your wife, who's telling you to get your butt out of there!"

Brian laughed, wondering if Harry had told her he was persona non grata with the prime minister. If he had, she'd know that as soon as the airports opened, leaving wouldn't be up to him. He'd be out of here, one way or the other.

Despite what little time was left, Brian was determined to leave this country with a television deal in his pocket.

CHAPTER NINETEEN

It was time to come clean with Abdel; it wasn't right to keep his intentions secret when Abdel was fulfilling his side of the bargain. He'd struggled between his own selfish desires and doing what was morally right. He couldn't stop thinking about the treasure and how incredible it would be if he were the one who revealed it to the world. It wasn't the money, although he was sure the show would be immensely profitable. He was wealthy already. It also wasn't the thing he had chased long ago – fame. Now he had plenty of that too. This was different. This trove wasn't just golden objects. Each was a masterpiece in its own right, fit for a king – the King of the Jews. Revealing this secret was personal, like none before had been. These were the treasures of the Bible.

He'd promised to help Abdel; that help was a trade-off and Brian was about to renege. That decision had led to sleepless nights. Brian had proudly been a man of his word – always. In his business, a handshake among two dealers who trusted each other was as good as any contract a lawyer prepared. It took years to build that kind of trust, and Brian was about to go back on his word.

They met for coffee and pastries in the Armenian Quarter not far from Abdel's shop. Atypically effusive, Abdel reported the he had packed six large crates so far and there would be only two more. "I will be ready for the cartage company to pick them up tomorrow morning if you can arrange it. I will feel much better when everything is in London. Thank you so much once again –"

Brian interrupted, placing his hand lightly on Abdel's sleeve. "I haven't been completely honest with you. I thought I knew who you were and what you were made of, even after you admitted you had once worked for al Qaeda. I could see how a poor Syrian kid could become enamored with a group of freedom fighters. I've known you by reputation for years and I've admired what you've accomplished in our field. Knowing your background, I selfishly wanted to overlook anything negative and focus on the incredible treasure you showed me. I was willing to help move your relics to safety because I wanted to treat the world to the same experience as when I first walked into that cavern. But all that changed when one of the most dangerous terrorists in the world invited you to sit by his side. He called you a brother. That was it for me. I won't be a part of that, no matter what it means to me personally."

"But I explained that to you. I am not Tariq's follower any more. All that was for show –"

"No, it wasn't! I saw it with my own eyes. You're afraid of him; I don't blame you – I am too. And you'll do anything he commands. You know that and so do I. You might not agree with what al Qaeda has become these days, but you can never walk away from it. I think if he asked you to kill me, you'd do it – not because you wanted to, but because of what he would do if you didn't."

"Brian, you are wrong. You must believe me. I will not obey Tariq."

"I don't believe you. I'm not sure I ever can. I'm not going to help move your goods and I'm not going to ask for anything else from you. As much as I regret it, this association is over."

"Brian! Please ..."

But Brian was already walking away.

———

When Tariq became the leader of al Qaeda in Syria, Abdel had decided to distance himself from the group he once served loyally. Abu Mohammad al-Joulani had been head of AQS when Abdel was recruited as a young Syrian boy. Joulani was a man of integrity, strength and honor. He was a jihadist, but his wrath was reserved for the infidels. He was guided by his interpretation of the Quran and he was committed to mayhem worldwide against those who refused to serve Allah.

Tariq was on everyone's radar. Mossad was offering millions of euros for his capture, dead or alive. Tariq's murderous acts were the wrong way to prove that Islam was the true faith, Abdel believed. Tariq had no compassion, no conscience and no concern for anyone but himself. Thanks to him, many considered al Qaeda a band of murdering thugs who should be eliminated like roaches in a kitchen. And as far as Abdel was concerned, that assessment was correct, but he couldn't convince Brian to believe him.

While Tariq was alive, there would be no peace effort, no negotiating, no understanding of others' beliefs and hopes. There would be more horrific sprees of killing like the ones in Nice, Brussels and Manchester. It didn't matter whether ISIS or AQS claimed responsibility. At this point, nothing of that magnitude happened without the involvement of Tariq the Hawk.

Since Brian's revelation yesterday that he wouldn't help move the goods, Abdel had made call after call, trying to find another way to get eight heavy shipping crates out of Israel and to the West. The freight forwarders all had the same answer – the country was in turmoil, the main airport was in ruins, and everyone's focus was on protecting Israel from its enemies. Except for essentials coming into the country – armaments, food, communications equipment, medicine and the like – there were no ships arriving or leaving. Call us back when things settle down, they told Abdel, but for him that would be too late.

He sat in the back of his gallery, racking his brain for a solution. His phone rang and he sat quietly as the caller berated him endlessly.

"You're a spineless traitor," Tariq ranted. "You are no friend to al Qaeda – you promise you are still loyal to the cause, but you chose the American over your obligation to me. You are playing me against Brian Sadler, but you are a fool. You cannot imagine what my capabilities are. My eyes and ears are everywhere and I know every move you make. You are planning to escape, to take your precious artifacts to the West, and your new friend Brian Sadler is going to protect them for you. You think you are going to run away, but you took an oath long ago. No one leaves. You know that.

"I should kill you, but I gave you a task. I asked you to find out who the Zulqarnayn is and where the treasure is hidden. Instead of finding answers, you have worked on your own needs and goals. You have twenty-four hours to give me the answers I want. Do you understand?"

Abdel swallowed a lump in his throat and answered, "Yes, sir. I will not fail you ..."

"Since you have failed me so far, you will do one more thing. I want Brian Sadler. I could have him seized at any time, of course, but this is a test of your loyalty. Twenty-four hours from now you will hand your American friend over to me. Do not fail me again, Abdel, or you will face the sword."

Abdel lit a cigarette and shook his head as if that would clear away the fears and danger. He had to think of something, but he was so jittery he couldn't get his thoughts together. He locked the store, walked to a restaurant down the block and ordered wine. The waiter filled Abdel's glass and left the bottle on the table. Abdel took advantage of the man's gesture, resulting in the sale of a bottle instead of a glass. Despondent and desperate, he had drained a second glass, then another and then one more until the bottle was empty.

He made a phone call. "We have to meet. Everything has changed and you are in danger. You must arrange protection for yourself every moment." He listened to Brian's response and said, "All right. I will see you at my shop tomorrow at twelve."

The man at the next table heard every word.

CHAPTER TWENTY

A phone was ringing and ringing. Was it a dream? He moved his hand to the nightstand and found the phone's receiver as his room was illuminated by a bright light. He saw more bright flashes and realized he'd forgotten to close the drapes. Was it a thunderstorm? His mind was still muffled from being jolted awake. He answered the phone and glanced at the clock. It was 2:25 a.m.

"AIR RAID! AIR RAID!" the recorded announcement screamed in English and Hebrew, repeating in a continuous loop. "Move to shelter on the lower level immediately! Take the torch in your nightstand and use the stairs. Do not take the lifts!"

He heard activity in the hallway and became aware of wailing sirens rising and falling outside. He jumped up, pulled on a pair of shorts and a T-shirt, and walked to the window where his sandals were. There was a plume in the sky that reminded him of a giant pop bottle rocket on the Fourth of July. But he knew it was no firecracker. It was a surface-to-air missile and this was war.

"Right this way, right this way, everyone," a man in a dark suit said in a calm, reassuring voice as anxious guests entered a hallway at the bottom of the stairs. "There's coffee and Danish in that room. Please make yourselves comfortable." Down here the walls, ceiling and floor were constructed of solid concrete. The entire basement had been built as a bunker. Brian and the others walked into a massive room where a couple of the girls he'd seen waiting tables in the restaurant yesterday were manning a coffee bar. There were round folding tables and chairs set up around the room. Many of the guests took chairs in front of a large-screen television in one corner of the room, where CNN was broadcasting a news alert.

"What's going on?" Brian asked the concierge who had helped him many times in the past ten days.

Instead of answering, he waved at a man across the room who began making his way over. "Brian Sadler," he said, "this is our general manager, Mr. Wegman."

"Ah yes, Chaim, thank you for letting me know Mr. Sadler had arrived," Wegman replied. To Brian he said, "I was asked to patch you through to your ambassador as soon as you arrived. Please come with me." He guided Brian back into the corridor and to a smaller room down a narrow hallway that appeared to be the hotel's underground command post. There were two soldiers using laptops, typing furiously while their rifles sat nearby. The manager ushered Brian to a desk, placed a call and handed him the phone. Then he left the room.

"Mr. Sadler, this is Ambassador Sheller. President Harrison called as soon as the attacks began and asked that I find out if you were safe. You know I would have preferred you were here at the embassy, but since you declined the president's offer earlier, there was nothing I could do but contact the hotel manager. Our personnel are in our shelter and a squadron of Marines has set up a perimeter around the property. Your hotel also has excellent facilities to protect its guests and I hope you're already in the basement."

"Thanks for asking, sir. I'm in a kind of underground safe room. Things seem to be fine and I'm sorry for all the trouble I've caused the past couple of days. Are you still in Jerusalem?"

"I must be brief; the president's waiting for my call. I sent three-fourths of my staff – mostly nonessentials – back to Tel Aviv yesterday. The facilities are more secure there, and as soon as the sun's up, the rest of us are going too. Right now we're holed up in a storage room two floors below our temporary headquarters."

"What's happening?"

"I'm not privy to information firsthand; the only word I get is from Washington, so consider this between us unless

146

you see it on TV or hear it from the president. This intel's not classified now, but things are in turmoil and it may end up being so later. Israel was attacked around 2 a.m. by missiles launched from a base in Lebanon. They targeted four sites: Haifa, Jerusalem, Tel Aviv and the Dimona radar center in the Negev Desert. That last one's ours, in case you didn't know. From what I hear, Israel successfully took out those missiles. I have to go; I'll tell the president that you're safe. Good luck."

Brian returned to the room and joined others watching a wall-mounted TV. He found it bizarre to be sitting in a basement while CNN replayed a missile attack on a city where he was. He wished he'd asked the ambassador to contact Nicole, but he knew that was asking too much. Too many people had gone far over the limits of propriety and reasonableness to deal with his issues. He'd call her when he could.

Twenty minutes later the "breaking news" banner scrolled as the anchor announced, "There's been a new attack!" He pressed his fingers on his earpiece, listened for a moment and said, "Six missiles were launched from a location in Syria a few minutes ago. Four were intercepted and destroyed by Israeli surface-to-air Iron Dome rockets, but there's an unconfirmed report that two have struck buildings in Jerusalem."

The news reports continued for several minutes and then the announcer returned. His facial expression gave away the somber news he was about to report. As he spoke, video from a helicopter filled the screen. "I must warn you," he said, "the footage we are about to show you contains graphic images." There was a walled compound with several buildings. The largest, a four-story structure, was engulfed in flames, its top two stories a ruined mass of concrete and steel jutting through clouds of black smoke. Floodlights around the perimeter highlighted the carnage and destruction. The bodies of several soldiers lay on the ground near the gated entrance.

"This is a live shot from the new American embassy compound in West Jerusalem," he reported. "Moments ago, two Syrian SCUD missiles struck the building, causing major damage. Several United States Marine guards appear to be down, but there is no word about the whereabouts of Ambassador John Sheller, his deputy and more than one hundred and fifty employees, many of whom have been living inside the compound while they arranged housing elsewhere. It is early morning in Jerusalem and we can only pray that most of the staff was not there when the missiles struck.

"There has been criticism over President Harrison's decision to move the embassy to Jerusalem three months ago. The president of Syria was one of those who denounced the move and promised retaliation for it." He paused again to listen to his earbud; then the screen switched to a reporter on the scene in West Jerusalem. She advised that the main building – the one that was now on fire – had an underground bunker, although there was still no information on whether people were inside.

Brian knew the ambassador and others were in that room. For a moment he considered calling Harry, but he decided against it. Ambassador Sheller would have called him right after they spoke, at least thirty minutes before the missiles hit the embassy. Harry would already be aware that there were people hunkered below the building.

The ambassador had said that their shelter wasn't really a bunker at all. It was simply a basement room and Brian hoped it had protected them. *If I'd done what everyone insisted, I'd have been there myself,* he thought. He recalled Tariq's first demand, giving Harry three days to announce he was moving the embassy out of Jerusalem. But it hadn't been that long. Had Tariq jumped the gun and ignored his own timetable, or was this something else entirely? Whoever planned it, Brian knew that reprisal would be swift. This was an act of war. What would Harry's response be?

It was hours before CNN reported the grim results of the strike. Unlike the embassy compound in Tel Aviv, the one in Jerusalem had far less provision for security and protection because it was a temporary home for the ambassador and his staff. A new complex was planned, but for now the only semi-secure hideout was a storage room in a subbasement. It would have provided safety from a windstorm, but it was no match for a missile strike. After daylight, a search-and-rescue team had dug through the rubble and reached the underground room. The scene was more horrifying than anyone could have imagined.

John Sheller, the US ambassador to Israel, was dead. So were his deputy and fifty-one other American employees. Fourteen Israeli citizens who were contract workers also perished. Eleven Marine guards were dead and twenty-four others were injured, many critically. The survivors had managed to escape the direct hit because they were in other locations, not the shelter. Only one structure – a maintenance building – was undamaged. Five civilians and eight Marines who had been inside were not injured.

Surrounded by loyal followers in a secure room of his base in Edlib, Syria, Tariq watched the scene unfold on CNN Headline News. Regardless of how or why, or that the timing was off, the consequence of his first demand had been carried out. He had nothing to do with the missile strike, but in Tariq's warped mind, the attack had proven he was a man of action and would make America cower in fear. He was overjoyed at the news.

His three demands had been issued in increasing order of importance and this one – requiring the president to move the embassy – didn't really matter. He couldn't have cared less – he only said it to stir the pot – as a show of strength. If the president had failed to comply in seventy-two hours, Tariq would have dispatched suicide bombers to the compound. It would have been the act of terror he promised but nothing on the scale of what had been carried out.

The only demand important to Tariq was his third one. He wanted his fourteen loyal brothers out of Guantanamo. So far none of them had given any information to the Americans – at least as far as Tariq could determine – but each had vast knowledge of al Qaeda's inner workings and about Tariq himself. He wanted them released both for security reasons and because he needed the help of these senior members of the jihadist movement.

———

The president and his advisors were in the Situation Room along with General Nelson Barker, the chairman of the Joint Chiefs of Staff. Harry addressed the group, assuming full responsibility for the tragic loss of American lives.

"I should have ordered the ambassador to move everyone to safety the minute there was a threat," he lamented. "Thank God many of the staff were already gone. John told me he and the rest of his people were moving to Tel Aviv at 7 a.m. That's just three and a half hours from now, dammit!"

Defense Secretary Vernon said, "Sir, I understand how hard this is for you, but no one could have expected AQS to ignore its own timeline. No terrorist has ever issued a threat with consequences and then followed through without waiting to see what the response was. Your final order to me when we met yesterday afternoon was to ask Ambassador Sheller for his assessment. He suggested moving the nonessentials before nightfall, and that happened. Thank God nearly two hundred people were moved out of harm's way. We had seventy-two hours to answer Tariq's demand, Mr. President. No one – the ambassador included – had an inkling this might happen if we took sixteen hours to get the rest of our people out. I polled each person in this room by telephone after I spoke with Ambassador Sheller and we unanimously agreed with the ambassador's plan. You can't blame yourself, sir. That's what I'm saying."

"But the buck stops here. That's the way it was for Harry Truman and that's still the way it is today."

CIA director Stan Kendrick was the only one in the room who was a friend of Harry's. They'd grown up in DC politics together, first in the House and then the Senate. He and his wife had spent many hours with Harry and Jennifer over the years. He knew what this man was made of and what he stood for.

"Mr. President," Kendrick said, "you're right. The buck stops with you. There's nobody above you in the pecking order. But if you took that literally, you wouldn't get much done around here. There are tough decisions that must be made every day. Our men and women in the armed forces bravely serve around the world. Every day some of them die. It's tragic that the world is like it is, but it's not this way because of what America has done. Like it or not, we are the world's policeman. Leaders around the world look to us for protection because they know we will do what's just, fair and right – not just for America, but for all nations. Ambassador Sheller was a good man. I knew and respected him and so did you and the others in this room. He knew what it meant to sign up for government service, just as our soldiers know and just as each of us who serves the United States knows. Based on the best information we had, Ambassador Sheller made a rational decision about his people. We signed off on it and it backfired. In memory of him, the deputy ambassador and the scores of others, we have to choose our reaction and decisively implement it."

The room was silent until the president spoke. "Stan, everything you said is right, of course. President Obama once spoke about how lonely the office is. He called the White House a great white jail. And in many ways, it is. I'm fortunate to be surrounded by the best and most competent leaders in the world. Join me for a moment of silence for our fallen comrades, and then let's move forward."

The room was quiet as six of the most powerful men in America and four United States Marine guards bowed their heads.

"Okay," the president said, breaking the reverie. "Back to the real world. Don't be reluctant to toss out anything you're thinking about all this. We have to think outside the box because nothing about this makes sense."

His team laid out what little they knew and tossed out theories and ideas. The underlying question was who was responsible. Tariq had promised to inflict terrible casualties on the workers if Harry didn't announce the removal of the embassy from West Jerusalem. But the attack came less than

151

twelve hours into a seventy-two-hour deadline. He hadn't given Harry time to respond, and a surprise strike against American interests was certain to provoke a response just the opposite of what the al Qaeda leader wanted.

"We know the missiles were launched from a site in Syria," Cruickshank added. "Regardless of the timing, we know Tariq promised to inflict casualties. He really might have been behind the attack." Some of the others thought that Tariq would have claimed responsibility by now, but so far neither ISIS nor al Qaeda had made an announcement.

"I have a question for you, Ken," General Barker asked the NSA director. "When Tariq made that threat, I wondered if he could back it up. As far as you guys or the CIA knows, do they have missiles and a launch platform? I don't want to underestimate them, but I still doubt they could pull this off."

"There's nothing we have to indicate that ISIS or al Qaeda have this kind of capability," he agreed. "What do you think, Stan?"

The CIA director agreed, but pointed out the enigma. "Are we talking about an angry terrorist who said he's going to kill people at the embassy, but someone else in Syria beat him to it? The government itself or another terror group blasted our embassy instead of Tariq? That's too much of a coincidence for me. There's something we're missing here."

They spent the better part of two hours trying to answer that last question – what was this about? Then President Harrison wrapped the meeting. It was time for him to speak to the people.

———

He addressed the nation from the Oval Office, calling the strikes acts of radical jihadists against both Israel and America, and promising a swift response. As so many other leaders have said in trying times, Harry declared that the attacks only served to bring the country closer together and make America stronger. He offered condolences to the families of those whose lives were cut short and praised Ambassador Sheller, his deputy and the staff for their dedicated service to their country. At the end of his speech, he pointed a finger at al Qaeda and its leader Tariq the Hawk, calling him a despicable coward who killed innocent civilians without compunction. Harry didn't know for sure who'd done it, but the words described Tariq regardless.

Tariq watched the speech. He jeered, snickered and joked during parts of it, but his laughter turned to violent cursing when Harrison called him a coward. "This is not over," he sneered. "*You* will be the sniveling coward soon, when you see what I do to my enemies. Your friend Brian Sadler is a dead man, Mr. President."

Tariq would waste no more time on Abdel Malouf. He was a traitor and he would pay the price for his sins. It was time to bring Abdel and his American friend in. He turned to a lieutenant. Fire blazing in his eyes, he commanded, "Put your most trusted people on this. I want Abdel Malouf and Brian Sadler, and I will pay a million euros for each. Force them to reveal where the Israelite treasure is hidden, but keep them alive. Once I have them and the treasure, the Israelis and the Americans will give me everything I want."

Within hours, al Qaeda operatives had received their orders. A team embedded inside Israel was on the Sadler mission while the task of finding the Arab was given to two men in Jordan, who were now heading to the Israeli border. Once Malouf and the American were captured, the terrorists would learn where the treasure was hidden. Tariq's interrogators looked forward to that part. Extracting information from prisoners always provided an interesting diversion. Tariq had taught them their trade, and he had prepared them well. It would be pleasurable for everyone concerned ... except the prisoners, of course.

CHAPTER TWENTY-ONE

The war raged on. Israeli defense forces successfully took out most of the surface-to-air missiles raining down on Jerusalem from Egypt and Lebanon, but others hit their targets, killing civilians and destroying neighborhoods. For a day and a half, air-raid sirens blared almost constantly in the larger cities and the night sky glowed with barrages of enemy activity and Israeli responses. Convoys of Jordanian and Lebanese armored tanks and troop carriers breached the border, rumbling across the Allenby Bridge into Palestinian-controlled Jericho. Israeli pilots flew mission after mission, systematically taking out one enemy battalion after another. When Egyptian jets entered Israeli airspace from the west, antiaircraft artillery units blasted them from the skies over the Negev Desert.

There were only a handful of guests left at the David Citadel Hotel. Once the airports briefly reopened, most had left. By now many had been able to get on flights out, and the rest still camped out in the terminal buildings or in hotels near the airports. All deliveries to the hotel had stopped, so the daily breakfast and lunch buffets were replaced by meals served at seven a.m., noon and six. Everyone – staff and guests – ate together. Breakfast consisted of bread, cheese and fruit. Lunch and dinner were whatever meat was still on hand plus potatoes and onions, which were in plentiful supply in the hotel's larder. There was also plenty of coffee, tea and thousands of bottles of wine, the latter now supplanting water as a primary drink after the main filtration system for Jerusalem had been damaged by a doomed Jordanian fighter jet that crashed into it.

Electricity was still working in most of the city and two television stations remained on the air, although there was speculation how long they would last if the shelling continued. Telephone and Internet connectivity was fine in parts of Jerusalem and nonexistent in others.

After the embassy attack, Congress had acted quickly. Now squadron after squadron of USAF bombers rained pure hell on Damascus and Syria's border installations until they were obliterated. Although Syria was no longer a threat, the other border nations still fought with determination, and Israel's military handled itself with the same poise and precision as it had done in the Six-Day War fifty years previously.

Once America had responded to Syria's attack, US forces withdrew. Shigon and Harrison agreed that so long as Israel could successfully defend itself, the United States would stay on the sidelines, although two more nuclear aircraft carriers had joined the *Harry Truman* in the Mediterranean off the coast of Haifa.

The battle raged for thirty-six hours, but at three p.m. the afternoon after things had begun, the residents of Jerusalem noticed an eerie silence. There were no planes, no antiaircraft gunfire, no screams and no air-raid sirens. News that it was over spread quickly. Their resources depleted, air forces destroyed and troops demoralized by the intensity of the response by the Israeli military, its enemies withdrew. An uneasy calm settled over the city and people hesitantly popped out of shelters to assess the damage. It was Sabbath afternoon – a time when families traditionally spent time together – and before long friends were gathering in parks and homes. People had died – no one yet knew how many – and their country had been attacked once again, but the resiliency of this brave nation was what shone forth in the aftermath of war.

In the unusual, brief call yesterday, Abdel had instructed Brian to come to his shop at noon. Brian had tried to call, but there was no service. It was now four p.m. and he was anxious to check on Abdel. Brian was torn; he regretted how he had left things; despite Brian's distrust of him, the man had upheld his side of the deal and Brian had reneged on a promise.

Because of previous hotel bombings – the King David decades ago and the American Colony recently – security outside Brian's hotel remained very high. Until an hour or so ago, guests had not been allowed to leave, but word spread that enemy troops had withdrawn, and everyone who had been cooped up was anxious to get outdoors. Armed security personnel outside the hotel still examined documents for every person coming or going, and the porte cochere was still closed to vehicles. It was chaotic, but everyone accepted the inconvenience because it wouldn't last much longer.

Brian was surprised to see how few cars there were in the streets. There were no taxis; he guessed there had been no fares to be picked up during a battle. He wouldn't have taken a cab now anyway. The conflict was over, the skies were clear, and there was a warm breeze. He wanted to walk. As he saw other pedestrians, he realized how tough these people were. The war hadn't been over four hours, but a few bars had already reopened, and he could hear music and conversation from inside them. In another hour or so it would be dark and Sabbath would be over. As usual on a Saturday night in Jerusalem, the streets would be filled, as they had been last Saturday evening. It was a comforting feeling knowing that things were going to be all right. Life was already returning to normal, whatever normal meant to citizens who lived knowing there could be more conflict at any moment.

He entered the Old City through the Jaffa Gate and strolled down the street that divided the Armenian and Christian Quarters. Above him, the Dome of the Rock stood grandly. Tonight, he stopped to gaze upon its beauty as the setting sun's rays emblazoned its roof. As he walked to Abdel's street, he gathered his thoughts. As conflicted as he was about the man, he wanted to know why he'd told Brian he was in danger. When he arrived, he saw that the gallery was dark. The front door was locked. He knocked a couple of times, but there was no answer.

As he turned to leave, he spotted Abdel coming around the corner. He waved and noticed that the man looked surprised – maybe even upset – to see him.

"Brian," he said sharply as he took out a ring of keys and unlocked the door, "what are you doing here?"

"You asked me to come at noon, but obviously I couldn't. As soon as they let us leave, I came here. What did you mean when you said I was in danger?"

"Everything is fine now," he said, his eyes darting nervously down the block. "I made a mistake, that's all. I'm sorry, but I must go now. I have a client who will be arriving at any moment."

"Your clients are still doing business in the middle of all this?" Brian joked, but Abdel didn't smile. Once again, something wasn't right.

"Abdel, you sounded really worried when we talked yesterday. Are you in trouble?"

"You must leave now," he stammered, glancing anxiously down the block. "I will contact you tomorrow." Brian saw two men dressed in black robes a block away. Abdel went inside the gallery, leaving the front door open behind him. Brian walked down the street, turned and saw the men go into Abdel's shop. In the gathering gloom, it was impossible to see their features, but there had been no mistaking Abdel's distress. Whoever they were, Abdel knew them and they weren't clients. He was terrified.

CHAPTER TWENTY-TWO

The three men sat around a table at the back of Abdel's gallery, drinking tea and smoking as he attempted to make small talk until they were ready to divulge what they were doing here.

"How difficult was it to cross the border?" Abdel asked the junior one, a Syrian he had known for many years.

"It was nothing," he replied, explaining that they had joined a convoy of Jordanian troops that crossed the Allenby Bridge and went into Jericho. "We left the soldiers and became just two more Palestinians caught in the battle. Last night we sneaked around an Israeli checkpoint, and today we hitched a ride from a farmer with a donkey and a cart. We arrived in Jerusalem just as the fighting ended."

The other man – the one with the six-inch scar on his face – was also a Syrian. His name was Ibrahim. Abdel had met him once or twice many years ago, but they had never worked together. Ibrahim had a commanding presence that demanded respect and a frightening reputation for violence. Rumor had it that he was a ruthless jihadist who had been trained by the best – Tariq himself.

Why were they here? Did Tariq send them? He had a growing sense of uneasiness and a knot in his gut that was getting more painful by the minute.

"What brings you to Jerusalem during a conflict?"

The cordiality was over. Ibrahim snapped, "We have no time to chatter like women. We have come to protect the treasure. You must take us there."

Now I understand, Abdel thought to himself. *Tariq didn't send them. He doesn't even know they are here. They're acting on their own and they want to steal the treasure!*

Abdel felt more comfortable now. One call to Tariq and he would be the hero while these two faced his wrath.

Abdel shrugged. "Me? Take you where? What treasure?"

"Who was the man you were talking with when we turned the corner?" he said with a twisted grimace that would have been a smile had the scar not pulled it roughly to one side. "Was it Brian Sadler?"

Abdel looked up in shock. "No, no," he responded too quickly. "No, just a friend."

Ibrahim's job wasn't to find Brian Sadler; his responsibility was to capture Abdel, and accomplishing that mission had been simple. Another team would be sent for Abdel's friend, but he could earn twice the ransom if he delivered them both.

"Tariq wants to talk to the American. Where is he staying?"

He shuffled nervously at the mention of Tariq's name. Maybe his visitors wanted something other than he had thought.

"How should I know where he is staying? I hardly know him."

Ibrahim let the lie pass. Soon Abdel would tell everything he knew, and there was still the matter of the treasure. He pointed to the crates sitting nearby. "What are those large boxes? Are you planning on going somewhere without telling your friends?"

Once again Abdel fumbled for an answer. "I'm shipping some things to someone ... uh, a dealer who wants to buy them."

"A friend in America, I'm sure. Those crates are quite large and your store is almost empty now. What are you and Mr. Sadler planning? Are you leaving, Abdel? Al Qaeda inserted you into Israel long ago and you have gotten rich and lazy from the rewards of living among the infidels. Would you give up the cause of jihadism and go to live with the Great Satan?"

Abdel said nothing. He wasn't sure now why they had come or what they wanted from him. He didn't know what to think, but this discussion wasn't going well.

Ibrahim shouted, "Answer my question! Are you planning to run away? Because you know the consequences for that. Each of us does. You know who sent us here and you are afraid – I can sense your fear from across the table. And you are right to be afraid. I sense you are too weak to be one of us! The leader senses it too. You know how he deals with weakness, do you not? Perhaps I should tell him ..."

Abdel was struggling to keep down the bile rising in his throat. He shook his head violently and wailed, "No, no. There is no need to tell him anything. You misunderstand my caution for weakness, my brother. It is good to be wary of the infidels. I am steadfast, as are we all. Give me a little time and I will find out where the treasure you seek is hidden."

"Enough!" Ibrahim roared, standing up, overturning the table and sending the teapot and cups crashing to the floor. "Your words are lies! You have been to a cavern somewhere in the north. You took the infidel there. Tariq knows everything! He knows what you are and that you have betrayed our brotherhood. You are not one of us. You are a lying fool and your days are numbered. Cooperate with me and perhaps the leader will grant you a quick death. Continue your deception and you'll die slowly as I pull your intestines into your lap while you watch." He looked at his partner and said, "Restrain him!"

Abdel wept as the other man jerked him to his feet and secured his hands behind his back with a twist-tie. Now he knew this was about Tariq. He was doomed. But when he heard the man's next words, he knew it wasn't just about the jihadist – they were here to steal the treasure too.

"At daybreak, you will take us to the treasure," Ibrahim said, wishing they no longer needed this despicable piece of dung. He had no time for weak people and he was looking forward to presiding over the brutal interrogation that faced Abdel whether he cooperated or not.

Abdel trembled like a beaten dog. "Yes, sir," he said submissively, "but how will we get there? I have no car."

"With Allah's help, I will procure a vehicle. Leave that part to me." Ibrahim instructed his partner to take Abdel upstairs to his bedroom and remain by his side every moment. Then he left, walking through busy streets and quiet, dark ones. At last he found what he wanted. He hot-wired a rusty 1970s Chevy parked in front of a boarded-up house and swapped license tags with a car a few blocks away. Forty-five minutes after he had left, he parked his new ride two blocks from Abdel's gallery. Soon he was getting some sleep while his partner watched Abdel toss and turn in his bed. The junior man could catch up on sleep tomorrow while Ibrahim drove.

Shortly after dawn the door to Abdel's shop opened and he emerged, his hands still tethered behind him. The men took him by each arm and walked to the place where the car was parked. Ibrahim shoved Abdel into the backseat and locked the doors. The old sedan coughed to life and they were off.

Brian watched them leave from a darkened alley across the street. He had stayed behind last evening to find out what was happening. Through the unbroken storefront window, he watched the men talking in the back of the store. He watched one of them angrily rise, saw the china crash to the floor, and noted Abdel's terror-stricken face as one man yelled while the other tied his hands. Then one of them left the gallery.

Brian had followed him as he strode purposefully to the busy Via Dolorosa without taking in anything around him. There were hundreds of people in the area enjoying the peaceful evening after two tense days of conflict. Street cafés were filled with laughing couples eager to resume their lives. With all the pedestrian traffic, it was easy for Brian to keep his target in sight without getting too close. The man abruptly turned from the well-lit avenue into a darkened, narrow street. Brian carefully glanced around the corner before creeping into the gloom himself. Although he couldn't see his quarry now, he could hear his footsteps. When he heard a car door open, Brian hesitated. A minute or two later headlights bathed the deserted street in a glow and an engine coughed to life. He stayed in the shadows as a vintage Chevrolet sedan passed him, turned at the corner and disappeared.

Brian arrived back on Abdel's street just in time to see the man enter the gallery and lock the door. Soon the light at the back of the shop was extinguished. All that was left was a faint glow through tattered curtains on the second floor – the place Abdel earlier had said was his living quarters. He glanced at his watch, saw it was nearly midnight, and settled in for a long, chilly night in the alley.

The lights in the shop came on just before six. The three men came out and walked two blocks to where the old Chevy was parked. They shoved Abdel into the back, got in front and drove away as Brian watched everything.

Having no way to follow them, he returned to the alley and stayed put for another hour. When nothing happened, he walked to the gallery, tried the door and found it unlocked. Acutely aware that they could return at any moment, he quickly looked around for anything that might show who Abdel's captors were. There was an ashtray full of cigarette butts and the smashed tea set. Upstairs he noticed that two people had slept in separate bedrooms, but there were no clues to tell him what had happened. For now, there was nothing he could do. He'd come back later and hope that they brought Abdel back. If they didn't, he had an entirely new set of issues to consider.

He returned to the hotel and saw the message light flashing on his room phone. Cynthia Beal had called to let him know that the regional airports would reopen tomorrow morning. She advised that every flight was booked solid, but she had used embassy privilege to snag one coach seat on a 2 p.m. flight from Haifa to Athens. She asked that he return her call as soon as possible to confirm he would be on that flight, but he couldn't leave yet. He had to help Abdel if he could.

He stepped into the shower and turned on a stream of water as hot as he could tolerate. As it rushed down his back, he pondered what to do. Earlier he had decided to stay in Israel just long enough to ensure the treasure was safe. Now it was much more than that – it appeared Abdel had been kidnapped and he had to do something about it. There was a time the embassy could have helped, but that was no longer possible. What little staff had survived was back in Tel Aviv, attempting to put their lives back together.

He could call the police or the Mossad, but every agency was overwhelmed, trying to get the country back on track. He might find someone who would listen to him and investigate what had happened, but all that would take up valuable time – time that Abdel didn't have.

After thirty hours awake, he could fight it no longer. He had devised a plan – maybe not a good one, but the only one he could think of. But first he had to sleep. He closed the blackout shades, advised guest services to hold his calls, and put out the Do Not Disturb sign. He set an alarm on his phone for two p.m.; that would give him what he hoped would be six uninterrupted hours of sleep.

When he awoke, it took a moment to remember where he was. He glanced at his watch – it was one. One a.m. or one p.m.? Trying to clear his brain and focus, he went to the window and pulled open the drapes. Bright sunlight flooded his room – it was daytime. He'd slept for five hours and felt sufficiently refreshed to implement his plan.

He visited a couple of stores, made some purchases and walked to a seedy, run-down hotel he'd noticed last night when he followed Abdel's kidnapper. As he walked into the dingy lobby, he couldn't help contrasting it to the opulence of his hotel. The desk clerk wore a dirty muscle shirt. His face was a mass of stubby facial hair and a cigarette hung from his lips. Brian asked for a kitchenette and paid a hundred and twenty-five shekels – about thirty-five dollars – in cash.

"Passport," the clerk grunted, and Brian explained he'd lost his. He palmed a US hundred-dollar bill across the counter and said he hoped there wasn't a problem. The man said nothing; he simply handed over a key and pointed to an ancient lift across the lobby. He noticed his guest's only luggage was a grocery sack, but there was nothing unusual about that. This guy wasn't typical; most people who checked in were either strung out or horny. They were here for drugs or hookers. Maybe this guy wanted both. Maybe his sack was filled with whips and chains. Who knew? Who cared?

The bedroom was nasty and the bedspread stained and ragged. *Thank God I don't have to stay here*, he thought. He smiled at what Nicole would have said about it, but he had to concentrate. He must work quickly. He had no idea how much time he had before – or if – Abdel and the thugs returned. If they did, he had to be ready.

He had chosen this hotel solely because it had a kitchenette. He needed the tiny stove and dented pots and pans. Ignoring roaches scurrying about, he put his purchases – a bag of sugar and a bottle of stump remover he'd picked up at a garden center – on the counter and followed instructions he'd found on the Internet. He mixed up a concoction, cooked it on the stove, and by five p.m. he had left the hotel without either checking out or getting even a glance from the clerk.

Abdel's shop was exactly as he had left it – no one was there. He slipped inside, went up the stairs, arranged everything on a bed beside him and sat down. He' would wait until twenty-four hours after Abdel's abduction had passed. If he didn't come back, Brian would have to think of the next step, whatever that would be.

CHAPTER TWENTY-THREE

A couple of hours later Brian tensed as he heard the front door open. He arranged everything he needed beside him – the stuff he'd cooked up on the stove, some matches and an ax handle. He held one of the flat patties he'd made and got ready. There were the sounds of people walking through the store and then he heard Abdel speaking in Arabic. He didn't have to understand the language to sense the fear in his friend's voice.

The men were in the back of the store, at the bottom of the stairwell just below where he crouched. He gathered what he needed, stuck a match to one of the patties and tossed it into a room across the hall. In seconds, thick black smoke poured out the door and down the stairs.

There were shouts from below. Through the haze, he saw one of the men rush up the stairs. As he reached the top, Brian swung the handle and caught him squarely on the back of his head. He crashed to the floor next to Brian. Downstairs, both Abdel and the other man were shouting now. He readied himself and mentally crossed his fingers. The smoke was filling the area where he stood and he hoped he could see which of the two came upstairs next.

A head popped up from the stairwell and a man looked straight at him. Brian had seconds to react. It wasn't Abdel! He took another mighty swing and heard it connect with a sickening crack.

Brian ran downstairs and found Abdel on the floor, weeping. Brian cut him loose as Abdel cried, "Are they dead? How could you be here? Is my store on fire?"

"It's fine! No time!" he yelled, pushing him toward the front of the gallery and out onto the sidewalk. He closed the door behind them to trap the smoke inside the building so passersby wouldn't call the fire brigade and possibly damage Abdel's antiques. He knew from the Internet that the grenades he'd created would burn out quickly. The smoke would be gone minutes later.

"I'm pretty sure one of the guys I hit is dead, but I don't know about the other one. Your store's fine. It's just a smoke bomb – no lasting effects. We must get away from here. Lock the door and let's go!"

They walked briskly so as not to attract attention to themselves and exited the Old City through the Lion's Gate. As they walked, Brian asked Abdel if there was someplace they would be safe. Too many people knew Brian was at the David Citadel Hotel, and Abdel's store certainly wasn't an option any more.

"My cousin has a place," Abdel suggested. "It's a flat in the western part of the city, not far from the museum. I don't know the address, but I can get us there."

They hailed a cab and went to the Israel Museum. From there Abdel led the way a few blocks to a row of modern townhouses. He explained to Brian that his cousin lived in New York and came to Jerusalem maybe six times a year. "He may be in town, but if he isn't, I still can get into his flat," he added.

They rang the buzzer several times, and no one answered. Abdel reached up to a porch light, ran his fingers behind the fixture and withdrew a key. Seconds later they were inside and it was clear his cousin was not around. All the drapes were drawn tightly shut and the place had a musty odor. They raised the windows and Abdel opened double doors leading to a small patio on the back side of the building. Soon a pleasant breeze wafted through the apartment.

Abdel had refused to say anything about what had happened until they could be alone. Now they sat at the kitchen table, sharing a bottle of red wine they had found in the pantry. Abdel pointed out once again he wasn't a big drinker, but Brian assured him after what he'd seen, Abdel needed one.

Abdel asked Brian if he'd explain how he happened to be at the shop at precisely the right time. Brian described his overnight surveillance mission and how he'd seen them take Abdel this morning. He'd found a recipe for smoke bombs on the Internet and made some in hopes he could take the captors out during the confusion. And things had worked perfectly.

Now it was Abdel's turn to talk. In the time since his rescue, Abdel had concocted a story that he hoped would be good enough to explain things. He was grateful for his friend's perseverance and that he'd been rescued, but he also knew that Brian now was in the same danger as Abdel himself.

A lot of people in Israel knew the rumors of the treasure mentioned in Isaiah 45:3, he began. It was a Loch Ness-type legend that sparked the imaginations of those with pure motives and those without. For years Abdel had researched the legend and began to believe it might be true. He had made many inquiries throughout Israel, Jordan and Syria before he was finally contacted by a man who knew where the cave was. The men who had abducted him had captured that man and forced him to talk. They had come to his shop, pretending to be customers, but instead they threatened to kill him if he didn't show them where the cavern was.

"You took them to the cave?" Brian asked, fearful about the safety of the treasure.

"I had no choice. They would have killed me."

"Why did they bring you back? Surely they didn't intend to just let you go." That didn't make sense to Brian.

Abdel's mind raced as he made up another answer. "Because I told them there was another cache of treasure besides this one, in a place I had never been myself. I was convinced it was real, I told them. I offered to give them a map."

"There isn't really another treasure hoard – right? How did you intend to deal with that?"

"There isn't, but it was the only thing I could think of. I have hundreds of old maps at the shop. I would have given them one that would occupy them long enough for me to get away somehow. Speaking of that, I owe you a huge debt, Brian. You surely saved my life."

Brian knew he was right. These men wouldn't have let Abdel live. If he hadn't made up the map story, he was sure they'd have killed Abdel after he showed them the cavern.

"What do we do next?" Abdel asked. "I cannot go back to my shop now."

"I'm glad you realize that. I was afraid you were going to convince me we still had to rescue your objects. Nothing's worth dying for, Abdel, and you must let that go. The thing I hope we can salvage is the treasure itself. Do you think these two men were working alone?"

"I believe so," he lied.

Brian laid out a plan. "The most important thing right now is to get you out of Israel," he began. "I got a call from Washington. I have a seat on a flight tomorrow from Haifa to Athens. I want you to take that flight. Your safety is critical. If the men weren't working alone, there will be others looking for you, but they don't know about me. I'll get out as soon as I can and meet you in Greece. Then we'll go to London. There's an extra bedroom in our flat, and you'll be safe there."

It was truly a good plan, Abdel concurred, insisting that they stay here for tonight, which made perfect sense to Brian. He called Cynthia and explained the situation. She said the president wouldn't be pleased, but she promised to relay his request. Fifteen minutes later she called back and confirmed Abdel's seat on tomorrow's flight and Brian's on a morning flight the day after. Less than twenty-four hours after Abdel left Israel, Brian would meet up with him in Athens. He booked a room online at a small hotel on the harbor, where Abdel could stay until Brian arrived.

Abdel said there was a market on the corner, where he could buy food for dinner, but Brian insisted on going himself to keep Abdel safe. Soon he returned and they prepared fish and vegetables with couscous and opened another bottle of wine. During dinner, Abdel said there was one problem.

"My passport is at the shop. Before I go to Haifa Airport, I will have to get it."

"You can't go back there. It's too risky."

"I have no choice. It's hidden and you'll never find it yourself."

It was a dangerous move, but Brian agreed he couldn't leave without documents, so they'd go there together in the morning. Brian called the hotel concierge and arranged a car and driver for 9 a.m.

He was there by eight. He packed his bags, checked out and gave the driver the address of the flat. They picked up Abdel and went to his shop, where everything appeared totally quiet. Abdel wanted to go in by himself, but Brian insisted on coming too.

"Didn't we lock the door yesterday?" Brian said when Abdel turned the knob and opened it. Abdel nodded. They listened for a moment but heard nothing. While Abdel got his passport, Brian crept up the stairs and looked around. A body lay in a pool of blood, its shattered skull a grim reminder of the encounter yesterday.

But the other man was gone.

Brian bounded down the stairs. "Let's get out of here!" he shouted.

After an uneventful ride, they were in Haifa by eleven and Brian dismissed the driver at the airport. He wasn't staying here, but he didn't trust anyone. Once the car pulled away, he told Abdel goodbye, promised they'd meet in Athens tomorrow, and caught a taxi to a nearby hotel, where he would stay until his flight tomorrow. A few hours later Abdel called Brian to report that he had checked in the hotel and he was on his way to a late lunch and to buy some clothes and toiletries.

Brian spent the afternoon in his room, ate dinner in a nearby restaurant, went to bed early and caught his flight out the next morning. The plane arrived on time in Athens and Brian was at Abdel's hotel before eleven. He called the room, but there was no answer. He had the same result when he called his cellphone. Increasingly worried, he convinced the manager to allow a bellman to accompany him upstairs.

A Do Not Disturb sign hung on the door. The employee rapped loudly, announced he was coming in, and inserted the key. The room was empty, the bed had not been slept in, and there were no personal items anywhere. The only signs anyone had been there were a raised toilet lid, a damp washcloth by the sink and a bar of soap that had been opened and used.

Abdel Malouf was gone.

CHAPTER TWENTY-FOUR

Brian unsuccessfully scoured the room, looking for a clue to Abdel's whereabouts. He spoke to the desk clerk, who remembered Abdel from yesterday. Brian asked if he had recommended a restaurant. He had, and he'd also given him the address of a men's clothing store nearby. Brian took down the information and left the hotel, hoping to trace Abdel's movements.

This time of day, the tiny restaurant was quiet. The maître d' recalled the man Brian described. He had come in around five yesterday evening, eaten a leisurely dinner and stayed over an hour. He had been on his phone some of the time, the headwaiter remembered. No, he did not appear concerned or edgy. He acted as though everything was fine.

The clothing store was a mom-and-pop place, which also helped. A clerk who'd worked yesterday evening didn't specifically recall Abdel, but he agreed to look through the sales receipts to see what they could find. Sure enough, there was a cash purchase for two pairs of pants, two shirts, a sweater, socks and underwear. That had been at 6:48 p.m. Had he gone back to the hotel after that?

Brian tried his cell again and left a message. "Please call me if you can. I want to help you."

———

"Mr. President, Director Kendrick's on line one."

"Hello, Stan," Harry said. "What do you have for me?"

"Word on the street in Jerusalem is that Tariq has offered a million-euro reward for the capture of Malouf and Mr. Sadler. He wants them brought in alive. I think he's in danger, Mr. President."

"I'll call him right now."

Five minutes later Brian heard the news and advised that he was safely in Athens.

"You're not safe," Harry replied. "Al Qaeda has tentacles throughout Europe, especially there. You need security immediately. I'll ask Cynthia to have the embassy arrange it."

Brian couldn't argue his way out of it this time. He was in Europe, but Harry still was worried. He'd accept the security and the restrictions that came with it until he could get home.

———

The hardest part of it all was the deception. *Brian has been nothing but a friend, and this is how I responded to his generosity. What kind of wretch have I become?*

Abdel turned on his phone and listened again to Brian's voicemail. The words saddened him. The choices he had made long ago had trapped him now and he couldn't allow his friend to be caught too. He truly regretted not being able to tell him what it was all about. Part of him wanted to return the call, to explain why he'd left, to confess his secrets and to make amends. But as quickly as those thoughts came, he dismissed them.

Brian had done him a huge favor by getting him this far, and he had made up his mind how he would return the favor, as much as the thought of it saddened him. He was safely out of Israel and – at least for the moment – out of Tariq's clutches. But in truth there was no place to hide. The ruthless leader would stop at nothing to hunt him down and slaughter him like a cheetah after a gazelle. Putting miles between him and Tariq might help for today, but soon he would be a dead man.

He had taken his kidnappers to the treasure trove. Brian had killed one of them and that was good, but the other had disappeared. He had to assume that by now the leader knew everything. And that meant the treasure would be gone soon. The one thing that was positive was the location of the cavern. If it had been in an Arab nation, Tariq would have had the relics already. But it was in Israel. The logistics of recovering and transporting it to Syria would require time and assistance from locals. The Palestinians might help, but would they really put their lives on the line for Tariq? Did the leader have connections with people at the border who would look the other way while truck after truck loaded with priceless relics rolled unimpeded across the Hussein Bridge? Abdel simply didn't know.

If he had spoken with Brian, his primary message would have been the urgency of securing the cave. Never mind that it was inside a national park. It needed iron bars, padlocks and armed sentries around the clock. Perhaps Brian was already working on it. He hoped so.

Before he put his old life behind him, Abdel had one more thing to do. He found an attorney, went to his office and instructed him to prepare a document. He went to the nearest FedEx office and bought a padded envelope. He took something from his backpack – a small object wrapped in cloth that he'd grabbed in his shop yesterday while he was getting his passport. He put the object in the parcel along with a handwritten letter and the legal document. He gave the clerk an address he had found on the Internet and paid to ship the package to Jerusalem. Another loose end was tied up, and this one affected him deeply.

He sat in the smoking area of the immense train station in downtown Athens, puffing away as he waited for the overnight Pullman service to Skopje, Macedonia, fourteen hours to the north. He would go to another country in a day or so, and then he assumed he'd move again before it got too risky. It was sad to think this was his life now, a man on the run, always looking over his shoulder, but he had made his choices and he must live with the consequences.

Since he was already in Greece – a European Union country – it would have been good if he could have gone from here to another EU venue. But he couldn't keep using his real passport. He had decided to travel to Eastern Europe – Macedonia being the closest country – and try to find a way to get new documents. He didn't know how one went about creating a new persona. If he'd still been part of al

Qaeda in Syria, he would have known who to ask, but now al Qaeda was the enemy. He'd once seen a movie where a man on the run went to a store, used a password and was granted entry to a back room where a master forger sat plying his trade. Euros had been exchanged for new documents. But that was a film and this was real life. He had no idea where to start.

Shortly after four in the afternoon, his train was announced and he walked to the platform. He had nothing but his backpack containing the clothes he had bought yesterday, a toiletry kit and a thick stack of euros he'd taken from the safe with his passport. He was afraid to use credit cards any more, and money was the least of his worries. He had maintained secret bank accounts in the names of shell corporations in London and Geneva for twenty years, quietly moving funds now and then just in case a day like this arose. Today those accounts held more than two million euros, and nothing could tie them to Abdel Malouf. He could buy a new identity, set up a new business somewhere and start over.

It sounded simple, but he knew it wouldn't be that easy.

He boarded the train and handed his ticket to a porter, acutely aware that this ticket symbolized the start of a journey to a new and different life. He was completely lost in his own thoughts, consumed about what would happen tomorrow, the day after and the day after that. The attendant touched him lightly on the sleeve, asking him to step aside so others could board, and directing him to his room – a private sleeper compartment down the narrow hallway.

Twenty minutes later the train rumbled out of the station. By nightfall he had eaten a satisfying meal in the dining car, enjoyed a couple of glasses of wine and was ready for bed. It had been an exhausting, gut-wrenching and terrifying twenty-four hours, but he was beginning to feel just a twinge of optimism. Maybe all this would really work. Maybe tomorrow would be a better day.

Abdel awoke before 5 a.m., completely rested and refreshed for the first time in as long as he could remember. For over an hour he lay in his berth with the curtain raised, marveling at the majestic snowcapped peaks of southern Macedonia. He shaved, dressed and padded down the hall to use the common toilet. The aroma of coffee wafted in from somewhere nearby, and it smelled wonderful. Back in his compartment, he rang for the porter and ordered some. It was delivered quickly, along with a pastry and some grapes. "We will be arriving in Skopje in less than an hour," the man advised. The train pulled into the station on schedule and he stepped onto the platform.

He went to a little hotel he'd found online. He checked in and handed over his Israeli passport, hoping it would be the last time he had to use it. He didn't know if the Israeli authorities would be looking for him because of the body in his upstairs hall with its skull cracked open, but even if they did, would they follow him all the way to Europe? He decided it was unlikely they'd be on the trail this quickly. Regardless, he had to change identities. If it wasn't the authorities he needed to worry about, it was Tariq's men. Even Brian Sadler might be trying to find him, unaware of the danger he would face if he did.

He showered, put on his set of new clothes, sent the others to the hotel laundry and went out for a walk. Even with its six hundred thousand inhabitants, the streets of Skopje felt quiet compared to the hubbub of Jerusalem. He knew the city had been virtually annihilated in a massive earthquake in 1963, which explained why there were few historic landmarks. Instead he passed street after street of drab, unremarkable modern buildings. As he crossed a major thoroughfare, he saw a side street that was closed to vehicular traffic. Street vendors sat behind tables filled with everything from fresh fruits to woolen mittens, from tourist souvenirs to bootlegged DVDs of American movies.

He walked through the busy lane, dodging shoppers speaking half a dozen languages and pawing through a plethora of things for sale. He bought a few more items – socks, underwear, Polo shirts and fake American-branded jeans. There was no need to exchange his euros since every vendor accepted them. He stuffed his purchases in his backpack and felt a sense of relief that he had more clothes now, another step in his new life. He saw a table to his left and an idea came to him.

Two scruffy young Arabs were selling roach clips, rolling papers and bongs. He selected a pipe and one of the salesmen quietly asked in English, "Do you need anything to go with it?" He took a baggie from his lap, cupped his hand over it and showed it to Abdel.

That was what he was hoping for. "I do," he replied in Arabic, a tongue to which the young man quickly switched.

"Twenty euros for the bag."

Abdel gave him the money and was handed a grocery sack. "I need something else," he said, venturing into a place that made him very nervous indeed. "I need a passport."

The men glanced at each other and one whispered, "Passports cost a lot of money."

"The question is, do you know where I can get one?"

The youth shook his head. "But I know someone who does. That will cost money too."

How much money? Abdel wondered. He didn't want to appear to be the novice he was, so he said, "Tell me how it works."

"You pay me a hundred euros and I will give you a phone number."

"How can I trust you?"

"You can't," his companion sneered. "But you appear to be a man who needs a passport, so you must pay the money."

Abdel peeled off five twenties and handed them over. The vendor grabbed his phone and walked away for a moment. When he returned, he tore a piece from a paper sack and wrote a number on it. He handed it across the table and said, "Nice doing business with you."

Abdel's heart raced. He had never done anything like this in his life. Even his work for al Qaeda had been low-level spying – passing along information about things he saw and heard in Jerusalem. He had taken the first step and he was terrified. But, he rationalized, there was no risk in making the call. He could hang up if he got nervous. He punched in the numbers and waited.

A voice answered in Arabic. Abdel said what he wanted and the man asked him a series of questions, including his name and birth date, both of which he made up on the spot. He was told to bring two passport photos and ten thousand euros to a certain sidewalk café where he would meet a woman dressed in a red sweater. She would join him for coffee, take the photos and his money and meet him exactly twenty-four hours later in the same spot. At that meeting, she would give him a European Union passport issued in Greece that would allow him to travel within the EU.

"Will the passport be real?" he asked, and he was told again that it would work perfectly for travel throughout the EU. Countries with customs officials, such as those in Eastern Europe and the United States, could be riskier.

"So how then do I get into the EU? Won't I be stopped when I leave Macedonia?"

"Not if you go by train," the forger answered. "Your documents would be closely examined at the airport. But if you take the train to Sofia, the only check will be a quick pass-through at the Bulgarian border. You will have no problems."

Abdel was almost free. All he had to do was get into the EU. After that he could move about Europe with a new name and new documents. He considered ten thousand euros a small price to pay, although he told the man he would pay half the money up front and half upon delivery, which was agreed.

He went to the café early, ordered lunch and a glass of wine, and he waved when a pretty girl in her twenties, her red sweater accentuating a nice figure, came through the entryway and walked to his table. She smiled as she sat and whispered, "Talk to me as if we are good friends."

They chatted casually in English about how beautiful the mountains of Macedonia were and what a pleasant day it had turned out to be. He put an envelope on the table next to her and she ignored it. She accepted his offer of a glass of wine, and when it arrived, she moved the envelope to her lap, looked inside and sent a brief text on her phone. They continued the small talk until her wine was finished.

"I'm concerned about the passport," he confessed as she gathered her purse. "Are you certain it will be good enough for safe passage within the EU?"

She smiled at him as if she hadn't heard. "See you tomorrow," she said gaily, giving him a peck on the cheek as she departed. To the other diners, they were simply an older man and a young girl, perhaps a niece, who had met for a quick drink. The routine was repeated the next day. This time the girl handed him a passport. He flipped through it and was pleased to see it wasn't brand new. It had his photo and new name, but it also had several border stamps from countries in Europe. It looked good to him, and he hoped it would be as reliable within the European Union as he'd been promised. He slipped five thousand euros across the table in an envelope. She glanced inside, sent another text, finished her wine and said goodbye with a friendly wave.

As simply as that, Abdel Malouf from Syria, an Israeli citizen, was gone. In his place was a Greek named Constantin Stefos.

CHAPTER TWENTY-FIVE

"Where is he?" Tariq fumed. Abdel hadn't been the only asset al Qaeda maintained in Israel. He had instructed his lieutenant to call a man at the transportation ministry, a friend who could search the database for the missing gallery owner.

"Our source advises that the Americans arranged an airline ticket for him. Two days ago, he flew from Haifa to Athens."

"Was Brian Sadler with him?"

"Not then, sir. The seat was originally held in that name, but someone in the American government changed the reservation."

"Where is the American now?"

"He also went to Athens but not until the next day. Our people in Greece are attempting to learn more."

Tariq was livid. He cursed himself for not dealing with Abdel sooner. The moment he saw a problem, he should have eliminated him. Tariq had always considered Abdel the weak link in his council, but killing him would have meant losing a valuable agent who had free movement inside Israel. Now his intuition had been proven correct. He should have dealt with Abdel long ago. His men would find the traitor, and he would wish he had never been born.

"Find him, whatever it takes. Allah will reward you greatly and so will I. Put out the word that he who captures Abdel, dead or alive, will be a millionaire."

And so the net was cast.

———

Abdel – Constantin now – sat in the first-class lounge of the cavernous downtown station, waiting for the train to

Sofia. It left in thirty minutes, and if everything went well, he would be inside the European Union by dusk. He had thought of one more thing he needed to do. His cellphone had been turned off since he left Athens, but now – for the last time ever – he clicked it on. He saw a few work-related calls that no longer needed returning. There was also a new message from Brian. He pondered if he should listen. He knew it would do no good, but his pent-up guilt and remorse won out. He played the voicemail.

"Abdel, it's Brian again. I'm really concerned about you. I came to Athens to meet as we agreed, but you were gone. If you get this message, please call me and let me know you're okay. If you don't call, I must tell the authorities about the treasure. I hope you understand – there's too great a risk leaving it unattended. The historic significance alone makes this an unprecedented discovery, not to mention the potential value of the individual objects. If I don't hear from you by six p.m. Athens time, I must call the head of the Antiquities Authority. Be safe, my friend."

Anguished, he turned off the phone. Everything in his life had been shattered the moment he walked away. It was good that Brian was going to the authorities. Now it was the only way to ensure the treasure's safety. He dabbed away a tear as he thought of that truly monumental hoard and the role in its unveiling that he deserved but would never have. Abdel only had himself to blame that Brian alone would reap the benefits of a documentary presentation. There was no question the TV show would happen. In exchange for Brian's revealing the location, the government would be only too pleased to grant him exclusive rights to show it to the world. After that, the priceless relics of Isaiah would end up in some museum.

Unless Tariq got there first.

———

"He's in Macedonia, Leader!"

In hopes of collecting a million-euro ransom, people sympathetic to al Qaeda in a dozen countries were feverishly making inquiries. Two things had emerged – Abdel had traveled by train from Athens to Skopje two days before, and he had activated his cellphone yesterday for a brief time.

Tariq sent his best soldiers to the Macedonia capital and they scoured the city. They discovered the hotel where he had stayed, but that was all they found. Generous bribes sprinkled around gave them access to air and rail manifests, but there was no listing for Abdel Malouf. There were video cameras in places, but it was nothing like the security found in major Western airports and train stations. It would take weeks to get the grainy black-and-white videotapes and they would provide nothing useful. For now, he had escaped, but Tariq vowed that the search for the traitor would never end.

CHAPTER TWENTY-SIX

The porter examined Constantin Stefos's ticket and directed him to the first-class section.

"Where's the bar car?"

He offered to fetch a drink and bring it to Constantin's compartment as soon as the train left the station, but he wanted it now. Until the last few weeks he hadn't been much of a drinker, but now alcohol was the only thing that soothed his rattled nerves. It was a hundred and fifty miles to the Bulgarian border. That was where the first test of his new passport would happen – and if things went wrong, it would be the last.

"I'll go there myself," he snapped, then softened his words, deciding not to call attention to himself. "It's been a long afternoon and I've worked up quite a thirst."

The porter laughed and said he understood. He pointed Constantin in the right direction and turned to the next passenger in line. He dropped his backpack in his compartment, went to the bar and purchased a bottle of Greek wine. Back in his cabin, he poured a glass as the train began to move out of the station, gradually picking up speed as it moved through the capital. Soon they were passing through green fields, well on their way to Bulgaria. As he sipped his wine, he crushed the cellphone under his shoe. He opened the window, finding the fresh air cool and invigorating, and tossed pieces of the phone out every so often as the train click-clacked northwest. He estimated he had about two hours before he reached the border and he wanted all evidence of his phone gone by then.

Before long the train began decelerating and finally it came to a complete stop. He could see a platform with a different flag on each side, presumably one Macedonian and the other Bulgarian. There was an announcement in two languages he didn't recognize and then in English. This was the border and inspectors would now pass through the train to examine documents.

He was slightly more inebriated than he'd have preferred, but thankfully downing three-fourths of the wine in his bottle had calmed his anxiety. There was a quick knock and the door slid open. A man in a uniform said something.

Constantin replied, "English?"

"Documents, please." He glanced at the passport and said more words Constantin didn't understand.

"English?" he asked again.

"You carry a Greek passport but do not speak Greek?" the officer asked.

Damn! He hadn't thought about that little issue. He wiped a bead of sweat from his brow.

"I am Greek by birth," he stammered as he created a story on the fly. "I was born there and I maintain a residence in Greece, but I have always lived in the UK. My parents ... they emigrated there before I was born and ..."

The inspector raised a hand. "Enough," he said affably. "It just seemed odd at first." He handed the passport over, wished Constantin a pleasant journey and left.

He poured the last of the bottle into his glass and tossed it back in one gulp. His heart was beating as if it would pop from his chest and now he was sweating copiously. He waited anxiously until he felt the train lurch forward. Within moments, the border was behind him and he was in the European Union!

"Sir, sir, we have arrived."

Constantin jerked his head up, coming out of his alcohol-induced slumber as the conductor touched his shoulder. "Sorry. I must have fallen asleep," he mumbled.

The porter looked at the empty wine bottle on the table by his passenger's seat and understood what had happened. He helped the inebriated passenger off the train and told him where the taxi stand was. Constantin had planned on arriving in Sofia sober, buying a burner cellphone, and researching and selecting a hotel, but he was in no condition to do any of those things now. He walked outside, saw a hotel across the street and went straight to it. Twenty minutes later he was sound asleep on top of the bedcovers, still fully clothed.

He woke around two a.m. with a throbbing headache. He'd never experienced a hangover before, but this novice drinker, who had consumed a 750 ml bottle of wine without eating anything, had a doozy. He made it to the toilet before he vomited, although in his condition he wouldn't have cared either way. He took two ibuprofens, stripped off his clothes and crawled under the covers. He visited the toilet twice more, but he finally managed to fall asleep.

After a shower and a shave the next morning, he felt a little better. He was ravenous, although he wasn't sure what he should put in his stomach. He remembered almost nothing about the hotel he was in, so he went to the lobby, hoping to find a dining room. He was in luck and he ordered coffee, bacon, eggs and toast. When the coffee arrived, the smell of it caused something to rumble in his stomach, so he switched to milk instead. That did the trick and soon he felt considerably better.

He hazily recalled the episode with the border inspector and realized he had to come up with a good story about why this Greek didn't speak Greek. He didn't really recall what he'd said on the train, but the tale he ultimately concocted was close to the earlier one and believable. He'd been to London many times and he could toss out names of streets and areas of town well enough to pass as a resident.

He bought a cellphone with prepaid minutes and went to an Internet café to search the web for a hotel. The one he was in was decent enough, but just in case someone came looking, he didn't want to be staying adjacent to the train station. He found a nice small one and tried to book a reservation online, but without plastic, he couldn't. He'd torn up all his cards back in Athens and was living strictly on cash now, which was fine for a lot of things but almost impossible for airline tickets and accommodations. Decent hotels required a credit or debit card. It would be simple to get one

– he already had bank accounts in the EU – but the logistics were an issue.

He walked to the new hotel and explained to the desk clerk that he'd misplaced his wallet, but fortunately he'd kept his cash separate from his cards. He rented a room for four days and paid in cash. He was required to put up an extra thousand euros just in case anything went wrong, and that was fine. He promised to provide his card as soon as a replacement could be sent to the hotel by his bank.

Back at the Internet café, he chatted online with a representative of the bank in Geneva where a fictitious corporation maintained an account stuffed with euros.

He answered a series of security questions, entered a password and ordered a debit card for a new corporate officer named Constantin Stefos. The card carried a daily limit of ten thousand euros, which he knew would be more than sufficient. The card would be shipped to his hotel by overnight courier, and he would be back in business.

Everything went perfectly. On the fourth morning he checked out, took a taxi to the airport and boarded a flight to London. He was anxious when he stepped up to the passport control booth, but his papers got nothing but a quick inspection. As the plane flew across Europe, Constantin Stefos prepared himself for the new life ahead.

CHAPTER TWENTY-SEVEN

Brian was on the phone with the director of the Israel Antiquities Authority. Although they hadn't met, several years ago Dr. Rebecca Kohl had been cited as an authority about the Dead Sea Scrolls in one of Brian's documentaries. A woman in her late thirties with a master's degree in Middle Eastern history from the University of Chicago and a PhD in archaeology from Cambridge, she was an internationally recognized authority on the subjects over which she was now in charge. Brian had considered her appointment a remarkable coup for the government – she could have made far more in the private sector – but she supplemented her income by writing. Her four books on Israel and its ancient cultures were used in classrooms at universities worldwide, but her real fame and fortune had come from two novels that had been published in the last couple of years.

The most widely known was the first book, a story about a young Jewish girl caught in the Six-Day War. The other was popular among mystery and thriller readers. It was set in biblical times and followed an archaeologist who wanted to demonstrate that the prophecies of Isaiah were literally true. Brian felt that was a perfect lead-in to his reason for today's phone call. He had been deliberately cryptic when he requested a telephone meeting, but given his stature in the world of antiquities, she had been only too happy to speak with him.

"Do you recall the words of Isaiah 45:3?" he asked when the pleasantries had been dispensed with.

"Of course, but rather than generalizing, let me grab my Hebrew Bible." Dr. Kohl took the book from her desk, thumbed through it and read the verse aloud first in Hebrew, then in English. "And I will give you treasures of darkness and riches hidden in secret places, in order that you know that I am the Lord who calls you by your name, the Holy One of Israel."

She paused and he could feel the smile on her face in the words she said next. "That sounds like something you'd be interested in, Mr. Sadler. I think I've seen every one of your amazing documentaries and I must say you and your production team know how to captivate an audience. The shows are fascinating and the thing I appreciate is the depths to which you go to avoid sensationalism. I can respect the opinions of others, even as farfetched as aliens building the pyramids of Giza, but you have a way of weaving legends into facts that make yours legitimate documentaries even a pragmatic archaeologist like myself can appreciate. But back to your call. What about the words of Isaiah brings you to me?"

Explaining the need for background, Brian told her what had happened since his arrival in Israel. He said that Abdel had shown him a cave in Beth Shean National Park and he explained what was in it. He told her about the men who had abducted Abdel and then brought him back. He added that he had been kidnapped, although he thought that had to do with his friendship with President Harrison.

"Abdel's disappeared," he continued, dismissing his own involvement in the situation as not relevant. "He took me to the cavern, and until he went missing, I respected that it was his site to reveal. But now I'm afraid he's dead. I'm calling to urge you to put guards at the cave. Other people know about it and the treasure may already have been stolen. You must move quickly."

She posed question after question, revealing both her intrigue about the discovery and her deep concern for the safety of the artifacts. "If I may be so inquisitive," she asked when he was finished, "what was your reason for coming to Israel in the first place? I know you have a burning desire to protect the things that reveal ancient history, but are you looking for a documentary out of all this?"

He explained that originally the trip had merely been about a visit to the Holy Land with his wife, and of course the auction of the Canaan wedding cup.

"Ah, yes, I recall that now," she replied. "I was the one that allowed that piece to go under the gavel. It was a beauty, wasn't it?"

Yes, he agreed, telling her he regretted losing it, but that those things happened in his business.

"After Abdel showed me the cavern, my reasons for staying in Israel changed. My wife returned to the States, but I've been here ever since. I'm interested in producing a show, but I also believe the relics must not leave Israel. With your help, I'd like to be the one to show the world that Isaiah's prophecies are true. For that – or even without it – I'm willing to show you where the site is. That's more important than anything: regardless if I get anything out of this, you must protect these treasures."

"I'm going to start the process immediately," she agreed. "Can you go with me to Beth Shean this afternoon?"

"I don't see how. I'm in Athens and I'm persona non grata with your prime minister. I doubt he'll let me back into the country." He briefly explained why.

"Book an afternoon flight to Haifa," she instructed. "I'll handle the PM. Call me when you know your arrival time and I'll meet you there."

He eagerly accepted, hopeful that things might finally come to fruition. He told her about the situation with Tariq and advised he needed security in Israel. No problem, she assured him.

———

Nicole listened in silence as her husband explained that instead of coming home from Athens as he'd promised, he was planning to go back to Israel this afternoon. At least he'd been assigned a security officer for protection – that gave her a sense of relief for the first time in all this craziness. He had gotten out of harm's way, and he was safely in the European Union. Unlike anywhere in Israel right now, he could simply board a plane in Athens and fly to the United States. The danger appeared to be behind him but now he was going back into the middle of it. How could he?

She understood that he wanted to lead the archaeologist to the cave. She understood how much this meant to his career and him personally, and she understood that Brian was on the scent again. He asked for her blessing, but she refused to go that far. She could have demanded he drop this crazy quest – and maybe he would have – but she still couldn't bring herself to do it. What she wanted – what she hoped and prayed for – was that he'd make that decision himself.

"Are you angry with me?" he asked when she told him flippantly to go off and get himself killed if he wanted to.

"Angry isn't the word for it. Angry is how I feel when you don't put the toilet seat down for the hundredth time or you forget my birthday. I'm terrified, Brian. I know how much this means to you and God knows I understand why you want to do it, but for as long as I live, I don't think I will ever see things from your perspective. Your mind has the power to let adventure block reason. Even though you've had problem after problem in the past, you convince yourself things will be different this time. Everything will be okay, and the risk of ... whatever the risk is, death or whatever ... is worth it because of the excitement. To answer your question, no, I'm not mad. I'm livid, to be perfectly honest, and any sane person would feel the same way. It's insane, irrational, unreasonable and totally bizarre how you twist reality. I just want my husband. That's all I want. I love you but I hate this part of you. Go do it, Brian. Just get it over with."

"I promise everything will be all right –"

She sniffled, "Stop it. Don't say that, because the words mean nothing. I may sound like a broken record, but so do you. Just come home."

She hung up, leaving him with swirling thoughts of regret and shame. He loved that woman more than he loved the life he was living to the hilt, and he knew the right thing to do. He should become a real husband, settle down with a wife who loved him the same way, and run the immensely successful business that would allow them financial freedom for the rest of their lives.

After this, he promised himself. *After this I'll stop.* He reflected that his words sounded like those of an addict.

———

The security guard he'd hired stayed with him until Brian went through the security area. His plane left on time, and just after four p.m. he walked to the immigration desk in International Arrivals at the Haifa Airport. Dr. Kohl had assured him everything would be fine, but he couldn't help wondering if he might be detained. When the man stamped his passport and handed it back without a word, he knew she'd fulfilled her promise.

He passed through the green line and went out to the sidewalk where a mob waiting for arriving passengers stood in the blazing heat. He saw an attractive woman wearing a Tilley jungle hat over her jet-black hair and holding a sign with his name. As he waved, she and a young lady in a skirt and blue blazer walked over.

"Welcome back," she said with a sincere smile. "I'm Rebecca Kohl. Let's dispense with the formalities. You're Brian; I'm Becky, and this is Elisabeth. She works in the security detail in my building. She's also a soldier in the Israeli army and I'm told she's a crack marksman!" The girl smiled and offered her hand.

A sedan was waiting at the curb. Elisabeth went in front as they climbed into the backseat for the hour-long drive to Beth Shean.

"I've arranged for armed soldiers to be at the site by the end of the day," she advised. "You and I can instruct them how best to stand guard, and they'll be on hand around the clock for as long as we need them."

They arrived at the national park entrance and Brian showed the driver the road that led past the ancient city and up the hill. They left the driver and Brian led the two women along the path, down the rope and to the entrance.

193

"This is it," he said quietly. "I hope to God everything is still here."

"As do I," she replied enthusiastically. "I can hardly wait to see it!"

She handed them flashlights as they entered the tunnel. They shuffled through the narrow passageway, and when they emerged into the cavern, he saw the same glint of gold that had captivated him before.

"It's here," he whispered, moving the beam of his light around the room. "It's all still here."

Elisabeth stood in stunned amazement as Becky gazed in wonder, gasping at first one thing and then another. Buoyed by their excitement, he too experienced it as though it was his first time. She walked to the nearest pile of objects, picked up a twelve-inch-tall golden chalice with a ram's head carved on it and marveled at its beauty.

"This truly is a special place, isn't it?" The words in accented English came from the darkness behind them.

Startled, they whirled about and saw two men emerging from the shadows, each holding a pistol. A third had an automatic rifle trained on Elisabeth; he ordered her to drop her weapon. When she paused, he brandished his AK-47 menacingly.

"He will kill you," the first man said evenly. "You have no part in this. Don't be foolish."

Becky nodded, giving Elisabeth her approval. She had no choice. She removed her pistol from its holster and dropped it to the floor.

The first man – their leader – barked orders while he held his gun on the three of them. The others tied their prisoners' hands behind their backs, searched their pockets and tossed their cellphones aside.

"You'll never get away with this," the archaeologist snapped. "I have soldiers coming –"

"I'm certain you do," he snarled. "That is why we have no time to spare. Allah willing, we will be gone before they arrive."

Brian glanced at Becky. Her eyes were wide with terror and for once the indomitable adventurer was beginning to feel the same way. Despite the security precautions and their careful planning, he knew what this was about. There was a bounty on his head – Harry had said that. Tariq's men had caught up with him and he'd put another person in danger because of his indifference to reality. For once, he was truly, deeply afraid. He had used up his nine lives; it was time to pay the price for his folly.

They were prodded back the way they had come until they were on top of the bluff. The leader paused, gave a whistle and got a faraway one in response. "We will go now," he said. "It is safe."

About an hour later, a truckload of Israeli soldiers arrived at the archaeological site. The lieutenant in charge was surprised that Dr. Kohl wasn't there to meet them, as he'd been told would happen. When darkness fell and she still hadn't arrived, he tried her cellphone several times. He waited two more hours and then contacted his superior. He and his squad were ordered to return to base until someone could figure out the apparent miscommunication between the army and the director of antiquities.

Brian and Becky lay on their sides in the bed of a pickup truck, bound, gagged and covered by a filthy tarp. It was just the two of them – they had no idea where Elisabeth was. They were driving on a road with enormous potholes, and they felt every jarring bump. After fifteen minutes the truck stopped; someone removed the tarp and prodded them with rifles. Despite the tethers on their hands, they managed to sit up, stretch their aching legs and get out.

The truck sat in front of a boarded-up building that had been abandoned for some time. Judging by junk strewn about, it could have been a mechanic's shop. The sun was setting and they could see a dim floodlight every twenty feet or so that did little to illuminate an eight-foot-high fence that ran as far as they could see either way.

"That's the border with Jordan," Becky whispered.

They were shoved into a bay that reeked of motor oil and grease. Its floor was sticky and there was trash everywhere. A single low-watt bulb hanging from a wire provided the only light.

A door opened and a man entered. Brian quivered when he saw who it was.

"We meet again, Mr. Sadler," Tariq began, his words smug and satisfied. "I see you've brought a guest. Dr. Kohl, welcome. Like Mr. Sadler, you're a famous person too. Today seems to be my lucky day. I have won two prizes for the price of one. What do you think your government will be willing to trade for your safe return?"

"Who is this?" she asked Brian.

Brian mustered every ounce of strength he could. If he was going to die, he wasn't going to do it sniveling around and begging for mercy. He was responsible for everything that had happened, and if he could get Tariq into a conversation, he might think of some way out of this. That possibility seemed remote, but it was worth a chance. He pulled himself up straight and looked the terrorist in the eyes.

"He's a punk who's crazy with power, that's what he is. That's Tariq the Hawk, the leader of AQS. He's also a liar – he told me he kidnapped my wife, but the US government got her first. You were a little slow on that one, Tariq."

Tariq flashed an evil grin. "I don't want to hurt you too badly while you're my guest," he said to Brian, "but if you continue to provoke me, I will be forced to return you in, shall we say, somewhat less pristine condition than when you arrived." He looked at Becky Kohl. "You, my dear, are a different story. When I have received what I want, perhaps I will allow my men to have you."

Despite being a strong, determined woman, his words made her shiver and Tariq picked up on it. "I do not wish to alarm either of you," he continued without emotion. "If you and your governments do everything I ask, both of you will be returned safely and with minimal inconvenience."

"Where's the girl who was with us?" she demanded.

He laughed. "Your guard? She proved to be completely ineffective, didn't she? I regret to advise you that she is wherever Jews go when their time on earth is completed. I can't imagine it's Heaven – I believe that place is reserved for the followers of Allah."

Becky gasped in horror. She looked at Brian, her eyes glistening with tears. "He's serious?" She sobbed, torn apart inside at having put one of her young people into this deadly, terrifying situation.

Brian nodded, knowing this warped animal's love for killing.

Tariq issued a command and the guards untied their hands. They rubbed their aching wrists as the men handed them bottles of water.

"Where are we? Where's Abdel Malouf?" Brian asked.

"Here we go again with the questions. You are in Israel, but shortly you will go to Syria. I hope you're looking forward to the trip as much as I am. As far as Abdel, I was going to ask you the same question. You helped him escape and you met him in Athens. Where did he go from there?"

Nothing about Tariq should have surprised Brian by now, but he did wonder how the man had found out so quickly that Abdel was gone. "I never saw him. He was gone when I arrived."

"You'll forgive me for not believing you," Tariq responded coldly. "He isn't what you think he is, Mr. Sadler. You may think Abdel is a man much like you – a respected antiquities dealer and a friend – but he is something else entirely. Have you heard of the Zulqarnayn?"

Brian didn't want to disclose that Abdel had mentioned the name earlier, so he shook his head. "Is it a man?"

Becky answered, "It's a title."

"I thought you would know," Tariq said with a smile. "Explain it to Mr. Sadler."

Her voice was shaky, but she was determined to show strength, not fear. "The Zulqarnayn is a title that's been passed down since biblical times. According to legend, there's a person – usually an Arab – who is the leader of a band of brothers. One of their missions is to guard a sacred treasure. Some think it was the sacred objects that King Cyrus returned to the Jews around 540 BCE."

"Yes," Tariq added. "I believe he was the Zulqarnayn at that moment in history. There were others before and since."

One thing about this ruthless bastard, Brian conceded, *is that he's highly intelligent. He's a student of history.*

The terrorist continued, "I knew a scholar such as yourself would know the legend. Today you saw the treasure. I cannot imagine what a pleasure that must have been, at least until the time when my men showed themselves. But please continue. Enlighten us with the rest of the story. When was the treasure actually hidden at Beth Shean?"

She answered, "There's a difference of opinion on that. I believe it didn't happen until the final destruction of the temple in 70 AD. The high priests moved the treasure there as the Romans sacked Jerusalem. Others believe it was the same cave where their valuables had been stored five hundred years before, when the Jews were taken into captivity. But it makes more sense to me that King Nebuchadnezzar took the treasure to Babylonia along with the Israelites."

Tariq smiled, enjoying the debate. "I disagree. I think Cyrus brought the Israelites to the cave and showed them the hidden treasure. They took it to Jerusalem and rebuilt the temple. Five hundred years later the Romans burned it and the treasure was hidden back in the same place – the cavern where the golden idols are today. And soon I too will be a part of history, when I remove the temple relics. I doubt any biblical prophecies will be fulfilled this time because I'm taking the hoard for myself! How many gold ingots do you think there will be after I melt down that pile of Israelite rubbish?"

Brian's mind was spinning, torn between the knowledge that he and Becky Kohl were in terrible danger and the understanding that this priceless cache of artifacts was in the hands of a man whose delight in destroying history had been proven time and again. He had to think of something and he had to keep Tariq talking until he did.

Abdel had also believed the treasure had been hidden in the cavern not once, but twice. But something nagged at Brian. Something about this Zulqarnayn account didn't make sense. Why would a band of Arabs be the guardians of an Israelite treasure?

Tariq appeared to be enjoying himself very much. He said, "The first Zulqarnayn was Alexander of Macedonia. King Cyrus was another, as you said. He and his men safeguarded the treasure until it was returned to the Jews. There has been a Zulqarnayn ever since."

"And are you the present one?" Brian asked.

Tariq burst out in laughter. "Quite the opposite! Why would you think such a thing? Were you not listening to your friend describe the Zulqarnayn? He is the protector of the treasure, while I intend to destroy it. Your precious goblets and chalices will soon be bars of gold.

"You know what I'm about, Mr. Sadler. The president must have told you what a dangerous man I am. And he is right. But I have noble goals. I am not protecting treasure on earth; I am destroying everything that drives men away from Allah. Men worship ancient ruins, statues, mummies, and golden objects from the past. I cleanse the Earth of those things. I defend the Arab people against infidels everywhere, but especially those in Israel and the United States. I will find my storehouse of treasure in Heaven, Allah willing."

The more they kept him talking, the more time someone might have to rescue them. "How admirable," Brian replied sarcastically. "But something doesn't make sense. Cyrus gave the temple treasure back to the Jews twenty-five hundred years ago, right?"

Tariq nodded.

"When that happened, didn't the Zulqarnayn's obligation to safeguard it end? It wasn't hidden any more. It was in Jerusalem once again."

"From the first, each Zulqarnayn has assumed responsibility for safeguarding the infidels' treasure. It has been carried out to this day. When the Romans were about to occupy Jerusalem in AD 70, the Jews hid the temple relics again at Beth Shean. And they stayed there for two thousand years, until Abdel Malouf decided to tell you about them."

"But Abdel said he's known about the cave for a long time. Someone else showed it to him."

"Your friend's a liar, Mr. Sadler. Haven't you figured that out by now? He's one of the Zulqarnayn's men. He was one of the people entrusted to safeguard the treasure, but instead he revealed its whereabouts to an infidel. That would of course be you."

Brian was astounded. "I don't believe a thing you're saying. He never said anything about Zulqarnayn. He admitted he had done bad things in the past. He said he had been part of al Qaeda –"

"Bad things? He is a fool who was part al Qaeda once, long before I became the leader!" Tariq exploded. "I would never have asked a weakling like him to join me! That is why I have never called upon him. He was unreliable; a Jew could have done al Qaeda's work better than Abdel. Only when you arrived did I ask him to perform tasks for the cause. They were simple – tell me who the Zulqarnayn is, lead me to the treasure and hand you over to me."

"And who is the Zulqarnayn today?"

"Abdel disappeared without telling me that. I will find him, Allah willing, and then I will know who that enemy is. In the meantime, I am taking control of things. I will destroy every single idol to the false god of the Israelites."

He glanced at his watch and issued an order in his language. "There is a bathroom in there," he told them, pointing to a door. "You should use it now." Then Tariq ushered them outside. "We will continue this enjoyable conversation tomorrow," he said as politely as if he were bidding old friends goodbye. "Now you must go."

Tariq's soldiers retied their hands, put duct tape over their mouths and took them outside. They were jostled and marched along the fence into the darkness. There were no buildings now; they walked in scrub brush and saw a light pole every hundred feet, dim bulbs barely illuminating the fence to their right.

They heard the soft bleat of sheep and saw a group of Bedouins sitting around a fire on the other side. There was no fence here; someone had knocked it down so the animals could graze on either side. The nomads ignored the activity as their captors whispered and got a response. Two men sitting in a Jeep walked over, took Becky and Brian and shoved them roughly into the backseat. Seconds later they were speeding down a dirt road with their headlights off as the moon's soft glow guided them on a rutted path toward the lights of a town far in the distance. Brian turned around, gazed into the darkness behind them and wondered if he would see Israel again.

CHAPTER TWENTY-EIGHT

An hour later the Jeep pulled up beside a long strip of dirt that functioned as a runway. They parked next to an ancient twin-engine Beech airplane. They were put in the backseat and a guard took the right front one. The pilot flew off into the starry skies over Jordan. If Tariq was telling the truth, they were on the way to Syria, one of the most dangerous places imaginable for an American millionaire and an Israeli government official.

The first light of dawn was breaking as they landed on another makeshift airstrip outside a dusty, war-torn village. They were shoved into another Jeep; now there was no attempt to hide the fact that they were hostages. Their mouths taped and hands bound, they rode along dirt streets filled with rubble from bombed-out buildings. There were no people – the town appeared to have been abandoned for a long time.

The Jeep stopped in front of the only structure in the tiny village that had four walls and a roof. It had a door, panes of glass in its windows, and a satellite dish. Three men in their early twenties milled about in front of the building, each with an AK-47 strung across his chest. They were ushered inside, where a swarthy, unkempt man in a filthy uniform jerked the duct tape from their mouths, untied them and handed them water.

It had been hours since they last had a drink, and they gulped it down. He gave them another and pointed to a door, indicating that Becky should open it. She cautiously looked inside and found a small room with a barred window. Flies buzzed around a hole in the floor. It was a bathroom, and as horrible as it was, it was a welcome sight. She closed the door. When she was finished, he took his turn.

For two hours, they sat in a stiflingly hot room ten feet from an overweight guard who hadn't bathed in days. He had a rifle in his lap and wore earplugs connected to a wire running to an old MP3 player. Neither of them was sure what Tariq's demands would be; they simply prayed for rescue. Brian was aware of America's longstanding policy of not negotiating with terrorists, but he also knew Harry would do whatever he could. His greatest concern was for Nicole, and he grieved inside that he had selfishly let her down once more.

Becky was consumed by her own thoughts. Her prime minister harbored a deep hatred for those who sought to destroy his nation, and she had no idea whether he'd negotiate or not. When she became head of the Antiquities Authority, she'd never imagined being a kidnap victim and a possible pawn in the war between Israel and its neighbors, but that was exactly what had happened.

God, if I get out of this, I'll never let it happen again, she prayed, even though she knew there could have been no way to predict this dilemma. It had been a simple trip to see a recently discovered treasure hoard, until everything went wrong.

Brian suggested they concentrate on other things than their situation until they knew what was going on. They talked quietly about the treasure and what would happen to it now that Tariq had them as prisoners.

Half an hour went by and Brian touched her sleeve gently. He nodded his head in the direction of the guard. The man's head fell forward and snapped back up now and then as he struggled to stay awake. They could hear faint sounds of music from his earplugs and his fingers tapped his leg in rhythm. At one point, he closed his eyes for a particularly long time and Brian moved to the edge of his chair. He wasn't sure himself what he thought he was going to do, and anything was risky since there were armed men outside, but in here it seemed it was just the three of them.

The guard's head jerked back up and his eyes popped open. He yawned and rubbed them with his grimy fingers. He satisfied himself that his prisoners were doing nothing alarming and went back to the reverie of his music. Seconds later his eyelids closed again.

Brian rose quietly and tiptoed across the room. In a single move, he grabbed the rifle by its barrel, pulled it out of the man's lap and swung it in the air, the stock connecting solidly with his right temple and sending him crashing in a heap on the floor. Brian aimed the weapon toward the door in case one of the guards had heard the man fall, but no one came inside. He felt for a pulse, but there was none.

Becky's face was filled with terror. "What have you done?" she cried as he shushed her. "There's no way out of here. Tariq will kill us now for sure."

"I had to do something," he whispered. "I couldn't sit here and let them kill us. We have no idea how much time we have. See what's in the other rooms."

He kept the rifle trained on the door while she was gone. In a moment she returned and said, "Someone's been living here. There's a kitchen and a bedroom. There are three handguns in there and some knives in the drawer. There's an old cellphone in a charger in the bedroom. There's also a back door, but how can we escape? We don't even know where we are!"

"Bring me a pistol and take one yourself. Be sure they're loaded. Bring the phone too." She came back and he told her to be ready to shoot anyone who walked through the door. The phone was an old flip version, grimy and scratched. Wondering if it would work, he entered 01 – the country code for the USA – and dialed a number he'd committed to memory long ago. It was evening there, but he hoped she'd get the message.

He prayed for a connection as there were numerous clicks and pauses. His face lit up as he heard the ringing. He didn't expect her to answer even if she was still at her desk. God only knew where they were, and a foreign cellphone number would go to voicemail, but it was better than nothing.

"Cynthia," he said quietly, "tell Harry Becky Kohl and I have been kidnapped by Tariq's men. I think we're in Syria, but I don't know where." He explained what had

205

happened with Tariq and how he'd overpowered the guard. "Please send help fast."

CHAPTER TWENTY-NINE

While Brian stood guard, Becky peeked out a window next to the back door. She told him that there was no means of escaping that way. It opened into a sandy yard enclosed by decaying fence posts and a strand or two of barbed wire. Getting out would be easy, but there was no place to go. They would be completely exposed. They were trapped.

Brian racked his brain for ideas, but he was out of time. There was a noise outside and they heard another vehicle pull up to the house and voices. Someone was talking to the guards.

"Get ready," he whispered, motioning her to join him behind the front door. "If there's more than one, I'll take the first. Can you shoot a pistol?"

"Are you kidding?" she replied. "I spent my two years in the Israeli army like everyone else. I can handle myself."

"That's good." He figured she'd be better with a gun than he was. "Stay focused."

The door opened and Tariq walked in alone. He closed it, saw two revolvers aimed at him, glanced at the dead body on the floor and smirked, "What have you done? All I need do is shout and you'll have three to deal with. You may kill me, but they'll kill you. I'd wager neither of you knows much about guns. I doubt you have ever held one. Put them down, I'll forgive your little indiscretion and we'll get on with things."

He took a step in their direction and Brian said, "I'll kill you if you move another inch! I may not make it out of here, but I'll make damned sure you don't either. And I grew up in Texas, just so you know. Shooting guns was a part of my childhood. Don't underestimate me or you're a dead man. Sit down in that chair."

Becky kept the gun trained on Tariq while Brian ran in the kitchen, returning with something that appeared to be a staple for terrorists in this country – a roll of duct tape. He told Tariq to wrap it around one of his wrists tightly and then pass it around the chair and his body. After three times around, the man was sufficiently constrained for Brian to step behind him and finish the job. The terrorist was tightly bound to the chair.

It was then that Tariq made his move. He yelled something in Arabic and Brian swung his pistol, hitting him solidly in the head. He slumped forward in the chair and the front door flew open. Only one guard at a time could pass through the narrow doorway. The first one burst in, saw Tariq and looked around in surprise. Becky shot him in the face and the second guard jumped over his body and raised his weapon. Brian fired at the second man's torso, but the shot went wide, striking him in the left forearm. Still gripping the rifle, the man turned to the door. Becky fired two shots into his back. He collapsed into the sandy street just outside.

Brian ran out, grabbed the man's weapon and made sure both guards were dead. They waited hesitantly to see if anyone else would respond to the gunfire, but there was silence. The village really was deserted.

"You handled yourself well," he told her. "That military training came in handy. My shot went wild. I haven't held many guns in my lifetime, to be honest."

She started to reply, but he saw a panic-stricken look on her face as she fell into a dead faint.

He dialed Cynthia's number again. This time it was answered on the first ring.

"Mr. Sadler?" He didn't recognize the voice.

"Who is this?'

"I'm with the CIA. We've monitored Ms. Beal's phone since your last call. Are you still in danger?"

"I'm in Syria. We captured Tariq."

The man paused for a second. "What? You've captured him? How?"

He quickly explained and said everything was quiet, but it couldn't last. They needed help immediately and were told that an extraction team was already in the air.

"How do they know where we are?"

"We pinged you from the phone's GPS when you called before. You're in an abandoned village in the Syrian Desert a hundred miles from Damascus. There's an ISIS training camp twenty miles from your location. That's the biggest danger for you and for our inbound chopper."

"Tell them to come quickly." He watched closely, aiming his pistol as Tariq raised his head and shook it. He saw one of his guards lying on the floor and the other just outside, both dead.

"You have no idea what I'm going to do to you," he hissed. "It would be best to kill yourselves now. It's a far better fate than what's in store for you. You're trapped here, miles from civilization in an area I control. The only people within a hundred miles are *my* people."

Brian pulled the other guard's body inside and swept the sand to cover his blood. He left the door ajar. The sun was directly overhead now and the temperature was soaring. He found more water bottles in the kitchen and knelt, cradling Becky's head with his arm. Her eyelids fluttered and she took a sip. She asked if he'd help her stand, and took his arms, steadying herself on wobbly legs. She held the back of a chair to steady herself and proclaimed she was better. She finished the bottle of water.

"Give me water," Tariq demanded.

"Go to hell," Brian answered. "I wish I had killed you already, but I didn't because you're going to stand trial for what you've done. It'll be fair, and that's the one thing I'm disappointed about. You should have the same fate you've dealt so many innocent people. You should have to stand by an open pit and beg for your life as an executioner prepares to cut off your head with a scimitar. But in a free society things don't work that way. And that's unfortunate."

"All your banter is entertaining," Tariq said coldly, "but aren't you getting ahead of yourselves? It will take more than two amateurs to stop me." He jumped from the chair and grabbed Becky, pulling her body in front of his as a shield and twisting her wrist until she dropped the pistol. Brian held his weapon on them, but there was no chance to fire without hitting her.

"Check your prisoner's pockets next time, you piece of dung," he chortled, displaying an eight-inch knife he'd taken from his back pocket and used to cut the tape. Now he held it tightly against Becky's neck. "Are you ready to go to hell, lady?"

"Shoot him, Brian! Shoot!"

The next seconds were a blur. Brian heard a noisy truck approaching. It wasn't the helicopter, so it had to be Tariq's men. Tariq heard it too. He smiled, shifted his body slightly and turned toward the door. Brian seized the opportunity. His last shot had missed its mark; if this one did too, she would die. He had to do something; this was his only chance.

He fired and Becky uttered a gasping, shrill scream as she fell to the ground, blood pouring from a gash in her throat.

Oh, my God! I killed her!

Brian struggled to maintain his composure. Everything seemed surreal, as though he were watching a scene from a movie. He saw himself running across the room as Tariq collapsed on top of her.

As the truck pulled up, he could hear shouts in Arabic. In seconds, they'd be inside and he would be heavily outnumbered. He checked the cylinder – there were four shells left. Becky's gun was on the other side of the room; he'd have to cross in front of the open door to get it. It was a chance he'd have to take. He lunged for the gun.

He'd made it halfway across the room when an enormous blast shook the house, knocking him off his feet. He lay on the floor, dimly aware that his eardrums hurt like hell and that he wasn't holding the gun any more. Everything went blurry as he tried and failed to understand what was happening. Now there was a piercing white light invading his brain, followed by peace and stillness.

CHAPTER THIRTY

"Mr. Sadler! Mr. Sadler, wake up!"

Brian tried to open his eyes, but it was hard to do. The pain in his ears was excruciating and it felt as if someone was beating a hammer inside his head. He was lying on a rough concrete floor and some man's face was hovering just above his. His eyes widened in fear as he recalled the enormous explosion he'd heard. Then he saw a United States flag sewn onto the man's cap. With a huge sigh, he relaxed.

"Where ... where am I?" he slurred, finding it difficult to put thoughts and words together.

"You're in Syria, sir. I'm Marine Staff Sergeant Todd Jenkins. I'm a medic and we've come to rescue you."

"What about Becky?"

"My partner's attending to her now, sir. She has a knife wound to the throat. There's a lot of blood, but it's not that deep. It looks like she'll survive."

Thank God. "How ..."

"We were inbound in a chopper and we saw a truck racing across the desert. You couldn't miss it; it threw out a cloud of dust for a mile behind it. We followed it in and realized they were heading for the same place we were. They got here a second ahead of us, but things worked out fine. Those ragheads almost made it to the front door before our Hellfire missile took out the truck and them too. No survivors among the bad guys."

"Is Tariq dead?"

"No, sir. It appears he'll live. I reported that to my commanding officer back in ... well, I can't tell you where we came from. But I'm wasting time. My major's orders were to patch you in to President Harrison as soon as you woke up. I guess I'll catch hell for that when this is all over!"

"Not if I can help it," Brian replied sincerely. "You guys saved my life. Becky's too."

As the soldier left the room, Brian sat up and slid on his butt to Becky's side. He held her hand as a medic applied ointment and Steri-Strips to protect the wound until she could be transported to a hospital. He had given her an injection to deaden the pain, and she was woozy. She smiled weakly and gave his hand a tiny squeeze.

The sergeant returned with another man. "Mr. Sadler, this is Major Fulton. Let me patch you through, sir." He spoke on his radio for a moment and then everyone in the room fell silent as they heard the familiar voice of the president of the United States crackling through the mobile unit.

"Brian, are you all right?"

"I'm a little woozy, that's all. Thank God for the Marines. They got here just in time. Literally just in time." His body trembled as the realization of how close to death he and Becky had come finally sank in.

"I hear you shot Tariq but left him alive. I couldn't have asked for more. We need to have a talk with him."

I didn't "leave him alive," Brian confessed to himself. *I had intended to shoot him in the head, but I missed.*

"There's someone on the line who wants to talk to you," Harry revealed. Brian heard a few clicks as another line was added.

"Brian! Brian," Nicole choked. "I'm so glad you're all right!"

Now the emotions became too much. He sobbed. His chest ached and he gasped for breath as he tried to speak. "Nicole," he managed at last, "I'm so sorry. I'm just so sorry."

"Don't waste words, sweetie. Don't worry – just come home soon."

He promised – a real promise this time – and said they'd talk as soon as they could.

Harry came back on the line. "Thanks to you the threat from Tariq's been eliminated. Nicole, you can go back home. As far as you're concerned, Brian, you owe her more than you can ever repay. She's been a real trouper and you owe her big time. She's your biggest supporter and you can't keep on doing this to her."

Nicole cried, Brian cried, and after a moment the president of the United States was crying too. The hardened soldiers in the room averted their eyes. This was a deeply personal moment and each of them wished he was someplace other than this.

Brian fought through the pulsating fury of the worst headache he'd ever had. "I'm a reformed man," he joked weakly.

Half-jokingly, Nicole said, "Don't say words you might have to eat later. Just come home and I'll forgive you."

As they signed off, Brian heard a thumping sound that was growing louder and louder. Eyes wide with fear, he looked to the major for reassurance.

"That would be the Israelis," the officer advised. "We got a little head start on them. When we reached the border, the Syrians demanded we turn back and we told them – very politely, of course – to go to hell. After the damage we inflicted on them earlier, their air force couldn't have responded if it tried. Shigon told the Syrian president we and his troops were coming in to rescue our people and ordered him to back off. Personally, I like this new prime minister. He doesn't mince words, and thanks to him no one stopped us from getting here."

The major spoke by radio to his Israeli counterpart in one of the two choppers that were now hovering overhead. The Marines loaded Brian, Becky and Tariq onto theirs and everyone headed back to Israel.

———

Brian's shot had been a lucky one, narrowly missing Becky's body as Tariq had moved slightly when he heard his men arrive. Brian hit him in the side, puncturing his kidney and spleen. He would recover to stand trial. At this point it was merely a matter of where – Israel or the United States. Until the details could be worked out, he was imprisoned under heavy guard in the hospital bay aboard the USS *Nimitz* in the Mediterranean Sea, just twelve miles off the coast of Haifa.

The chopper carrying Brian and Becky went directly to a hospital in Jerusalem. They were the only ones on their floor – all other patients had been moved. Eight Israeli soldiers with automatic rifles stood guard at the elevators and in the corridors. Two more were outside each patient's door.

With no external injuries, Brian's hospitalization was for observation. The concussive effect of the Hellfire missile strike on the Arabs still caused him intermittent pain in his head and ears, but a low dose of sedatives had allowed him to sleep.

Brian walked down the hallway to Becky's room. She lay in her bed, wearing a brace to immobilize her neck and tubes ran from her arm to an IV tree.

"Can you talk?" he asked.

She smiled, nodded from her bed and thanked him for saving her life. Her voice was soft and raspy, but she said that speaking didn't hurt thanks to localized anesthetics the doctor had injected around her wound.

"I shouldn't have taken the shot," he said. "I could have killed you."

"Thank God you did. He was a second away from slitting my throat," she said, struggling a little with the words. "I prayed that God would guide your hand. I knew He would let your aim be sure and true and keep that murdering terrorist alive to stand trial."

"What about the cave? Do you think the relics are safe?" He knew anything could have happened in the thirty-six hours since their kidnapping.

"My deputy minister stopped by earlier," she answered. "I told him how to get to the cave and instructed him to post round-the-clock security. I've also sent a team from the Antiquities Theft Prevention Unit to be on the scene. They're hybrids – part archaeologist and part cop. The doctor says if things go well, we will both be discharged tomorrow. What do you say we make a trip to see for ourselves if the treasure is still there?"

"Are you up to it?" he asked. "I don't think ..."

"You don't understand. I'm going, period. I'm simply asking if you want to come too. I don't care if I go in an ambulance and I don't care that it's the Sabbath. I *must* go back. Everything must be there – it simply must. I choose to believe that God has protected my people's treasures."

"I know exactly how you feel," Brian replied. "Once you've seen the cavern, it's as though you can't wait to see it again. Count me in!"

In the afternoon, the embassy sent over a new iPhone Brian had ordered from the Apple Store and he spoke to Nicole for almost an hour. She sounded calm and relaxed for the first time since she'd left Israel. He explained that he and the antiquities director were heading to the cave again tomorrow and – presuming things were still in place – he was going to petition her to allow a documentary about the hidden treasures of Isaiah. There was lots of security at the cave, he added, and he promised to stay at the embassy compound in Tel Aviv until his work was finished in Israel. For once, she agreed with everything. With Tariq in custody, the worst was over and, barring a new outbreak of hostilities, her husband could wrap things up and come home at last.

Around six that evening a representative from the consulate in Jerusalem called Brian to report that a FedEx package intended for him had arrived. A courier dropped it off at the hospital an hour later.

As he opened the thick padded envelope, he noticed it had been sent from a FedEx office in Athens, but it had no sender's name. There were two things inside. Wrapped in a cloth was a thin plate made of solid gold, about ten inches square and filled on both sides with tiny words. The ones on its obverse appeared to be in a different language from those on the back. It reminded him of the Rosetta Stone – a stela found in 1799 that was inscribed in three languages, which was the key to deciphering Egyptian hieroglyphs.

The parcel also contained a small envelope with two things inside. One was a letter written in Arabic, a language Brian recognized but couldn't read. The other was a legal document written in English. On its last page he saw Abdel's signature, attestations and a seal. He was barely able to contain his emotions as he read it.

Brian still didn't know if he should have trusted Abdel. Regardless, he wondered what intense grief Abdel must have experienced as he signed a notarized affidavit transferring ownership of his gallery and all its contents to Brian. Abdel had been an enigma – a self-proclaimed member of al Qaeda, a prominent merchant and Brian's colleague. He also had been a friend – maybe. Whatever he was, this document was a testimonial that he wasn't coming back. For whatever reason, he had given away the thing that was most important to him.

Speaking of what Abdel had done, Brian needed to arrange protection for the gallery immediately. He called the security firm he'd used earlier and hired round-the-clock guards for Abdel's shuttered shop.

Next, he called Nicole. Unlike the upbeat conversation they'd had this afternoon, now she was far less exuberant. Abdel's actions made her sad because she, like Brian, knew it was a last resort. And now, despite the anguish over Brian's adventure in Israel, now he owned a shop there. He would be back to Jerusalem on a regular basis. She asked him about that; he promised that coming home was still the immediate thing on his agenda. Before he left, he'd go by the gallery, make sure everything was good, and leave it locked and guarded until he could plan another trip.

"Promise you'll come home this time?" she asked. "Please, Brian. Do you promise?"

"Yes, I do." And he meant it.

He put everything back into the FedEx package, walked down the hall and knocked lightly on Becky's door. She looked perkier than when he'd last seen her.

"I told my doctor I was going to the cave tomorrow morning," she said slowly, wincing when she tried to grin. "He wagged a finger at me but also said there's no reason I couldn't. I can hardly wait!"

He showed her the parcel he'd received from Athens and told her that Abdel had transferred his gallery and contents to him. She agreed with Brian that it was a final, tragic move for the Arab dealer. Brian regretted that he might never know the fate of this man who had been his colleague and perhaps even his friend.

Becky knew Malouf by reputation and commented that he had handled some extraordinary pieces in the past several years, a few of which she had hoped could have been displayed in a museum. Brian said he was open to that discussion – there would be time for that once the most pressing issue was dealt with. They had to see where things stood with the treasure. But that was tomorrow, and right now he had one more revelation.

He handed her the golden plate. She turned it over and over in her hands, watching its surface glisten from the reflection off the overhead light.

"It's incredible," she murmured. "Close the door, pull up a chair and tell me where you found this fascinating object."

He explained that it had come in the same parcel and handed her the letter, saying he didn't know if it pertained to the relic or not.

"I'm fluent in Arabic," she said. "I can read this if you wish. It may take time because I'm not moving at full speed right now."

"If you're up to it, I'd like that very much. I'm really excited about the plate, and I hope this explains what it is."

My friend Brian, she began to read.

I am grateful for your willingness to help someone you barely knew – a man whom you thought was your business associate but who instead was something entirely different. Yes, as you pointed out, I am al Qaeda even today – one can never be a "former" member. Please understand that when I was a young man, al Qaeda was a noble cause. It fought for purity, the sanctity of Islam against the godless peoples of the world, and it appeared to follow the teachings of Mohammed. I believe its followers back then were devout supporters of what was good and right.

Long ago I was sent to Jerusalem on a secret mission and I carried it out with loyalty and dignity. I became an Israeli citizen and a part of the community. I integrated myself completely into my new life and my new country. Yes, you can call me what I was – an infiltrator, a mole and a spy – but my superiors rarely asked anything of me, and even then, only in the beginning. For many, many years I heard absolutely nothing from Syria. I chose to think they were finished with me, although in my heart I knew someday I would hear from them again.

Tariq learned that you were coming to Jerusalem for the auction. He called me the day we went to the cave at Beth Shean and gave me orders. He wanted to see you in person – to give you a message for your president. I knew from the news that Tariq had ordered the assassinations of your vice president and Israel's prime minister, but I was afraid. I did as he commanded. I admit my weakness, my friend, and I trust that Allah will grant you safety even though I betrayed you.

Becky paused and glanced up at Brian. "He was a good man after all," she said quietly.

"He really was."

I now will reveal a secret that I have kept since 2005. It was then that I learned of the hidden treasure of Isaiah and saw it for myself. Before it was purchased by Israel as a national park, most of Beth Shean – including the cave – belonged to one man. My cousin, a poor Arab shepherd boy who worked for the owner, stumbled upon the cavern much as the discoverers of the caves at Qumran did. Bedouins there found the Dead Sea Scrolls, while my cousin found the treasure of Solomon's Temple, something I hope your documentary will demonstrate was an equally astounding discovery.

In 2005, the United States had invaded Iraq and ISIS was just beginning to show its true colors. Its leaders were not friends and protectors of the people, I observed, and al Qaeda was quickly becoming just like ISIS. These were extremists bent on destroying history, defacing monuments, stealing anything that was important to civilization and promoting terrorism against both infidels and their own people. It mattered not if civilian men, women and children of Syria or Iraq were brutally murdered in the name of

Islamic radicalism. It was Allah's will, they would have you believe. But their actions speak the truth. They twist and distort the Quran. And I was determined not to allow them to get their hands on the Israelite treasure. If they did, the priceless memories of a civilization would be destroyed.

To protect the valuables, I became the Zulqarnayn, a title once held by Alexander III of Macedonia and later by Cyrus, the king of Persia who freed the Israelites and brought this very treasure back to Jerusalem. The Zulqarnayn is Allah's direct representative, empowered to protect the world from the evil Gog and Magog until the end times. I know now that ISIS and al Qaeda are Gog and Magog and I have done my part to keep them at bay, but now my time is finished.

My cousin, the one who found the cave, became my partner and for these many years we have kept the secret. I revealed it to you because ISIS and al Qaeda have become more vicious than ever. The destruction of monuments at Palmyra, the looting of the museum at Mosul and hundreds of other travesties through the region convinced me that if the jihadists gain a foothold in northern Israel, both the ancient city of Beth Shean and the treasure itself are doomed.

Brian, I must leave now. I must create a new life and give up everything from my past. I cannot protect the treasure any longer. Please become the Zulqarnayn yourself. Read about him. Learn what he stands for and what treasures he guards. Who better than an "infidel" to fight Tariq? Save the treasure, I beg of you. Save Beth Shean's ancient temples from Tariq's destructive forces. Keep the tradition alive, my friend. Become the Zulqarnayn, as Alexander the Great and King Cyrus did. Save the treasures of God's chosen people. May good fortune and safety accompany your every move. I wish you well.

He asked her to pause for a moment. He was becoming emotional, finally seeing the torment his friend must have experienced. Abdel truly was ashamed of what he once had been. He really was a good, honest man, but Brian had refused to believe it. He couldn't be blamed for mistrusting the man, but he was remorseful that his negativity might have pushed Abdel to decide to leave his life behind.

"This is difficult to hear," he said, drawing a big breath of air.

"I can only imagine. There's more. Should I continue?"

She read the rest of his letter – incredible words that took them back thousands of years – and they realized the significance of the golden plate. It was the key that unlocked the secrets of the temple treasure. Abdel said it was the only thing he had ever removed from the cavern, and they understood why he took this one important object. If ISIS had found the trove and melted down this relic, a priceless chronicle of Jewish history would have disappeared forever.

"We'll feature this prominently in the documentary," Brian murmured when she was finished. "It'll be a tribute to Abdel."

CHAPTER THIRTY-ONE

They sat in silence for several minutes and then she whispered, "This plate is as important as the Dead Sea Scrolls, don't you agree?"

"Yes, but what if the treasure's gone?"

"All right, Brian. I have a confession. I'm afraid I've deceived you a bit. I briefed the prime minister about the site and what it contained. I told you I sent the Antiquities Theft Prevention Unit to the cave, but what I didn't say was that I sent their boss – a trusted aide of mine named Colonel Green – down into the cavern. I had to know if things were all right. I was going to keep it a secret until we got there, but now I realize I should have told you earlier. Take a look at these." She handed him her cellphone and he scrolled through a set of pictures. Everything appeared to be exactly as it was the last time they were there. Tariq's men hadn't gotten to the site in time!

She asked, "Is it all right if I send the plate to my office for translation and examination? I promise it'll be safe and secure."

That was exactly what Brian was going to suggest. He snapped pictures of the front and back, returned it to the FedEx package and handed it to her. She made a call and thirty minutes later the plate was in a safe at the Antiquities Authority. A linguist would work on it tomorrow while they were away.

The next morning Brian and Becky left the hospital. With sirens screaming and red lights flashing, Israeli military police led three black Range Rovers and an ambulance from Jerusalem and over to Beth Shean. A Jeep with four heavily armed soldiers brought up the rear, ensuring there would be no surprises during the visit to the cave today. The prime minister had approved the extra security and sent a photographer. Brian and two guards were in the middle SUV.

Becky slept in the ambulance. Her physician had allowed her to travel, but only if EMTs and a nurse went along. The ambulance made it easier for her; she could rest most of the trip and the attendants were there to apply fresh bandages, give her medications and handle any complications that arose. Her wound wasn't that deep, but the slice of the knife had cut the skin across her entire throat. It had required many stitches and she was on a light regimen of pain medication. The healing process was just beginning and it would be a slow process, her doctor had advised.

Obeying their orders not to enter, the soldiers were at their posts when the entourage arrived. She gave instructions and one of them led them down the corridor, cradling his M4 carbine as he sidled through the tight part. Brian went next, followed by Becky, her nurse, the photographer and a second soldier. Becky moaned as she was forced to bend her head to navigate the passage, but she wouldn't have turned back for anything in the world.

As they crawled into the cavern and turned their flashlights on, there were murmurs of astonishment. This was Brian's third time here, but it was as breathtaking as the first. The treasure lay everywhere in front of them, but considering the large number of individual pieces, it would be impossible to know if some had been removed. Becky led the photographer around, pointing out the things she wanted him to shoot, while Brian took a hundred pictures of his own on his iPhone.

————

At the White House, President Harrison made a hard decision, one that was as disappointing to him as it was necessary under the circumstances. He and the Israeli prime minister had conferred by phone for over an hour yesterday about a permanent location for the American embassy. Shigon implored him to stay the course and rebuild the compound in West Jerusalem. It was a matter of national pride for Israel and Harry understood the reasoning, despite the ever-increasing risk of danger from an incensed group of Palestinians.

The NSA had proven that the missile attack on the embassy was the work of the Syrian government and not al Qaeda, the leader of which had threatened to bring casualties on the infidels. But the American people saw no distinction between organized terrorists and state terrorism. Whoever was behind it, the mass murder of nearly a hundred American citizens at the compound had resulted in fervent patriotism and renewed Islamophobia.

Harry was on the same page as Shigon. He wanted to defy the terrorists and keep the embassy in Jerusalem, but he couldn't risk more lives in Israel and possibly at home for something that was more symbolic than necessary. He told Shigon he had sought input from leaders on both sides of the aisle, his national security team and the CIA, and everyone agreed that the security of American citizens came first. The embassy would stay in Tel Aviv, a new ambassador and deputy would be appointed, and hopefully the people of America could eventually put aside their rekindled anger at Muslims.

The Tel Aviv Airport reopened without fanfare only twenty days after the bombing, although on a vastly reduced scale. The part of the terminal building that was undamaged had been modified to provide the bare necessities of international ingress and egress. Existing tenants were forced out. A bookstore became the airport operations office, a coffee shop the customs and immigration area, and a large upscale duty-free shop now housed temporary arrival and departure lounges. For security and logistical reasons, only three airlines received authorization to serve the airport until it could be rebuilt. Their ticket counters were set up in a long hallway where kiosks once offered sunglasses, magazines and cellphone accessories.

Armed guards were posted every ten feet along two heavy security fences that encircled the building. The terminal was open to passengers only; no one passed through the three-tier inspection zone without a passport and a same-day ticket. Three miles from the airport, a huge parking lot had been hastily created to accommodate all vehicular traffic, including taxis and limos. Shuttles ran to the terminal every few minutes. People arriving to pick up inbound passengers waited in that lot, not at the terminal. Some were upset, but Israelis knew better than to fret. This country did things its own way and security – always a high priority – was an obsession now.

———

Since Brian could hardly wait to see Nicole, he and Becky crammed meeting after meeting into two long, grueling days, visiting with one official after another to hash out a thousand details. Each of them had to mesh to create a television documentary in a foreign country.

There were meetings with the prime minister, agency heads and Knesset leaders, who had to push through legislation approving the project. Everything went smoothly and Becky was instructed to issue permits allowing the ruined city at Beth Shean and the cave to be used for Brian's documentary.

Truly believing the relics must stay in Israel, he asked for nothing for himself. His payment-in-kind from the Israeli government for his role in revealing and protecting the treasure trove would be simple. He would own the documentary in perpetuity. That was an income stream that would give him millions of dollars for many years from royalties and broadcast rights.

They went to the American embassy in Tel Aviv to meet with the acting ambassador and a team she had assembled. Over the next few months this group would generate the paperwork required to bring Brian's production crew and tons of equipment to Israel.

Everywhere he went, Brian was pleased at the level of cooperation he was afforded. The Israeli government saw the documentary as a means of taking the world's collective mind off the never-ending politics of the Middle East. The discovery would make Jews everywhere proud that the lost treasures mentioned by the prophet Isaiah were revealed at last in majestic splendor.

After two tiring ten-hour days of administrative meetings, it was Brian's last night in Israel. He'd been staying at the embassy since his release from the hospital, but today's meetings were in Jerusalem, so tonight he was back at the David Citadel Hotel once more. Tomorrow afternoon he would fly to London Heathrow and before midnight he'd be in the arms of the wife he hadn't seen in eighteen days.

He and Becky Kohl would have a last round of meetings tomorrow morning, and he'd asked her to join him tonight for his last dinner in Israel. They were seated on the patio, he with his martini and she a glass of white wine. He pointed to the breathtaking picture of the Old City bathed in moonlight just across a small valley.

"Nicole and I were swept away by that view the first evening we were here," he said. "It's hard to believe that was nearly a month ago. I'll never forget my time here. Despite everything that happened, I think I've been closer to God in the past four weeks than in my entire life."

"Israel can have that effect on people," she agreed. "Whether you're Christian, Jew or Muslim, this is a holy city – *your* holy city. We all have our differences, but we all have things in common too. Take Isaiah for instance. All three religions believe that Isaiah was a prophet. He told us there were hidden treasures and that Cyrus would help the Jews rebuild their temple. Thanks to Abdel, you proved it true.

"He asked you to become the protector of the treasure – the Zulqarnayn. In a way, you did what he asked. You *are* the protector of the temple treasure. I can provide men with guns to keep out looters, but your role is far more significant. Your documentary will bring it to life for millions. Once that happens, I am hopeful we can raise funds to properly make it accessible to pilgrims who wish to see God's handiwork in person."

Almost twenty-four hours after their dinner, his trip was over at last. As the massive British Airways Boeing 777 rolled down the runway and turned northwest to cross the Mediterranean Sea, he took off his watch. He rolled the hands back two hours to London time. He'd land in six hours and be at the Stafford Hotel ninety minutes after that. He reclined his seat, ordered a glass of champagne and held it high, toasting the success of his journey, thanking God for safety, and remembering Abdel Malouf, wherever he was today.

CHAPTER THIRTY-TWO

The world soon learned that the full name of the thirty-four-year-old al Qaeda terrorist in custody was Tariq Majd Saada. It had been years since anyone had called him by that name. Since he was a teen, he had been known as the Hawk. A man who'd never been photographed, his picture now was plastered on every media outlet in the world, and everyone could see the defiant, arrogant, cruel demeanor of this ruthless killer.

He'd been patched up by American doctors on the USS *Nimitz* and given a couple of weeks to recover. Since his capture, he'd been the topic of conversation in extensive meetings between newly appointed US ambassador to Israel Ardelia Lloyd and Prime Minister Shigon. President Harrison joined the discussions by phone from time to time, trying to sway the Israeli leader to send Tariq to the United States for trial. The primary issue was that of capital punishment. Although the USA hadn't executed a federal prisoner in over a decade, the chance of Tariq's receiving the ultimate punishment for his crimes in Israel was even more remote. There hadn't been an execution there since Holocaust mastermind Adolf Eichmann was hanged in 1962.

Shigon at last reluctantly agreed to let Tariq go, not because of capital punishment but because he felt the attention directed toward such a public trial could create major problems. Tariq was a hero to militants, a brave warrior in the fight for jihadism. If his trial were held in Israel, there would be riots, bombings and acts of terror – a nightmare Shigon simply didn't care to tackle.

The logistics for Tariq's relocation were kept under tight wraps. By the time the news media learned that he would face trial in the United States, he was already behind bars at ADX Florence, a facility in Fremont County, Colorado, that was the most secure "supermax" prison in the country. Packed with extremely violent prisoners considered too unstable, high-profile or risky to be placed in other facilities, the men here faced the tightest security possible.

Two terrorists – Zacarias Moussaoui, one of the 9/11 conspirators, and Ramzi Yousef, who was behind the 1993 World Trade Center bombing – were currently incarcerated at ADX Florence. The warden was careful to assign Tariq a solitary confinement cell far from these men whose motives had been so like his own.

Four guards surrounded Tariq as he sat in front of a video camera during his arraignment. The district court in Denver had been selected for the trial, given its proximity to the prison should Tariq be required to appear in person. The courtroom was the same one where Oklahoma City bomber Timothy McVeigh was tried, convicted and sentenced to death in 1997.

Given the notoriety and importance of the trial, the judge was determined to make no mistakes. For most Americans, there was only one goal – justice followed by swift retribution. Tariq appeared on a huge screen in the courtroom and announced in English that he wished to plead guilty and waive all his rights.

"I did all the things I am accused of doing, and I am proud of my actions," he continued. "I only wish that I could have rid the world of more infidels, especially the leaders of the Great Satan. Allah has a special place for servants such as I, and I willingly submit to death, secure in the belief that Allah in his infinite wisdom will swiftly destroy the United States of America."

The judge told Tariq he was going to appoint an attorney to ensure he understood the implications of what he was requesting and the rights that were available to him under the American legal system. He spat on the ground and cursed the judge. He refused to speak to his attorney and muttered verses from the Quran as his legal counsel explained what options he had available.

Two weeks later the judge asked Tariq if he understood his rights.

"I have a right to justice," he screamed. "Kill me, you son of a whore!"

There was the mandatory presentence investigation, this one abbreviated by the defendant's fervent desire to be executed. Five months after his first court appearance, Tariq appeared on the screen. This would be his last visit to the courtroom. He was impassive as the judge sentenced him to death by lethal injection. He waived his right to appeal and the judge ordered him to be transferred as soon as reasonably possible to the US penitentiary in Terre Haute, Indiana, where his sentence would be carried out.

On a sunny day in June, the most wanted man in the world lay strapped to a gurney in a small room. "*Allahu Akbar!*" he screamed as the warden gave the order to start the drugs flowing. Minutes later, Tariq entered the place he would spend eternity.

Only five months had passed between the day Tariq's trial began and the day he was executed. It was the speediest trial since the Wild West era of "Hanging Judge" Roy Bean, and its swift conclusion was praised by everyone who had hoped for justice.

Tariq was gone, but others would take his place. Al Qaeda and ISIS were not dependent on one man, as awful a creature as he had been. The terror would continue and so would the hunt for Abdel Malouf and Brian Sadler.

CHAPTER THIRTY-THREE

Eight months later

The stately Roman columns standing amid the ruins of Beth Shean gleamed like huge white sentinels standing guard over the treasure of a nation. Brian used enormous floodlights to illuminate the beauty of this ancient city that was thriving three thousand years ago, in the days when biblical heroes like David and Solomon ruled Israel.

Brian had wisely chosen to film the show at night, the glow from carefully placed lighting casting a supernatural aura over the scene and adding to the feeling of mystery and intrigue. An estimated four million viewers worldwide were mesmerized as the documentary began. *The Hidden Treasures of Isaiah*, the deep-voiced narrator echoed as an overhead shot of the ruined city bathed in light faded into a panorama of golden objects that had been found in the cave.

And I will give thee the treasures of darkness, and hidden riches of secret places, that thou mayest know that I, the LORD, which call thee by thy name, am the God of Israel.

The show began with a tribute. Brian introduced himself and Dr. Rebecca Kohl and then the screen displayed a photograph. It was a street scene in the Old City of Jerusalem with a man standing in front of a building. On the awning above the shop's entrance were words in Arabic and English – *Abdel Malouf, antiquities dealer*. Brian had found the picture in Abdel's shop.

The camera zoomed in on the photograph as Brian acknowledged his friend's contribution to this project and explained that without Malouf he would never have known about the treasures of Isaiah. He described Abdel as a colleague, a worthy opponent in bidding contests for priceless objects of art, and a man genuinely interested in the preservation of history. There was no mention of Abdel's disappearance, his possible ties to al Qaeda or any speculation as to his whereabouts.

Brian explained how close Abdel's shop was to the Temple Mount – the place where Hebrew scholars believed the temple would be rebuilt someday. He and a film crew started in front of the gallery and then walked along the Via Dolorosa, a street Brian described as an example of how the various religions were intertwined. Today in what is called the Muslim Quarter, Jesus carried a cross on this very street on the day of His crucifixion. Brian walked up to the Temple Mount, where the Dome of the Rock and Al-Aqsa Mosque stood proudly on the same broad platform where the temple of the Jews was built, destroyed, rebuilt and destroyed again.

"The treasure we're about to reveal was here," he explained. "It was here when King Solomon built the First Temple, it was here when King Cyrus helped the Jews build the second one, and perhaps if it's God's will, those treasures will be in the Third Temple when it is rebuilt on this site in the end times."

Brian realized this part would highly offend the Muslims, who were always outraged at any thought of a temple supplanting the sacred shrine that had been there for thirteen centuries. But this part was important. This production was a history of the Jews and their treasure. He was lucky to have even been allowed to film on the Muslim-controlled Temple Mount. It only happened after Prime Minister Shigon himself made a formal request to the PLO. Brian wasn't sure how that had happened or if Harry had also been involved in discussions with the Palestinians, and he never asked. All that mattered was that permission was granted, the filming was done quickly in case someone changed his mind, and that was that.

The next forty-five minutes of the documentary was a *Ten Commandments*-style movie explaining the history of the Israelites and their treasure. It was a fascinating glimpse into the past. Production staffers who watched this part as it was being edited remarked of having goose bumps when the narrator relayed the history of a captive people released by a Persian king and given back the treasures of their temple – the most sacred and important relics of a civilization.

Jews, Christians and Muslims alike could relate to the next part of the story because it was woven into the religious history of each. The narrator spoke in a mysterious, haunting voice as viewers watched the great prophet Isaiah predict that someday far in the future a king named Cyrus would free the Jews from Babylonian captivity. A hundred and fifty years later that prophecy was fulfilled. Cyrus, the ruler of Persia, appeared next, speaking the words of Second Chronicles. "The Lord, the God of heaven, has ... charged me to build him a house at Jerusalem, which is in Judah. Whoever is among you ... may the Lord his God be with him. Let him go up."

This preview to the unveiling of the treasure continued with a clip showing Cyrus protecting the Jews, bringing them back to Jerusalem and returning treasures that had been stolen when the First Temple was destroyed. Brian's description of the building of the Second Temple – for which King Cyrus footed the bill – revealed a massive structure that stood proudly on the Temple Mount in Jerusalem as a tribute to the God of the Israelites.

After a commercial break, Brian and Becky Kohl were center stage. Dressed in the khakis they'd worn when they visited the cave and a scarf hiding her nasty scar, each of them spoke about the events leading up to the discovery. Brian turned to an easel behind him, where an object covered by a cloth rested.

"Abdel Malouf knew about the hidden treasure for years," he began, "but he removed only one piece. He was an Arab who spent years protecting the treasure of the Israelites. For Abdel, this wasn't about religion, or internecine conflict, or one man's beliefs versus another's. This was about history."

"This is the only piece Abdel removed from the cave," he said, pulling away the cloth with a flourish and revealing the golden plate. "He wrote a letter that explains what it is."

At this point the screen split; on one side was a close-up shot of the plate itself and on the other was a portion of Abdel's handwritten letter in Arabic. The narrator read the words in English, the last part of Abdel's letter that had affected Brian so greatly when Becky translated it that evening in the hospital room.

I doubt anyone will find anything in the cavern more significant than this golden plate. I took it from the cave the day I first laid eyes on the wonders of the hidden treasure of Isaiah. It is the most precious of all objects in the cavern, a chronology of the treasure from the very beginning, and it is the only thing I have removed in all these years. It is a priceless artifact that must always belong to the Jewish people. The inscription is in three parts. The first is the most astounding – the words of King Solomon himself, written by his scribe three thousand years ago. They describe the First Temple and the religious objects inside it.

A second set of words in ancient Hebrew is the work of an unknown person. He records the decree of Cyrus of Persia that the Israelites shall be freed from Babylon and the temple rebuilt in Jerusalem. These words proclaim Isaiah's prophecy about Cyrus and the treasure of the temple. "At last we restore these holy objects to their rightful place," it reads. Those words were written in the sixth century before the birth of Jesus Christ, two thousand five hundred years ago.

Last are the words on the reverse, written in Aramaic at the time of the destruction of the Second Temple in AD 70. They weave a woeful tale of treasure taken from the temple under cover of darkness as Jerusalem burns. The priests and followers piled wagons high, covering the sacred icons with cloths and guiding their donkeys through the crowded streets until they were at last outside the burning city. They turned and watched their beautiful temple go up in flames, then made their way to Beth Shean, where they had long ago created a hiding place in case of just such an event.

Did all the treasure make it? The golden plate doesn't reveal the ending. I am not a Jew, but I have witnessed a miracle. I have seen the temple treasure with my own eyes. For that reason, I believe the God of the Israelites gave His people protection as cart after cart moved along dusty roads until all that could be seen of Jerusalem far in the distance behind them were billowing clouds of smoke.

Another break followed that spine-tingling part of the program. They were ninety minutes in with just thirty to go, and they were reaching the climax. To demonstrate how he had found it on his first visit, Brian was led blindfolded from the hill above Beth Shean. He took off his hood, shinnied down the rope, stood on the ledge and pointed out the partially obscured entrance. Inside, he stood by the massive Egyptian statues and then started down the corridor, his headlamp the only illumination. As he maneuvered sideways through the tight passageway, he described his claustrophobia on that first visit. The camera recorded his surprise as he popped into the cavern. As he turned the dim light of his headlamp from side to side, the viewers got only a tantalizing glimpse of a glint of gold here and there in the darkness.

Then the scene switched back to the hill above Beth Shean. It was time to reveal the pièce de résistance.

He and Becky walked through the brush and weeds, went down the rope and entered the cave. Strings of lights illuminated the hallways as Brian and Becky walked past the statues and went single-file down the corridor. After squeezing through the cramped part, they emerged into the now brightly lit cavern. For the first time, the audience experienced the vastness of the jumbled piles of golden relics.

It had been almost a year since he and Abdel first set foot here. During that time, Director Kohl's team had painstakingly cataloged and photographed every item in the room. Hours of video footage had been shot. Once the fieldwork was done, some of the pieces were moved to allow access to the entire cache. Like visitors to the house of a hoarder, Brian and Becky had to move some of the objects, creating pathways so researchers could access everything. At times, they were literally knee-deep in the most beautifully crafted pieces ever assembled in one place.

There were almost two thousand things in the room, most made of gold, a few of silver, copper and bronze, and others bedecked with precious stones. The builder of the First Temple – King Solomon himself – had surely held some of these objects in his hands, Brian told the audience in a hushed voice that demonstrated his awe and reverence for the sacred relics. Other major figures from the Bible – kings, high priests and officials – would have seen these majestic treasures with their own eyes. Perhaps even Jesus Christ had prayed before them.

With a sweep of his hand around the room, Brian said, "Although it is not in this room, the Ark of the Covenant was once housed in the temple along with these priceless objects. It disappeared sometime before the Jews were exiled to Babylon. Where it was taken and by whom are questions that have never been answered, but just look at what Dr. Kohl and I found here."

He held up one of the two matching miniature arks, stating his opinion that the pair might have been exact replicas of the original. "Imagine this possibility," he said, his enthusiasm fueling the tempo of the show. "This three-thousand-year-old object might have been made by a man who sat in front of the Ark of the Covenant itself, copying its every line in painstaking detail."

Next he pointed to a large box with a golden Torah inside.

"Dr. Kohl, can you tell us where this stunning object might have sat?"

"Most likely it was prominently displayed on an altar in the Second Temple, twenty-five hundred years ago. It's unique, as are most of the objects in this room. Nothing remotely like this one has ever been found before."

For the last five-minute segment, Brian introduced Reverend C.R. Faulkner from Miami, a noted pastor and student of eschatology.

"Does the Dome of the Rock have to be destroyed before the Jewish temple can be rebuilt?" Brian asked.

"In my opinion, no," the pastor said. "I think the actual site is north of the Muslim shrine and there's plenty of room to build a structure worthy of King Solomon himself. All it takes is cooperation between two of the world's major religions, and I think everyone on earth needs to pray that that might happen."

Wrapping up, Brian thanked the audience for allowing him to walk with them through the most fascinating storehouse he had ever seen. He promised that soon there would be a museum to properly display the artifacts. The plan was to incorporate the cavern itself into the building, allowing much of the treasure to remain as it was today.

"You'll have an opportunity to be a part of history," he concluded, standing in the cavern. "I hope you'll join me in making it happen. Thank you and good night."

CHAPTER THIRTY-FOUR

Over the months, Abdel Malouf settled comfortably into life as Constantin Stefos. He opened a little antique shop in Camden Town, far from the ritzy parts of London – the West End, Mayfair and Knightsbridge – where the likes of Brian Sadler maintained their upscale galleries.

Occasionally on his way to a lunch or a meeting, his cab would turn down Old Bond Street and pass the show windows of Bijan Rarities. He wondered if Brian was inside, engaged in some exciting new project. He would have enjoyed walking in, greeting his old friend and catching up over a pint of ale at a nearby pub. Thinking about those streets in Jerusalem's Old City that he and Brian had walked – those streets he would never see again – made him wistful. That life was over. It had to be that way, but it was hard to accept even after all this time had passed.

He never chased after the important consignments, the ones that he would have jumped on in a second when he'd been Abdel Malouf. He steered away from pieces and auctions that would create publicity, for fear someone would recognize him. Every day that passed was another day that al Qaeda hadn't learned where he was – and one more day in his new identity.

He had watched Tariq's widely publicized trial and execution, but knowing the terrorist was dead didn't mean Abdel was free. People could still be looking for him. Maybe they weren't, but for a long time he couldn't shake the fear that something might happen. But as months of quiet days and nights passed, he began to feel a sense of peace at last. He stopped constantly looking over his shoulder, fleeing in panic from sudden noises or becoming startled and afraid when a stranger stopped him on the street to ask directions. His old life was behind him at last, he felt.

One day recently a client had given Constantin's name to a lady who wanted to consign a nice set of Georgian chairs dating to the mid-1800s. Her house was in Lowndes Square, Knightsbridge, and he had met her this afternoon to see the furniture. They agreed on a price, signed the papers, and he said he'd have the pieces picked up tomorrow.

Since it was a beautiful day, he decided to walk for a while instead of going back to the Knightsbridge tube station. He'd rather be outside than underground on a train. He strolled along Brompton Road, its sidewalks filled with pedestrians window-shopping, everyone darting here and there or just killing time like he was. He popped in to Harrods a couple of blocks away. Thanks to its Arab owners, the store always carried a good selection of books in his native language and he found one he wanted.

He left the store through its rear entrance and went down Basil Street. As he passed Pavilion Road, he glanced right and saw Sale e Pepe, a trattoria he'd enjoyed a couple of times in years back. He decided to stop in for a glass of wine, having nothing else on his agenda for the afternoon. Abdel Malouf had had good times here in the old days, but it had been long enough that the staff wouldn't remember who he once had been.

There were a few people finishing lunch in the tiny restaurant, but he had already decided to just have a drink. This time of day he was the only person at the six-seater bar and he ordered a glass of Saint Veran wine and an escargot appetizer. They had been his favorites once. Actually, they were *Abdel's* favorites, he thought nostalgically as he remembered what once had been. Constantin didn't have many favorite anythings, because he hadn't existed long enough and he was afraid to visit the same restaurants more than once. He had no habits anymore because habits could get you in trouble if someone was looking for you.

As he sat with his back to the entrance, he heard the door open and close. He was lost in reverie, remembering better times, when he heard the maître d' say, "Welcome back, Mr. Sadler. I have a nice table for you and your guest."

Constantin turned his head slightly as Brian and a younger man walked through the tiny bar and to the back without a glance his way. Part of him wanted to call out, to say hello to his friend and to explain everything. But that couldn't happen. Brian's table was out of sight around the corner, and Constantin did what he had to do. He finished his food and his wine quickly, paid the bill and left without telling his friend how painful it had been to see him again.

He was deeply saddened and he told himself for the thousandth time it was all his own doing. He only had himself to blame that he was lonely, bitter and depressed. If he weren't terrified of spending eternity in Jahannam, he'd probably have taken his life by now. But the Quran was clear about that, so he was doomed to hell on Earth instead.

As the months passed, Constantin became content with his new existence. He was making a living from the shop, he had enough euros to last a lifetime, and his life was peaceful and quiet. He lived in a modest flat in the Edgeware Road, a section of London near Paddington Station that was home to many Arabs. He felt at home in this area and he rode the tube to his shop and back every day.

One day he finally saw what he'd been expecting. A new Brian Sadler archaeological documentary would be broadcast soon. He wept as he watched the trailer. There was his friend standing in the cave Abdel had revealed. He was with a woman – probably an archaeologist, Constantin mused, thinking it should have been him. He watched Brian and the woman walk down the tunnel – *his* tunnel – and enter the low, narrow corridor off to the right. As they disappeared, he heard the deep, resonant voice of the announcer. "Join your host Brian Sadler for *The Hidden Treasures of Isaiah*, a fulfillment of prophecy and a fascinating look at biblical treasure hidden for a thousand years!"

Once he'd seen the teaser, his days became gloomy again. Everything he'd hoped for, worked for and dreamed about had been tossed away. Someone else was getting all the credit for what was rightfully his. Truthfully it never had been his, of course. He hadn't found it in the first place and the wonderful things that the cavern held were centuries old. But he should have had the glory, the fame and fortune. It wasn't Brian Sadler's fault; it was his own and he hated himself for it.

He tried time and again to put the documentary out of his mind, but instead – like millions of other eager Brian Sadler followers – he found himself counting the days until it aired. At last it was the day. Tonight at eight, it would happen. He told himself he wouldn't watch it. Then he talked himself into recording it in case he wanted to see it later. Then he decided he would have to see it tonight. But not alone. He was miserable enough already. He wouldn't sit in the darkness of his depressing flat all alone. He'd go out instead.

Constantin was drinking more and more these days. Although he didn't allow himself a routine, he occasionally stopped into a friendly Syrian place a block from his apartment building. He walked in, took a seat at the bar and noticed there was only a handful of customers. In his language, he asked if anyone minded switching the telly in a few minutes from a football match nobody cared about anyway to the latest Brian Sadler documentary. "It's about some lost treasure," he added, and nobody protested.

By the time the show aired, the pub was getting busy. Now every stool at the bar was occupied. Constantin was sandwiched between a chubby lady with her husband and a young man wearing a baseball cap, jeans and a dirty sweatshirt. There were a lot of working-class people in this neighborhood and he was one of those. He spoke briefly to everyone when they arrived and they dove into their pints.

He'd had a couple by now, and when the TV special began, he watched the first part in shock. There was Brian Sadler greeting his audience. The screen shot switched to a familiar place – his store in the Old City of Jerusalem. "Turn it up!" he shouted to the bartender, watching as the camera zoomed in on a man standing in front of the shop. Brian was acknowledging him – Abdel Malouf – as the man who'd led him to the amazing cache that was the subject of tonight's show.

Constantin began to weep, which caused those around him to cast an uncomfortable glance his way. The bartender asked if he was all right, but Constantin waved him away.

"That's me," he whispered to no one in particular. "That's me and that was once my store." He turned away, realizing it had been a mistake to watch this show in public, even though he couldn't have known his own picture would be part of the program. He threw a few pounds on the bar, got off the stool a bit unsteadily and walked out as the other patrons requested the channel be switched back to sports. Several of them wondered about the morose man who had asked to switch channels but left before his show really got under way.

The man in the dirty sweatshirt quickly tossed back his drink, paid his bill and followed the sad man home.

Weeks ago, Constantin had met a lady his age at a laundromat down the street, learned she was from the same part of Syria he was, and asked her out for coffee. Although he wasn't interested in a long-term relationship, he realized from spending time with her how starved he was for human interaction. They began to have dinner now and then.

A couple of weeks after the Brian Sadler documentary aired, he closed his shop early because he and his lady friend were going to a fancy restaurant in the Charing Cross Road for dinner. It would be the first time they were going for what might be considered a "date."

The evening went well and the time passed quickly. She was friendly and outgoing, easy to talk to and genuinely interested in him – at least the life he'd invented for himself. When the evening was over, they stood outside the restaurant and she advised him she was going to spend the night with her mother instead of returning to their part of town. He hailed a taxi, smiled as she pecked him on the cheek, and decided to ride the subway home because it was less expensive than a cab.

As he rode the crowded train under the streets of London, his mind was a million miles away. The train arrived at Victoria Station and a jostling mass of people exited the train as even more boarded. Constantin didn't pay attention to a rowdy group of youths who had entered, pushing and shoving their way through the car. There were no seats available, so they stood in the aisle. His nose wrinkled as he noticed the body odor of a man just beside him, his arm in the air holding a strap. He turned his head away and closed his eyes.

The train arrived at the South Kensington station, just three stops from Constantin's destination. As the doors whisked open, the young man standing next to Constantin jabbed a knife into his throat. "*Allahu Akbar*," the killer whispered as his victim's life drained away. With the confusion and so many passengers jammed like cattle into the car, it took a moment for anyone to notice the blood covering the Arab man's shirt. By the time the screams began, his killer was gone.

CHAPTER THIRTY-FIVE

The Monument Club in London was a refuge for Brian and other like-minded adventurers, and he made it a point to spend time there at least once during every trip. Built in 1894, the three-story building sprawled along the Thames River at the Embankment. A tranquil haven for its members over the decades, the club had been founded by a group of men linked by an interest in archaeology and adventure.

There were quiet, wood-paneled reading rooms, a bar that invited pleasant conversation, a four-star restaurant overlooking the river and a gentlemen's cigar room with an enormous fireplace. Brian enjoyed the latter immensely, sharing a before-dinner martini and afterwards a fine Cuban cigar with other members – anthropologists, archaeologists and armchair adventurers.

The club's expansive third floor housed a library of archaeological reference material unrivalled in the world. There were over sixty thousand volumes and Brian had spent many an afternoon there doing research on one project or another. It had a sister club in New York that was stately and refined, but Brian always had a special affinity for the original. It was a pleasure to sit in one's own club, fraternizing with others who were equally fascinated by ancient relics, exciting stories of treasure and suppositions as to what might appear at the next turn of a shovel in some faraway ruined city. It was a fraternity of kindred spirits.

Oscar Carrington, a good friend of Brian's and the owner of a well-respected gallery in the posh Knightsbridge area of London, had long ago sponsored him for membership and joined him often for a drink or dinner when Brian was in town. He was present tonight, as were fifty other guests who had gathered in a second-floor salon for a special tribute.

It was Carrington himself who walked to a dais in the front of the room, stood at a podium, clinked a glass and waited until the conversation stopped. "We're here to honor one of our colleagues," he began, beckoning to Brian and Nicole to join him. "Some of you are stodgy academics," he quipped to laughter from the audience as several pointed to others nearby. "Some are famous in your own right, such as Lord Aynesley here –" he pointed to a man with a cane sitting nearby "– whose work in Egypt in the 1970s led to the discovery of a long-lost pharaoh. There are those of you who were in the field long before modern irritants like cable television and alien documentaries became fashionable." Another outburst of laughter, this one more robust. "Many of you have been content to stay in the shadows, letting others receive the glory for conquests that belonged equally to yourselves. You've shunned the limelight and remained anonymous."

He saw nods and heard murmurs of agreement.

Carrington paused for a long moment and then put his arm around Brian's shoulders. "And then there's our friend Brian Sadler."

The room exploded in laughter and applause. As much as some of the members – especially the seniors – decried the commercialization of archaeology, everyone who knew Brian enjoyed his ebullient personality, his positive, cheerful outlook about every project or obstacle, and his passion for adventure. Some of the members felt people such as Brian portrayed archaeological expeditions as crass treasure hunts, but everyone had to admit that he had created a spark of interest and fascination among common people, who were caught up in the excitement every time they watched Brian's documentaries.

Carrington continued. "I'm remiss if I don't introduce Nicole, Brian's far better half and the woman who should be taming his wild spirit but instead finds herself hanging on to the tiger's tail, I'm afraid." She waved and flashed a big bright smile.

"Brian has outdone himself with the Israel documentary. Not only was the production spectacular, the revealing of the actual treasures of the Temple Mount is his crowning achievement to date." He continued with effusive praise peppered with a smattering of applause now and then from the onlookers.

Oscar motioned to someone in the back of the room and the lights were lowered. A video began playing on a screen behind the dais. Brian and Nicole turned as a familiar face appeared. There was President Harry Harrison sitting at his desk in the White House.

"Hello, my old friend. Greetings from this side of the pond and congratulations on a mission successfully accomplished. I have to admit I had my doubts about you now and then, and you put the fear of God into all of us more than once on this adventure, but once again you managed to ignore the advice of every sane person you know – including your wife, Nicole – and get yourself into and out of more jams than Wile E. Coyote and the Road Runner."

There was laughter in the room and a couple of men shouted, "Hear, hear!" in agreement.

"I'm proud to count you and Nicole as my friends and I wish you well tonight. I'm told there's some big news coming next, so I must say my goodbyes and let you get on with the festivities. Best wishes, Brian!" The video went to black and the lights came up as the group applauded.

Oscar resumed his remarks. "In closing, let me say that you've brought the wonders of Israel to millions of viewers. As your colleague and friend, and as a man who appreciates rarities just as you do, I know how much it would have meant to own some of the wondrous things you saw. I know the exhilaration I'd have felt if my gallery had offered some of them at auction. There were over a thousand items in that cavern. You could have pressured the Israeli government to part with a few as partial compensation for the work you did. But instead, you did something generous and unselfish. A little bird told me you made a pledge to the Israel Antiquities Authority, providing seed money for a new museum at Beth Shean. I'm told the building will be constructed on the hill above the treasure cave. Many of the finest items will be displayed there. The more adventurous and hardy visitors – people who want to see more than relics in glass cases – will be able to descend a narrow set of stairs to the ledge outside the cave. They will walk down the same corridor you walked, enter the cavern and experience the treasures of the temple just as you did."

Brian looked perplexed. "How could you know about that? That's not public information ..."

"I know you well." He laughed. "Ever since your return eight months ago, you've gushed about Israel, the spirituality you felt at sites you and Nicole visited, and your incredible adventures there. Observing how deeply the entire experience affected you, I had an idea that you might be doing something charitable behind the scenes. I put on my Sherlock Holmes hat, gripped my meerschaum pipe in my teeth and engaged in some detective work. It took a little persuading, but your friend Dr. Rebecca Kohl finally gave up your secret. Please don't be upset with her or me. I believe you'll find the outcome satisfying."

He picked up a large envelope from the podium as he continued. "Yours is a matching pledge; the Antiquities Authority must raise the same amount to get your donation. Well, my boy, get out your checkbook. On behalf of the Monument Club, its directors and officers, I'm pleased to announce that the club is matching your donation one hundred percent." He opened the envelope and showed everyone a large mock check payable to the Israel Antiquities Authority in the amount of one million dollars.

Usually not at a loss for words, Brian stood dumbfounded in front of his fellow members, every one of whom was on his or her feet and applauding boisterously. Carrington ushered Brian to the podium and stepped off the platform. He took Nicole's hand and they walked forward.

Wiping a tear from his eye, he said, "Words can't adequately express how important this contribution is. Not only am I personally awed by such a gesture, your immediate match of my pledge means that construction can begin far more quickly. The government of Israel has already agreed to fund everything over two million dollars, so the architects and engineers can start now instead of months from now. The museum will become reality months – maybe years – ahead of our original schedule." He held up the check. "This grant ensures that the hidden treasures of Isaiah will be safeguarded and appreciated by millions. Thank you, Oscar. Thank you, my friends, and may God bless this club and each one of you."

The after party went on until the wee hours. At last it was closing time and only Brian, Nicole and Oscar were left at the bar, finishing one last nightcap.

"What's next?" his friend asked.

"I'm hanging up my spurs, as we say in Texas," Brian responded. "I think it's time to stay home for a while. I'm afraid this time I've given Nicole enough worry to last a lifetime."

"You're absolutely right," she admitted, "but there's another saying in Texas about dying with your boots on. I know you well. Don't hang those spurs too far away. I have a feeling you'll figure out a reason to use them again before long."

———

Brian traveled to Jerusalem at least once a quarter. In these days of instant technology, it was easy to run a business from a distance, but owning a gallery required a personal touch. There were opportunities to acquire exquisite artifacts, a chance to broker a sale with a colleague in Europe or Asia, and the most important thing to Brian – on every trip he found something new in Israel, something he hadn't seen before.

He had kept the gallery in the same location where it had stood for twenty years. He enjoyed traversing the ancient streets of the Old City to get to work. Experiencing the sights, sounds, smells and tastes of the area and its teeming masses of Arabs, Jews and tourists invigorated him.

For this visit, Nicole had accompanied him. She hadn't been back since the documentary had aired, and she was surprised to see how many people approached her husband these days to meet him and thank him for showing the public the temple treasures. Due to his growing notoriety, he'd been forced to give up some of his privacy. An armed security person accompanied him every waking moment when he traveled outside the United States, and although it was an inconvenience, it was essential for his safety. The man stood casually to one side, respectful but always vigilant, as fans asked the handsome American TV personality for autographs or selfies.

"It seems so peaceful compared to when we were here during the conflict," she said as they sat on the balcony outside their room. "I don't see how these people get used to it, but somehow they do. They go about their lives in ordinary ways, but they must always wonder when the next attack might happen. Maybe today, maybe next week, maybe not for twenty years, but as sure as God's in heaven, it's going to happen sometime."

She glanced up and saw Brian lost in thought, gazing off toward the Garden of Gethsemane in the distance. When she saw his face, she regretted her words. The things she said described not only an Israeli, but also her husband. She and Brian pretended the reason he needed protection was because he was a celebrity. Even though neither discussed the real reason, it was always lurking somewhere deep in their minds.

Tariq the Hawk was dead, but the million-euro contract on the head of Brian Sadler still stood, as far as the United States and Israeli governments could determine. No one knew if Abdel had evaded capture; since his disappearance from Skopje, Macedonia, over a year ago nothing had ever turned up about his whereabouts.

Brian was an optimist. He chose to think that those days were behind him. The man who'd harbored such deep anger for President Harrison, the United States and Brian himself was dead. Hopefully the need for revenge had died with him. Perhaps Brian would never know. His last prayer every night was that God would protect Nicole and him.

So far, so good.

Thanks for joining Brian Sadler's
latest adventure!

We hope you enjoyed *Treasure*.
Here's what you can do next.

If you liked the book and have a moment,
I'd appreciate a brief review.

Even a line or two makes a tremendous
difference, so thanks in advance for your help!

———

My next novel will be available in the coming
months. You can sign up to be notified in
advance and get pre-release specials as
available.

Just go to
billthompsonbooks.com
and click "Sign Up for the Latest News"

———

Please join me on
Facebook
http://on.fb.me/187NRRP

Twitter
@BThompsonBooks